F SWA

PRAISE FOR JAMES SWAIN

"James Swain's *The King Tides* is a hundred percent adrenaline rush disguised as a detective novel. Its hero, an ex-detective named Jon Lancaster, is as adept at using the latest digital sleuthing software as he is shooting a gun. The pacing is terrific, the dialogue memorable, and the characters, including a tough-as-nails female FBI agent and some truly frightening serial killers, jump off the page. You will read this book in one sitting. It's that good."

  —Michael Connelly, #1 *New York Times* bestselling author

"Lancaster is a terrific new character and Swain's writing is better than ever—together they're smart, tough, suspenseful, and rewarding."

  —Lee Child, #1 *New York Times* bestselling author

"*The King Tides* takes off like a rocket and doesn't ease up until an edge-of-your-seat finale. Swain is a pro at creating memorable characters, but the duo of Jon Lancaster and Special Agent Beth Daniels might be my favorite yet—tough and confident, but utterly fresh and modern. More please!"

  —Alafair Burke, *New York Times* bestselling author of *The Wife*

"*The King Tides* is crime fiction of the finest vintage—fast and furious, with memorable characters and skillful plotting. Jon Lancaster is a great protagonist, and Jim Swain is a terrific writer. Don't miss this one."

  —Michael Koryta, *New York Times* bestselling author

"Jon Lancaster is a former Navy SEAL and a retired cop, who works rescues of abducted children and is a kick-ass private investigator. Tough as nails, Jon doesn't take no for an answer when searching for missing kids. As a private investigator he doesn't have to abide by the same rules of law enforcement officers, giving the perpetrators no rights. Author James Swain has created a protagonist who is real enough to be your next-door neighbor. I have read, and loved, many of Swain's books over the years, but I think *The King Tides* is his best work yet. The story is action-packed, tough, and believable. I hope the Jon Lancaster adventures will become a series."

—Cheryl Kravetz, Murder on the Beach Bookstore, Delray Beach, Florida

THE KING TIDES

THE KING TIDES

A THRILLER

JAMES SWAIN

THOMAS & MERCER

Published by Thomas & Mercer, Seattle

www.apub.com

Amazon, the Amazon logo, and Thomas & Mercer are trademarks of Amazon.com, Inc., or its affiliates.

ISBN-13: 9781503901698 (hardcover)
ISBN-10: 1503901696 (hardcover)
ISBN-13: 9781503901681 (paperback)
ISBN-10: 1503901688 (paperback)

Cover design by Shasti O'Leary Soudant

Printed in the United States of America

First edition

For Sarah E.

CHAPTER 1
The Old-Fashioned Way

Jon Lancaster sat slumped in a chair, fighting exhaustion. Dressed like a street person, he wore ratty jeans with holes in the knees and a stained Jimmy Buffett T-shirt. He did not have an athletic appearance, and his most prominent physical feature was his stomach, which was as round as a beach ball. He also smelled like low tide.

"No offense, Jon, but I really don't think you're suited for this job," Dr. Nolan Pearl said. "You're a little rougher than I'm used to."

Lancaster blinked awake. "You want me to leave?"

"If you don't mind. You need to go sleep it off."

"I'm not drunk. I've been up seventy-two hours straight on a job, and I hit the wall. I'll be okay in a few minutes. Think I could bum a cup of coffee?"

"There's a Starbucks down the street." Pearl rose from his desk. "I'll show you out."

Lancaster remained seated. "You said you were desperate."

"I am. I just don't think—"

"That I'm right for the job? Don't judge a book by its cover."

"These aren't your normal clothes?"

"No. They're a disguise."

"No offense, but your body odor is repulsive. Is that part of your disguise too?"

Lancaster's eyes narrowed and his lips parted, the movements hardly noticeable. Pearl shuddered, knowing that he'd stepped over an invisible line.

"Why don't you sit down, and tell me what the problem is," Lancaster said.

"Please don't order me around in my house," his host said.

"Look, I'm normally a nice guy. But I drove two and a half hours, and traffic was a bitch."

"I thought you were local."

"I was in Melbourne on a job. I'll be heading back once we're done."

Pearl suddenly looked ashamed of himself for treating his guest so rudely. He sank back into his chair and spent a moment gathering his thoughts. "Very well, here's the situation. A group of strange men are stalking my daughter, Nicki. I don't know what they want, but I want them to go away."

"How many men are we talking about?"

"Eight that I know of."

"That's a big number. Any idea who they are?"

"I don't have a clue."

"Have they tried to harm your kid?"

"Yes. Two days ago, two of them attempted to abduct Nicki at the Galleria mall. Luckily, I was there and managed to stop them. I filed a report with the police, who suggested I hire a private bodyguard until they can figure out what's going on. I contacted several security companies, who have pitched me on their services. They claim they can keep Nicki safe, but I want more. I want these men to go away."

"You want someone to put the fear of God into them."

His host nodded vigorously. "That's exactly what I want, and I'm willing to pay for it. I visited a local bar, hoping to find a person with the right credentials. The bartender mentioned you, and gave me your number. I did a search on Google, and saw the YouTube video of you saving that little girl from those kidnappers back when you were a policeman. It gave me hope, so I called."

The YouTube video that Pearl had seen was a car chase that had stretched over two counties, with speeds exceeding 120 miles per hour. A news helicopter doing a traffic report had started filming right as Lancaster had rammed the kidnappers' vehicle into a field, jumped out of his car, and shot them both to death. The victim, a ten-year-old child with flowing blonde hair, had climbed out and run into Lancaster's waiting arms. There were plenty of car-chase videos on YouTube, but Lancaster's video was different. Perhaps it was his willingness to risk his life in order to save a child and the "Dirty Harry–like" aspect of shooting first. Or maybe it was the indelible image of the girl clinging to her savior well after the danger had passed. At the end of the day, it really didn't matter. It had gone viral and made him famous.

"Well, you called the right person," Lancaster said.

"How so?"

"Security companies are licensed and bound by a strict set of rules in the state of Florida. I'm not licensed, which lets me do pretty much whatever the hell I want. I'll get to the bottom of this, and make these characters go away."

"Is that a guarantee, Mr. Lancaster?"

"Call me Jon. Yes, it's a guarantee."

"How do you plan to do that?"

"The old-fashioned way." He lifted his T-shirt to reveal a Smith & Wesson M2.0 handgun tucked behind a silver belt buckle. He produced a Beretta subcompact from his pants pocket, then drew a Heizer two-shot from an ankle holster.

"You're a walking arsenal," Pearl said.

"Yes, I am. And they're not for show."

"You mentioned you were on a job. May I inquire what it is?"

"A cocktail waitress in Melbourne disappeared over the weekend. The police think she's partying in Key West; her grandmother thinks it was foul play, and hired me to find her. I've been on the case for three days, and am convinced the girl was abducted. I was waiting for the bloodhounds to arrive when you called, so I drove down."

"You use bloodhounds?"

"Sometimes. I rent them from a tracker in Lake City. It's a long-ass drive, so rather than kill time, I decided to come see you. I'm heading back once we're done."

"Do you think the girl's alive?"

"I'd rather not go there, Dr. Pearl."

His host drummed his fingers on the desk, thinking. Lancaster knew that he hadn't made a good first impression, which was critical in his line of work. But Pearl had a bad situation on his hands, and desperate men sometimes resorted to desperate measures.

"You're on," Pearl said. "Can I interest you in a cup of coffee?"

"Now you're talking," he said.

- - -

"Last week, I became aware that strange men were stalking my daughter," Pearl said, blowing steam off his drink. "Every time our family went out, a man would appear, and start leering at her. They were everywhere. At the beach, in a restaurant, or just walking down the street, there was a guy following Nicki."

"How many times has this happened?" Lancaster asked.

"Seven times. Each time, the man was different. The last time was at the Galleria mall, when two men nearly abducted her."

"Do these creeps ever say anything?"

4

"No. But I know what they're thinking. It's written all over their faces."

"They want sex."

"Yes, they want sex."

"Can you describe them?"

"They're never the same. Four were white, three were Hispanic, and one was black. And their ages are different."

"Give me a range."

"Late twenties to late fifties."

"How old is your daughter?"

"Nicki just turned fifteen."

"So none of these creeps are her age?"

Pearl shook his head. "The situation would be understandable if my daughter's stalkers were teenage boys. Nicki is quite pretty, and boys in her age group are attracted to her, which is normal. These men are anything but normal."

"You said your daughter was nearly abducted at the Galleria mall. Is there a surveillance video of what happened?"

"There is. The police asked me to study it, and see if my wife and I could identify the two men. Would you like to see it?"

"Please."

Pearl opened the laptop on his desk and turned it so they both could watch. It was in sleep mode, and he hit the "Return" button, causing the screen to blink awake. He played with the mouse, and Windows Media Player filled the screen. He clicked on the "Play" button, and a full-color surveillance video started to play.

"Nicki is in the bottom corner of the screen," Pearl said. "Two days ago, I picked her up from school and took her to the mall to do some shopping. While we were outside Neiman's, I got a call from the hospital where I work, and was momentarily distracted. That's when it happened."

The coffee had brought Lancaster around, and he stared at the small screen with a frightening intensity. "Your kid's wearing the khaki dress?"

"Yes, that's her school uniform."

Neiman Marcus was a popular store, and there was heavy foot traffic by the entrance. Two middle-aged white males wearing sweatshirts and ball caps whose rims shaded their faces entered the picture. One of the pair held a metal flask in his right hand, a folded cloth in his left, while his partner pushed a wheelchair.

"What do we have here," Lancaster said under his breath.

"Do you know them?" Pearl said excitedly.

"Not personally, but I know their type. They're pros."

"That's what the police said as well."

The kidnappers' intent was obvious: they planned to knock Nicki out, and wheel her away in front of unsuspecting shoppers too distracted to pay attention to something sinister taking place right beneath their noses. On the video, Pearl ends his call and sees the danger. His paternal instinct kicks in, and he bravely tries to protect his daughter. The kidnappers throw the wheelchair in his path, knocking him down before fleeing.

"Nice job," Lancaster said. "Have you ever seen these creeps before? Maybe their clothes reminded you of someone, or the way they ran away. Think hard."

Pearl dredged his memory. "Sorry. They were strangers."

Lancaster asked Pearl to play the video again. As it ended, Lancaster pointed at the screen. "Our kidnappers used the mango exit for their escape."

"Is that significant?"

"It bolsters my theory that these guys have done this kind of thing before. The Galleria's parking garage is color coded: plum for the restaurants, lime for Dillard's, orange for Macy's, and mango for Neiman Marcus. Thieves who robbed the mall over the years have used the mango exit to park their getaway cars, since it takes a minute to reach, while a typical 911 call takes six minutes to respond to. Our kidnappers planned ahead. Did the police search the parking garage?"

"They did," Pearl said. "According to the detective handling the investigation, the officers at the scene conducted a search, and found a flask one of the kidnappers threw in a trash basket. It was filled with chloroform."

"You got lucky, Dr. Pearl."

"I know. My wife said I have an angel sitting on my shoulder. I just don't know how long that angel will keep protecting my child."

The memory was painful, and Pearl spent a moment collecting himself. Lancaster placed his empty coffee mug on the desk. "Where is your daughter now?"

"Nicki's outside by the pool," Pearl said.

"Do you think that's safe considering what happened?"

"I think she's very safe. I'll show you."

They crossed the study to a window facing the Intracoastal, where his host parted the blinds with a finger. The waterway was an endless parade of expensive watercrafts and Jet Skis and always busy. Nicki sunbathed on a towel by the pool, beside her a black German shepherd the size of a small lion. Nicki was dark-haired and stunningly pretty, but so were many teenage girls in Fort Lauderdale. Why was she being targeted?

"Does Nicki have a boyfriend?" Lancaster asked.

"No," Pearl said.

"Have you asked her?"

"I'll rephrase that. Not that I'm aware of. But I'm reasonably certain that there isn't a young man in her life. She doesn't have time for one."

"How about an ex-boyfriend?"

"Same answer. No."

"Does she hang out with a bad crowd at school, or run with a gang?"

"Of course not."

"Does she do illegal drugs or peddle them?"

"What are you implying? That my child's a criminal? To answer your question, my daughter doesn't do or sell drugs. Nor is she an assassin or a spy."

"You're not helping, Dr. Pearl."

"I don't see how this line of questioning is helpful."

"I'm trying to find a motive. Those two bastards in the mall had a good reason for trying to abduct your kid. If I can determine what they wanted, I'll be one step closer to putting a stop to this. Make sense?"

"Yes. I'm sorry if I sound short. This has been very hard."

"No need to apologize. Does Nicki chat with strangers on the internet?"

"We monitor Nicki's internet time. Going onto chat rooms is forbidden."

Lancaster nodded and moved away from the window. Pearl followed him until they were standing in the center of the study.

"Do you have any enemies, Dr. Pearl?"

"Not that I'm aware of," his host said.

"Are you being sued?"

"No."

"Any disagreements with other doctors at your hospital?"

"I don't think so. Do you think a doctor could be behind this?"

"It's a possibility. Chloroform is not available on the open market, but most hospitals have some in their pharmacies. That would indicate another doctor."

"I suggested that to the police. The detective handling the case said criminals can legally buy the chemicals to make chloroform from swimming pool companies, and mix up a batch in their kitchen."

"They can. The problem comes when a criminal tries to cook a batch and knocks himself out, which is what happens ninety-nine percent of the time."

"Your reasoning makes perfect sense. However, I only joined Broward General three months ago, which is hardly enough time to turn a colleague against me. I don't believe another doctor is behind this."

Lancaster frowned and shook his head.

"Is something wrong?" Pearl said.

"If you don't mind, I'd like to talk to your daughter, see what she knows."

"My wife and I have already done that. Nicki doesn't know a thing."

"You could be wrong. Every teenager has a secret life they don't reveal to their parents. It's part of growing up. Maybe she slips out at night, and moonlights as an exotic dancer at a local strip club, and a patron is infatuated with her. Or she's peddling weed and owes money to her dealer. My gut tells me your kid's in hot water, but doesn't want to admit it."

"You're out of line, Jon. No, you cannot talk to my daughter."

"Don't you want to know the truth? Your daughter's being targeted for a reason. Maybe she'll tell us what that reason is."

"Your gut is wrong. Nicki's an innocent victim."

"If you want to hire me, I need access to your kid. If not, sayonara."

Pearl's face grew red. "Then I'm afraid I won't be using your services."

"You sure about that? You're in a real jam here."

"I'm positive. Thank you for your time. I hope things go well with your other case. Let me show you out."

Pearl led him to the foyer. The house was huge and would have been easy to get lost in. Nearing the front door, Lancaster's cell phone rang, the ring tone Jimmy Buffett singing, "Why don't we get drunk and screw?" He pulled the cell phone from his pocket and stared at the screen. "Do you mind? It's my tracker."

"By all means," Pearl said.

He answered the call. "Hey, Shorty, you getting close?"

"I've got another two hours in front of me," Shorty said.

"What's the holdup?"

"There was a wreck on the turnpike. I'm going to be stuck for a while."

"Call me when you get there."

He ended the call. Pearl twisted the knob on the front door.

"If I do a search on Google, will I find out why you use bloodhounds to find living people?" Pearl asked. "I thought dogs were only used to find the dead. Or is that just something I saw on forensic crime shows on television?"

"You won't find it on Google. It's something new," he said.

"My loss. Goodbye, Jon."

"Are you sure you don't want to think this over?"

"I already have. You're the wrong person for the job. Have a nice day."

"Talk to your daughter, Dr. Pearl. She knows what's going on."

"You think my daughter's not trustworthy?"

"Your words, not mine."

Pearl's lips trembled in anger. Lancaster had gotten under his skin, and he hoped Pearl would accept that Nicki was somehow involved with the men who were stalking her. As he started to say goodbye, his words were interrupted by a piercing scream.

CHAPTER 2

SNEAKIN' AND PEEKIN'

Certain sounds set off chemical reactions in the body that turn normal men into heroes. A child's scream is one of those sounds. Pearl sprinted through the house like an Olympic runner chasing the gold while Lancaster struggled to keep up.

"Your daughter?" Lancaster asked.

"Yes," Pearl said over his shoulder.

They passed through the kitchen—where a small TV was tuned to a cooking show—into a laundry room that led to a door opening to the backyard. Coming outside, Lancaster did a quick sweep and saw everything that he needed to know. Nicki was gone, while the German shepherd purchased to protect her was snoozing in the grass, courtesy of the tranquilizer dart sticking out of its side.

"They're getting away," Pearl said.

"You see them?" Lancaster asked.

"Yes, I see them."

A Donzi classic was moored at the dock. Pearl got behind the wheel and searched his key chain for the key, which he jammed into the ignition. Lancaster untied the boat and hopped in, and they sped down the waterway. Two hundred yards ahead, a black cigarette boat was churning up the water. Lancaster shielded his eyes from the blinding sun to get a better look. Two men in shorts and long-sleeve T-shirts. Both wearing ball caps and shades. Their body language reminded him of the kidnappers from the Galleria. They worked in tandem, without having to resort to time-wasting verbal commands. They'd been doing bad shit for so long that it was second nature. The smaller one was at the wheel while his partner wrestled with Nicki, who was putting up one hell of a fight, kicking and screaming as she tried to break free.

"Hit your horn," Lancaster said.

"But they'll know we're following them," Pearl protested.

"That's the idea. Do it."

The Donzi's horn was electric and sounded like a fire siren. Both kidnappers' heads snapped to the sound, letting Lancaster get a good look at them. Late forties, deep tans, no visible tattoos or piercings, they looked like a couple of ordinary guys out for a day on the water. What wasn't ordinary was how they reacted to being spotted. Their boat sped up.

"They're getting away!" Pearl said.

Once they hit open water, the Donzi would be no match for the cigarette boat, and the kidnappers would disappear into the wind. Lancaster had learned long ago that when it came to emergency situations, he who hesitated was lost, and he drew the M2.0 from behind his belt buckle. Holding the gun with both hands, he went into a crouch. He had dealt with kidnappers before. As criminals went, they were cowardly and predictable. Rather than getting caught and going to prison, a smart kidnapper would dump his victim if being chased, knowing there were other victims down the road.

Not here. These kidnappers were hell-bent on keeping their victim, despite being seen. Nicki was the prize, and he felt certain there would be no ransom note or late-night phone call demanding that Pearl drop a suitcase stuffed with unmarked hundred-dollar bills at a specified location. These boys had something else in mind, and didn't care that they'd been seen. That wasn't normal. Lancaster cocked one eye.

"What are you doing?" Pearl shouted.

"What does it look like I'm doing?" he shouted back.

"You could kill my daughter!"

"Do you want to see her again?"

"Yes!"

"Then shut the hell up."

What Lancaster liked most about the M2.0 was its aggressive grip texture. Once a target was in his sights, he had no fear of the gun slipping out of his hands. It was as simple as point, aim, and fire. Which is what he did, three times.

He'd learned to shoot in the military and was a crack marksman. Pressure did not faze him, nor was he afraid of hitting an innocent victim, which he'd never done, despite having shot over a dozen very bad men as a cop and in the military. All three bullets found their mark and tore through the back of the smaller kidnapper's shirt, causing him to pitch forward onto the wheel. The cigarette boat slowed down. Seeing her chance, Nicki kicked his partner in the groin and broke free. There was no greater instinct than survival, and she took a heroic leap off the back of the boat and dove into the water.

"Go girl!" her father yelled.

Pearl pulled back on the throttle in order not to run his daughter over. The second kidnapper made a rifle appear and pointed it at the Donzi.

"Get down," Lancaster said.

Pearl killed the engine, and they both hit the deck. Instead of the rifle's blast, Lancaster heard a roar and lifted his head to watch the cigarette boat race away. The smaller kidnapper was at the wheel, no worse for wear. He must be wearing a bulletproof vest, Lancaster thought. There was no doubt in his mind it was the same two bastards from the Galleria mall.

"I could use some help," Pearl said.

Nicki had swum over to the side of the boat, and they grabbed her arms and hoisted her from the water. The poor kid was scared out of her mind. She sobbed as her father tried to comfort her.

- - -

Pearl motored back to the house. Nicki's mother stood on the dock, choking on her tears. She was ten years younger than her husband and not hard on the eyes. Nicki came off the boat into her mother's arms, and they shared a good cry. Lancaster tossed the M2.0 into the water, where it made a large plop.

Shooting a suspect had been no fun when he was a cop. Each time he'd shot a suspect, he'd been assigned to a desk while an internal investigation was conducted. The investigation included psychological testing and hours of questions, and was as much fun as having a colonoscopy. The shootings captured by the YouTube video had been worse, and the investigation had dragged on for months. He'd finally had enough and turned in his badge. Since then, he'd shot two people, and discovered the drill was different. If there were no witnesses or incriminating videos, the shooting came down to a he said/she said. This was an advantage for the shooter, especially if the victim died. The shooter could make up a believable story, and there would be no one to dispute it. Better yet, the shooter could ditch the gun, and make the whole thing go away.

"I can't believe you just did that," Pearl said.

"Pretend you didn't see anything," he said.

"Look, I plan to call the police, and file a report."

"You do that."

"Will you corroborate my story?"

"No, I'm leaving. There are two detectives with the sheriff's office named Vargas and Gibbons who hate me. It would be my luck if they responded to your call."

"We need the police to hear what happened."

"You tell them. Leave me out of it."

"But we need the police's help."

"Have they helped you so far?"

"They're conducting an investigation. What else can they do?"

Lancaster lowered his voice so Nicki and her mother couldn't hear. "The police can do any damn thing they want to, *if* they want to. But so far, they haven't. There's a reason for that. The police believe Nicki is tied into some type of bad activity, like drug dealing or selling her body, and is bringing this situation upon herself. So they're not interested in helping. You can file a report, but don't expect anything to come of it."

Lancaster jumped out of the boat and nodded at the mother before heading inside. As he neared the front door, Pearl appeared.

"My wife called 911," the doctor said.

"Then I need to beat it. I hope you get to the bottom of this," he said.

He did not want to have another encounter with Vargas and Gibbons. The last time, they'd run him in on a trumped-up charge, and made his life miserable before his attorney had bailed him out of jail. The charges had later been dropped.

He went outside. His Camaro was parked in the street beneath the shade of a cluster of royal palms. In South Florida, it was all about the shade when it came to parking a car, even if it meant walking half a mile.

Pearl came up behind him, breathing hard. "Wait."

"I can't. Sorry."

"But I need to explain something to you."

"All right, but make it fast."

"My family and I lived in Dubai for the past five years while I ran the neurology department of a large hospital. We only returned to the United States three months ago. Nicki hasn't had time to get herself in the kind of trouble that you're describing. I know this sounds trite, but she's an innocent child."

"You're saying your kid couldn't know who's behind this."

Pearl nodded vigorously.

"Where does she go to school now?"

"Pine Crest. It's the finest private school in the area. She's taking several Advanced Placement classes. All she does is study."

"I've heard of it. No time to get in trouble, huh?"

"She wants to be a doctor like her father. I told her it wasn't easy."

"Then who the hell are these guys stalking her?"

"God only knows."

A police siren blared in the distance, and he judged it to be less than a mile away. He said goodbye and started toward his car. Pearl's hand touched his sleeve.

"I want to hire you, if you're still interested," Pearl said.

As courtships went, this one had taken a while. Pearl had a situation that the police weren't going to solve, and he had money, and in Lancaster's experience those were the best kind of clients to have. If there was a problem, it was that Pearl was a doctor, and doctors were used to calling the shots. He decided to lay down the ground rules now, just so they were both clear who was in charge.

"I still need to talk to your kid," he said.

"May my wife and I be present?" Pearl asked.

"I don't see why not."

"Then yes, of course."

"Then you and I have a deal, Dr. Pearl. I'll call you once my job in Melbourne is over. In the meantime, keep Nicki inside the house. No more lounging by the pool."

Pearl nodded.

"And whatever you do, don't let strangers inside the house for any reason. Those two guys in the cigarette boat were real pros. They spent the afternoon cruising the Intracoastal, *sneakin' and peekin'*."

"What does that mean?"

"It means to case a place. It's a special ops expression."

"I see. Were you in special ops?"

"I was a Navy SEAL. Don't act so surprised."

The siren was drawing closer, less than a few blocks away. Pearl cleared his throat. "I don't mean to sound vulgar, but what are your fees?"

"I need a new refrigerator made by a company called Bosch," he said. "I've already got it picked out. I'll text you the details."

"Is that supposed to be a joke?"

"No joke. That's how I get paid. I also need to get reimbursed for the gun I tossed, seeing how it was your kid's life I saved. Are you good with that?"

"Whatever you'd like, Jon. It's your show."

"I'm glad we've come to this agreement. Goodbye, Dr. Pearl."

He hustled over to his car. His shirt lifted as he climbed in, exposing his big belly. He shut the door and glanced at his new client, who'd remained in the driveway. Pearl wore a frown that hadn't been there moments ago.

Get over it, he nearly said. He'd been born with a belly. Growing up, he'd been left off teams because the coaches thought he was overweight, and shamed by girls because of his looks. That had changed after he became a SEAL. No one in the navy had made fun of his appearance. All that had mattered to the navy was his ability to accomplish a dangerous mission in a hostile environment with an enemy who wished to kill him. On that playing field, he'd had no peers.

Pearl didn't know any of this. For all Pearl knew, he'd just hired a fat bum. He lowered his window.

"Stop worrying," he said, and drove off.

CHAPTER 3

JANEY

Driving toward I-95, he asked Google Maps for instructions to Melbourne so he'd have the quickest route. Shorty would be arriving soon, and he wanted to be there to supervise the search for the missing girl, Janey MacKenzie.

Janey's grandmother, an elderly lady named Sheila Dotson, had hired him to find her missing granddaughter. As payment, Mrs. Dotson had agreed to buy new dishes and cutlery for his apartment, which were sorely needed. Mrs. Dotson lived off her Social Security, so he'd told her to pick the items off the Walmart website, and not spend too much. But first he had to get there. Google was telling him traffic was standing still and that there was no estimated time of arrival. That had disaster written all over it, and he found a Starbucks and called Shorty from the parking lot.

"I'm thirty minutes away," the tracker said. "Where are you?"

"Stuck in Fort Lauderdale," he said. "Call me when you arrive. You can start the search, and I'll direct you with my laptop."

"Sounds like a plan. Did you tell the sheriff I'd be coming?"

"I did, and he okayed it. He also told me that I was wasting my time. I'm looking forward to proving him wrong."

"What an idiot. I'll call you when I pull in."

His next call was to Mrs. Dotson. She whiled away her days on the living room couch with a mangy mutt and a flat screen TV tuned to *The 700 Club*.

"Mrs. Dotson, it's Jon Lancaster. Do you mind turning the TV down?"

The volume was lowered. "Hello, Jon. I hope you're calling with good news."

"We're going to be starting our search soon. I was calling to see if you'd gotten any additional texts from Janey."

"Yes, matter of fact, I did get a text. It was from him."

"The kidnapper?"

"I'm sure of it. He's using Janey's phone and pretending to be her. He said *Grandmom, I'll be home soon.* That's how I knew. Janey calls me Grans. It's her special name for me."

"Did you share the text with the sheriff?"

"And have him say 'I told you so'? No, I didn't. The sheriff is a fool."

"I won't argue with you there. When did you get this text?"

"Two hours ago. Is that significant?"

"It may be. I was knocking on doors earlier today. Maybe our kidnapper found out and got scared. He could have sent you that text to throw me off the scent."

"I pray that you're right. Could Janey be nearby?"

He started to say yes, but bit his tongue. The evidence pointed to a patron of the bar where Janey worked following her home and abducting her, but sharing that with Mrs. Dotson would do nothing but raise her blood pressure.

"We'll soon find out," he said. "I'll call you in a few hours."

"I'll be here, praying," the elderly woman said.

- - -

Google said traffic still wasn't moving. He switched to an app called Waze, which let its users report problems, and saw that a tanker had overturned in the median of I-95 and burst into flames, stopping traffic in both directions. His alternative was to take the Florida Turnpike, but users were reporting more accidents there. He was stuck.

Inside the Starbucks he bought a cup of Pike Place, then took a table and connected his laptop to the free Wi-Fi. He recognized the bearded guy at the next table working on his laptop. Smart criminals knew to change their look. Not this clown.

"Hey, buddy, remember me?" he asked.

"Can't say I do," the bearded one said.

"Last November, Starbucks in Pembroke Pines. You tried to steal the personal information off my laptop while I was using the Wi-Fi, and I hauled you outside to the parking lot and beat the boogers out of you. Remember me now?"

The bearded one swallowed hard. "I'm not doing that stuff anymore."

"Got a job?"

"I'm unemployed at the moment."

"Those are nice clothes for a guy who doesn't have a job. And a really nice watch. I think you're lying. I frequent Starbucks a lot. If I see you again, I'll break something."

"You can't threaten me like that."

"It's not a threat. It's a promise that you can take to the bank."

The bearded one wanted to make a stand, but the beating was still fresh. He slurped down his coffee and went to the exit. Turning, he stared at Lancaster.

"Don't let there be a next time," Lancaster said.

Never turn your back on an asshole. Lancaster had learned that lesson the hard way in Somalia when a SEAL team member had turned his back on a little boy standing outside a hut and nearly gotten Jon and the rest of the team killed. Lancaster watched the bearded one walk across the parking lot, get into his black BMW M3—not the car most unemployed people drove—and leave.

He went back to work. When he wasn't doing private jobs, he worked rescues for Team Adam, a select group of retired law enforcement officers who helped the National Center for Missing and Exploited Children find minors who were victims of abductions. The pay was minimal and the hours long, but in addition to the satisfaction of being part of a team that had the highest success rate of any law enforcement group in the country, he got to use the latest crime-fighting wizardry, courtesy of Uncle Sam.

The most recent tool sat on his laptop, a software mapping program called Collector Application—CA for short. With CA he could supervise search missions without being present during the search. Best of all, CA took the guesswork out of the process, and allowed the search team to home in on what was important.

He pulled up CA and typed in the location where Janey MacKenzie had been last seen. A topographical map of Melbourne appeared on the laptop's screen with a red star indicating the location of the bar where she worked. It was called the Slip Slide. All set, he rang up Shorty. "Where are you?"

"I just reached Melbourne," the tracker said, his pack of bloodhounds baying in the back of his pickup. "You on the road yet?"

"I'm still in Fort Lauderdale. Looks like it's going to be a while before I can get to you. Let's get this party started, shall we?"

"Works for me. I've got my son Hollis and his friend Caleb with me. Hollis has a map of Melbourne on his iPad. Where do you want us to start our search?"

"A bar called Slip Slide on North Eleventh Street. Our missing girl is named Janey MacKenzie, and she disappeared three nights ago after leaving work. But first go to her grandmother's house and introduce yourselves. The old lady's name is Mrs. Dotson, and she has the sheets from Janey's bed that you can use to scent the dogs. Grandmom is super sweet. If you're polite, she'll give you a homemade cookie."

"Got it. You really think this girl isn't out partying somewhere?"

It was a fair question. Key West and South Beach were responsible for many missing-persons cases, their lure as strong as a siren's song, and Janey was a perfect candidate for such an excursion. She had a wild side, her arms covered in sleeves of tattoos, her face a pincushion of piercings. A visit to her grandmother's home, where Janey lived, told another story that had convinced him this was an abduction. Janey was studying business at the community college with the goal of marketing a line of beauty products whose fancy bottles and labels were scattered around the house. And she was helping pay her grandmother's mortgage by working at Slip Slide. Janey had accepted the responsibilities of adulthood, and people like that didn't run off on a moment's notice.

"That was what I first thought," he replied. "This young lady's different. She sent some texts, but they don't sound like her."

"You think the kidnapper's sending them?"

"I do. Call me after you go see Mrs. Dotson."

"You got it."

Lancaster ended the call. He was nearing the end of the hunt and could feel the mixture of elation and dread that always greeted him. If they found Janey safe, champagne for all. But if she was found dead or badly hurt, the ending would be as uplifting as a David Lynch movie. Thirty minutes later, Shorty rang him back.

"We just left Mrs. Dotson's. She let the dogs sniff the girl's bedsheets. We're ready when you are."

"Do your dogs have their GPS collars on?" he asked.

"Of course. This isn't my first rodeo, Jon."

"Sorry." He minimized the Collector Application program on his laptop's screen and then pulled up another program called Traccar. Traccar was a GPS tracking platform that let him monitor the bloodhounds' search for Janey in real time. None of these gadgets had been in use when he'd been a cop, which was why so many missing-persons cases he'd worked on had hit dead ends. That was then, this was now. A second map of Melbourne appeared on his laptop screen, courtesy of Traccar. He counted five tiny flashing red dots on the screen, all of them congregated around the same spot.

"How many dogs did you bring with you?" he asked.

"I brought six of my best," Shorty said.

"Only five are showing on my computer screen. One of the collars isn't turned on. Five bucks says it's one of Caleb's dogs."

"You think so?"

"I sure do. Go check."

"Hold on." Silence, then, "Damn, it was one of Caleb's. How'd you know that?"

"I've worked with you and your son before, and you've never screwed up. Caleb is new, so it stood to reason that it was one of his dogs that didn't have the GPS tracking device turned on. Now let's see if we can find this missing young lady. Start with the area around the Slip Slide. I'll be watching from my laptop."

"Sounds good. Wish us luck."

"Good luck."

He ended the call, then bought a double espresso and sucked it down. He was about to turn forty-two, and the late-afternoon caffeine jolt had gone from habit to ritual. But he had to be careful; too much caffeine made him as charming as a rattlesnake.

He stared at the flashing dots on his laptop's screen. Janey did not own a car and drove her grandmother's aging Corolla to work. On the night of Janey's disappearance, her grandmother had needed the car to go grocery shopping, forcing Janey to walk to work, a distance of about a mile. Melbourne was a sleepy burg with little crime, which was why her disappearance later, after she left work, should have been cause for alarm. But Janey's reputation for being flirtatious—"Only way a girl can make money in this town," her grandmother had declared—had been enough reason for the lazy sheriff to convince himself that Janey was shacking up down in the Keys.

The caffeine hit his system hard. There was always the chance that Janey was dead, but his gut told him that wasn't the case. Janey's abductor had done a good job of making his victim disappear, and that wasn't easy. If you were going to spend the time planning an abduction, you wanted a reward. Keeping Janey alive was that reward.

The red dots moved across his screen like a video game. Jimmy Buffett singing the virtues of drinking and screwing filled the air, and he answered the call.

"Hello, Jon. This is Nolan Pearl," his caller said.

He turned away from his laptop. "Is everything all right?"

"We're okay. I spoke to the police, and they wrote up a report and said they'd get back to me. I left your name out of it."

"I appreciate that."

"I know you're working another case, but could you come back to the house for a few minutes? I explained to my wife that I planned to hire you, and she got angry with me for not consulting her first."

"Your wife wants to talk with me?"

"Yes. Melanie's very protective of our daughter, as I'm sure you can understand. She was on the end of the dock and saw you shoot the man steering the boat. It scared the daylights out of her."

He frowned into the phone. "Then tell her to hire someone else."

"Please. It'll just take a few minutes."

"What do you want me to do, crack some jokes, make your wife feel better? That's not who I am, and quite frankly, that isn't what you need here."

"She just wants to talk with you and set her mind at ease."

He nearly told Pearl to take a hike, but he restrained himself. His business was word-of-mouth; every time he blew off a client, it cost him down the road. If he didn't go see Pearl, he'd just stay here, and get wired on more coffee.

"I'll come, but I want you to tell your wife something," he said.

"What's that?" Pearl said.

"I'm not your friend."

"Then what are you?"

"I'm your weapon. See you soon."

- - -

He'd worked undercover for the Broward Sheriff's Office for a decade and developed a sixth sense for sniffing out bad guys. Leaving the Starbucks, he spied a black BMW M3 with tinted windows parked in the corner of the lot. His instinct told him the bearded guy had returned and was itching to get back inside and steal the personal information of the next unsuspecting customer who booted up his laptop. That was the problem with people who stole for a living. They'd figured out that crime really did pay. To stop them, you had to punish them, and you had to do it in a way that they'd never forget. As a cop, he'd been restricted from doing that. Not anymore.

He circled the block and a minute later was back in the Starbucks lot. Through the front window he spied the bearded guy sitting at a table by himself and went inside. Coming up from behind, he boxed the bearded one's ears with the palms of his hands, causing him to pitch forward and smash his face against the keyboard. Boxing didn't leave any bruises, but it would make a person's ears ring for a while.

Going outside, he ran over the bearded one's laptop with his car, the crunching sound bringing a smile to his lips. He spied the miscreant standing in the window, holding a bloodied napkin to his face.

He waved as he drove away.

CHAPTER 4
SOFT SPOT

Pearl met him at the front door wearing the sheepish expression of a man who'd just lost an argument with his wife. "Thank you for coming back. Melanie is anxious to meet you. This situation has made her a nervous wreck."

Lancaster grunted under his breath. He didn't like kissing ass, but on rare occasions he made exceptions. He followed Pearl through the house.

"May I offer you something to drink?" his host asked.

"No, thanks. Look, I can't stay long. We've started our search in Melbourne and I need to focus my energy on that."

Pearl stopped and spun around. "You must think we're being very insensitive."

"No, you're being parents. I get that. I just happen to have another priority right now. Once it's over, which hopefully will be soon, I can give you my full attention."

"You seem confident you're going to find this woman in Melbourne."

"I am."

He didn't try to explain. He knew when his hunches were going to pay off, even when the rest of the world thought he was wrong.

Melanie Pearl awaited them on the lanai. She was an attractive woman with a short haircut and a trim figure, and he guessed she'd once been a nurse. It was only a guess, based upon the fact that nearly every male doctor he knew was married to a nurse, the profession producing a lot of couples. She looked her guest up and down and could not hide her displeasure.

"Thank you for saving my daughter's life," she said stiffly.

"Thank your husband. He called me."

"Very well. Please have a seat."

"No, thanks. I'm not staying for long. Your husband says you have a problem with his decision to hire me. Why is that?"

"How should I put this? You seem rather coarse. My daughter has been traumatized, and I don't want to make things worse for her. Do you understand?"

"Not really."

She chewed her lower lip, unsure of how to proceed. Her dilemma was written all over her face. Her vision of what her daughter's protector should look like didn't resemble the man standing before her.

"If I clean myself up and wear a nice shirt, will that work?" he asked.

"Is that an attempt to be sarcastic?"

"Look, Melanie, I won't pretend to be something that I'm not. What you see is what you get, warts and all. Take it or leave it."

She shot her husband a look. Pearl struggled to find the words that would convince her this was the right decision. Lancaster decided to help him out.

"Let's cut to the chase. The two men in the cigarette boat were not normal kidnappers. Kidnappers want ransom money, and if they sense a problem, they switch targets. These men have another reason for wanting Nicki. Once I understand what their motive is, I'll figure out a way to stop them."

"You've dealt with men like this before."

"Many times."

She hesitated. "Can I think about this?"

"Take your time. It's only your daughter's life."

"You're not making this any easier."

He'd muted his cell phone before coming into the house, and it now vibrated in his pocket. He excused himself and stepped off the lanai into the house to stare at the screen. Shorty had texted him. The bloodhounds had picked up Janey's scent five blocks away from Slip Slide in a quiet residential street, only to have the trail go cold.

A Traccar app resided on his cell phone. With it, he'd be able to see for himself where the red dots had converged. A blank screen stared back at him. No Wi-Fi service. He went back onto the lanai to find Pearl and his wife having a heated debate.

"Do you have a house Wi-Fi that I can connect to?" he asked. "My case in Melbourne is about to break open, and I need to see what's going on."

Pearl gave him the password. Lancaster went into settings on his cell phone and entered it. No luck. His phone had a mind all its own, while his laptop tended to obey its master. He went outside to his car and got on his laptop while sitting behind the wheel. He entered the password and this time had better luck.

Pearl appeared at his window. "Are you working your other case?"

"Yes, I am."

"Would you mind coming back inside? I want my wife to see you in action."

"She doesn't like me. I can't change that."

"But I can. Please."

Pearl had a pleading look in his eyes. Lancaster had only one soft spot, and it was for people in trouble. He caved and followed Pearl back inside to the study. Melanie stood by a window, staring out at the crowded paradise that was South Florida.

"Melanie, I want you to see this," Pearl said.

She moved to her husband's side. Lancaster placed his laptop on the desk so its screen faced his hosts. Then he opened the Traccar app, and the map of Melbourne appeared, the red dots converged around a single spot.

"What are we looking at?" she asked.

"A cocktail waitress named Janey MacKenzie went missing three nights ago," he said. "The local sheriff thinks Janey's shacking up with a guy, and will show up in a few days. Her grandmother is convinced she was abducted, and hired me to find her."

"Is the grandmother right?"

"Yes." He pointed at the red dots. "These are a pack of bloodhounds with GPS trackers attached to their collars. They picked up Janey's scent on a street between the cocktail lounge where Janey worked and her grandmother's house, then the trail stopped. Here's what I think happened. Janey was walking home after work and was approached by a patron offering to give her a lift. She accepted, and got into his car. He knocked her out and took her home. That's my guess, anyway."

"Do you think she's dead?"

He shook his head. Janey's abductor coveted her. Unless Janey angered him, he'd keep her alive until she no longer satisfied his perverse cravings, which might be several days or longer. Knowing that a patron was the culprit thinned the pool of suspects. But the bar was popular and had several dozen regulars.

He minimized the Traccar app and went into his video library. A black-and-white surveillance video taken of the Slip Slide's parking lot appeared on his screen. The video was time-stamped and had been taken three nights ago. He had an idea and hit the Play icon.

"This is the cocktail lounge's parking lot, taken the night Janey went missing," he said. "Unfortunately, the light's poor and it's hard to make much out."

"What exactly are you looking for?" Melanie asked.

"I want to determine the makes of cars that were at the bar. Most of the patrons live in town. Some walk to the bar after work, others ride motorcycles. Only a few drive cars. If I can learn the makes, I'll contact the bartender on duty that night, and see if he can identify the owners. That should narrow down our pool of suspects."

"Got it."

The video continued to play. After a minute a door to the bar opened and a patron came outside. Light from inside the bar flooded the parking lot, and Lancaster froze the frame. Four vehicles were parked in the lot, but he was unable to determine the makes.

"Do you have a magnifying glass?" he asked.

Pearl produced a magnifying glass from his desk. Lancaster used it to study the frame and was able to make out two pickup trucks, a Mustang, and a vintage Corvette. He borrowed a pad and pen, and wrote down the makes along with any identifying dents or bumper stickers. He started to shut down the video, then had another idea, and sped the video up so the time stamp said 12:00 a.m.

"What are you doing now?" Melanie asked.

"Janey MacKenzie got off work at midnight and walked home. I want to see if any of the vehicles left right after her. That may very well be our suspect."

"Got it."

The video played for several minutes. It was too dark to see much of anything, and he waited for another patron to leave the bar. At 12:10 a.m., a man stumbled out, flooding the parking lot in light. Lancaster again froze the frame and studied it with the magnifying glass. The Pearls leaned in as well, their breath tingling the back of his neck.

"I see four cars," Melanie Pearl said.

"So do I," her husband said. "Could you be wrong about this, Jon?"

Lancaster heard his own sharp intake of breath. He *was* wrong. Janey's abductor hadn't used a car, he'd been on foot, and had intercepted Janey during her walk home. Janey was petite, maybe a hundred pounds soaking wet. Light enough for a big man to throw over his shoulder and carry home down a darkened street. That was why the trail had gone cold. He called Shorty.

"She's in the neighborhood. Fan out, and start looking," he said.

CHAPTER 5

NIMBS

Lancaster leaned back in his chair, deep in thought. Carrying a one-hundred-pound woman on your back was tough, even for a man in great shape. To become a SEAL, he had been required to run a mile and a half in nine minutes. Then in training camp, he had to run the same time wearing boots and long pants. It had been brutal, and he could only imagine how challenging carrying a person on his back would be. He couldn't see Janey's abductor traveling more than half a mile before growing exhausted.

He used Google to check traffic to Melbourne. Interstate 95 was still a parking lot. It was more important that he stay connected to Shorty's bloodhounds on his laptop, which he couldn't do while stuck behind the wheel of his car. He needed to stay put for a while.

He turned around in his chair. His hosts hadn't moved, and were so quiet that you would have thought they were in an operating room watching open-heart surgery.

"I hate to impose, but can I stay here? We're close to finding her."

"Can you really find a missing person on your computer?" Melanie Pearl asked.

"Yes. With the right help."

"Of course you can stay. Would you like a drink? I just made some iced tea."

"Please. Spike it with rat killer."

She raised her eyebrows, his humor lost on her.

"Artificial sweetener, if you have it. It makes me think better."

"You have a strange sense of humor," she said.

Movement caught his eye. The red dots were all over his laptop's screen, the bloodhounds fanning out. In the old days, it would take a search party to find a missing person. Now, just a few dogs and the right software program. It was like playing a video game with life-and-death consequences.

A cold nose touched his wrist. The guard dog had snuck in and was checking him out. Nicki Pearl trailed behind it, her eyes glued on their guest. A nasty bruise on her forehead was the only sign of her recent brush with darkness. Her father motioned her closer. Nicki ignored him and kept her distance.

"Who is this?"

"This is Mr. Lancaster, the man who saved you this afternoon."

Lancaster petted the dog's head and smiled. Nicki's fear ebbed, and she stepped forward and offered her hand. South Florida was a tough place to raise kids with all the bad influences and sick degenerates running around. Nicki exuded a rare innocence, and he wondered how long her parents would be able to keep her this way.

"Thank you, Mr. Lancaster," Nicki said. "Are you a policeman?"

"Call me Jon. I was once. I work for myself now, helping people like you."

"I'm taking a CSI course at school. It's really cool."

"They teach CSI at your school? That's great."

"It's part of the biology curriculum. What do those red dots on your laptop mean? Are you working a case?"

"Those red dots are a pack of bloodhounds wearing GPS collars that are helping me find a missing girl in Melbourne."

"Wow. Can I watch?"

"That's up to your parents."

Nicki looked to her father for permission. Pearl glanced at his wife, who'd returned with a tray of iced teas. Melanie nodded, and Pearl said, "Of course, honey."

The teenager pulled up a chair next to Lancaster and stared at the screen.

"A young woman named Janey MacKenzie went missing three nights ago while walking home from the cocktail lounge where she works," he said. "I'm pretty certain that a customer abducted her, so I hired a tracker to use his bloodhounds to find her."

"Why are the dogs wearing GPS collars? How does that help?"

The kid was sharp. The GPS collars didn't help Shorty, but they did help him. Leaving the Traccar app running, he opened the Collector Application software program and began adding data overlays to the map of Melbourne on the screen. Each overlay was a different color that visually illuminated the screen. "This is a software mapping tool that lets me add layers of data to my search map. Do you know what the biggest problem finding a missing person is? Too much information. If the searcher can't bring all his information together, he'll miss valuable clues. Make sense?"

"Like putting all the pieces of a puzzle together," Nicki said.

"Exactly. The first overlay in yellow shows the areas where the police searched the night Janey went missing, so we can eliminate those. The second overlay in blue shows the addresses of registered sexual offenders in Melbourne. Each time the bloodhounds pick up Janey's scent, we'll be able to see if it's near any bad guy who might have hurt a young woman before."

"You mean a pervert," Nicki said.

"Correct. The third overlay in pink shows the locations where people have been abducted and killed in Melbourne in the past. If we find a match with that overlay, it might mean that we're dealing with a serial killer."

Nicki squirmed in her chair. "Do you think a serial killer did this?"

"No, I don't. There haven't been any abductions in Melbourne in over a decade, so the chances are slim that this is the work of a serial killer. But you can never be too careful, so I always include it."

The overlays softened the red hue of the dots so they were barely visible. Nicki pointed at the dot on the left side of the screen, on the western side of downtown.

"That one's stopped moving," she said. "Is that significant?"

Lack of movement could mean many things. A hit, or perhaps one of the dogs had stopped to relieve himself. "Let's check," he said. His cell phone lay facedown on the desk so he would not be distracted by incoming emails or news alerts. He turned the cell phone over to see if he'd gotten a text. As he did, it lit up. Shorty was calling him.

"We got a hit from a garbage can in an alley," the tracker said.

The breath caught in his throat. Had he been wrong? Had Janey been knocked over the head, killed, and thrown away? He'd been wrong on cases before, but this time it was different; he'd connected with the grandmother on an emotional level, and breaking the news to her that Janey had perished would hurt him deeply as well.

"You see a body?" he asked.

"Lid's off. I'm shining my flashlight in it. I see women's clothes."

The air in his lungs escaped. "Describe them."

"Black jeans, red halter top, a pair of pink Keds."

"Any sign of blood?"

"Not that I can see. No."

"Don't touch anything. The same for your son and his friend."

"You don't have to tell me that, Jon."

"No harm in reminding you. You said the can was in an alley. Any idea which house it might belong to?"

"It belongs to 1249 Rachel Court. It's spray-painted on the side."

"Beautiful. I'll call you right back."

He ended the call. Missing-persons cases were like roller-coaster rides that were filled with emotional highs and lows that came at you without warning. The low had become a high, and he planned to keep it that way. Janey's abductor had stripped away her clothes, knowing she was less likely to run away while naked. She had been turned into a sex slave, was his guess. Based upon everything her grandmother had said, Janey would play along until an opportunity to summon help presented itself.

"Is she still alive?" Nicki asked tentatively.

"I think so. Now we have to save her." His fingers typed the address into Google. A reverse directory site named Spokeo came up with the desired information. 1249 Rachel Court was a one-bedroom dwelling with a single-car garage with an appraised value of $85,550. The owner was named Ryan Wayne Nimbs.

"Is he the bad guy?" Nicki asked.

"Could be. Let's check the sexual offender overlay."

He single-finger-typed a command. Tiny stars appeared on the pink sexual offender overlay on the screen. Each star represented a current resident of Melbourne who'd been arrested for a sexual offense at some point during their life. There were enough of them to start a support group. None lived on Rachel Court.

"He's not there," Nicki said. "Maybe it isn't him."

Or maybe the sexual offender registry had missed Nimbs. The Sunshine State, home of endless sandy beaches and amusement parks, was also a breeding ground for sexual predators, and the state didn't have the resources to track all of them. He minimized the screen, got on the internet, and pulled up mugshots.com. If Nimbs had been arrested for sexual assault or kidnapping, a record of it would be here. He typed in his suspect's full name and hit "Enter."

"Wow, there he is," Nicki said breathlessly.

Nimbs's mug shot filled the screen. Spiked hair and a face like a blunt instrument with a Neanderthal slant. A hideous neck tattoo of a skull with a dragon's mouth spitting out a serpent. Thirty-four years old, six foot three, 230 pounds. One arrest for false imprisonment and rape, which had led to a stretch in prison. Additional arrests for lewd and lascivious behavior and assault. A really bad hombre.

"He must be your abductor," Pearl said, breaking his silence. "Are you going to alert the police, and have him arrested?"

Lancaster closed his laptop and stood up. He would make a call, but not to the police. Nimbs's absence from the sexual offender registry may have been accidental, or it may have been deliberately omitted by someone in the Melbourne Police Department who knew Nimbs or was related to him. Melbourne was a backwater town, and those things happened. He had friends at the Florida Department of Law Enforcement office in West Palm Beach. He'd call them instead.

"I need to run. Thank you for your hospitality," he said.

The Pearls followed him into the foyer. Their faces were filled with apprehension, and he thought he knew why. He had won their trust, and now they felt safe. As long as he was in their presence, no harm would come to Nicki. But the moment he left, the fear of Nicki being abducted would return with a vengeance.

"Goodbye," he said.

"Are you going to help me?" Nicki blurted out.

His eyes met Melanie Pearl's. She had teared up and nodded vigorously.

"Yes, Nicki, I'm going to help you," he said. "In the meantime, I want you to stay inside the house. No more sunbathing by the pool." She agreed, and he addressed her parents. "I want you to pull Nicki out of school until this situation gets resolved. One or both of you need to be with her when she's away from home. Preferably both of you."

Her parents said yes. It was all he could do for now. He shot Nicki a parting glance. He still had no idea why she was being targeted. Normally, he would have a clue by now. But maybe Nicki did. Maybe she was holding back out of fear that her parents would become angry with her. It was time to press her.

"Nicki, I want you to be honest with me. Why are these men after you?"

Nicki swallowed hard. "I don't know. I just know that they're evil."

Yes, they are, he thought, and said goodnight.

CHAPTER 6

DELUSIONS OF GRANDEUR

Pearl bolted the front door after Lancaster was gone. He glanced at his wife and daughter and managed to smile. This crazy situation was going to get worked out, he was sure of it. "What do you say we find a funny movie to watch on Netflix?" he suggested.

"But it's a school night," his wife protested.

"Jon said that Nicki needed to stay home until this situation gets resolved. No harm in staying up late if we don't have to get up in the morning."

"Aren't you going to work tomorrow?" his wife asked.

"I'm not scheduled for any surgeries. I'll ask one of the other neurosurgeons to check up on my patients and make sure everyone's okay. If there's a problem, I'll run over to the hospital and deal with it. Otherwise, I'm staying right here."

Nicki tugged on his wrist. "Can I pick the movie?"

"You most certainly can. Do you have something in mind?"

"*Blind Date IV*. I hear it's really funny."

Pearl shot his wife a look and saw Melanie roll her eyes. It felt fantastic to be talking about normal things again and not dwelling on the dangers that lurked right outside their door. He said yes, and his daughter squealed with delight.

The doorbell made them jump. Pearl stuck his eye to the peephole. A Latina wearing a tan-colored pantsuit stood on the other side, a detective's badge pinned to her jacket lapel. Her partner was a Caucasian male with afro-style hair.

"Who is it?" his wife asked.

"Looks like a couple of detectives with the Broward police," he said. "Maybe they've made a break in the case."

"From your lips to God's ears."

"Let me talk to them. You and Nicki have been through enough."

"I think that's a wonderful idea," his wife said. "Come on, Nicki. Let's go make some popcorn to eat with our movie."

Pearl waited until they were gone before ushering his visitors inside. The female detective was named Vargas, her partner Gibbons. They were about as friendly as a pair of junkyard dogs, and he got the distinct impression that they would have been happier belting back a stiff drink at a local watering hole than talking with him.

Vargas reeked of cigarettes, the foul smell pouring off her skin and breath. She produced a sheet of copy paper and held it up to Pearl's face. On it was a photo taken off a surveillance camera that showed Pearl and Lancaster riding in the Donzi.

"Your neighbor called 911 earlier and reported gunshots," Vargas said. "Same neighbor has a surveillance camera pointed at her dock, and got a video of you and your friend flying by in your boat. That's a Donzi, isn't it?"

Pearl nodded while staring at the photo. It had been taken before Lancaster drew his gun and shot at the kidnappers. "I filed a report with the sheriff's office about what happened. What does this have to do with it?"

His words carried the hint of accusation. The detectives stiffened.

"We read your statement, Dr. Pearl, and it didn't mention that you'd hired Jon Lancaster," Vargas said. "That was a mistake."

"Who said I hired Jon Lancaster?" Pearl said.

"He was with you in the boat. We assumed you had."

"Well, you assumed wrong. I've spoken to a number of security companies, including Lancaster's. Jon happened to be in my home when Nicki was abducted, and he jumped in the boat with me. He was actually quite helpful."

"Then why did you leave Lancaster out of your statement?" Vargas asked.

"I didn't realize that I had. My apologies."

"Did he fire his gun at the kidnappers?" Vargas asked.

"Not that I remember."

"I think you'd remember a gun being fired," Vargas said.

"The engine on my Donzi is quite loud. If Jon fired a gun, I didn't hear it."

The detectives looked stymied. They seemed intent on pinning a charge on Jon when none was warranted. Pearl hid a smile, feeling proud of himself. Jon had mentioned there was a pair of detectives he was on bad terms with, and he guessed this was them. Pearl didn't know what the dispute was, nor did he care. Jon's quick thinking had saved his daughter, and Pearl was going to protect him however he could.

"Are we done?" Pearl asked.

"Are you planning to hire Jon?" Vargas asked.

"Why is that any concern of yours?"

"Because hiring Lancaster is a bad idea," she said. "He's mentally ill and suffers from a delusional disorder. He thinks he's the greatest cop that ever lived, and is happy to tell you so. But it's not true. Lancaster was a terrible policeman, and had to be let go."

There were six common delusional disorders. The one Vargas had described was called grandiosity and was more common in men than it was in women. Jon had talked a good game, and was certainly good with a handgun, but had it all been a show?

"Why was he let go?" Pearl asked skeptically.

"He had a drinking problem and anger issues," Vargas said. "His folder was filled with complaints filed against him by citizens and by other cops that he worked with. It finally got to be too much, and he was asked to turn in his badge."

"He was fired, is what you're saying."

"Yes, he was."

"There's a video on YouTube of Jon rescuing a young girl from a pair of kidnappers. How do you explain that?"

"That was his shining moment," Vargas said, her tone softening. "Lancaster happened to be in the right place at the right time, and saved that little girl's life. He was a hero that day and did the sheriff's office proud. But trust me, Dr. Pearl, it could just as easily have broken bad, and that little girl been wounded or killed. He'll tell you he's the greatest marksman in the world, but he's not. It's part of his illness."

"But he was a Navy SEAL."

Gibbons laughed under his breath. Vargas shot her partner a disapproving look before turning her gaze on Pearl.

"Another delusion, I'm afraid," Vargas said. "Lancaster was in the navy and tried to become a SEAL several times but failed the physical exam. I don't mean to be cruel, but he doesn't have the physique. A SEAL is required to do a thousand push-ups in an hour, among other things. He simply isn't capable."

"You're saying he was a washout," Pearl said.

"That's right. Only he's convinced himself otherwise. That's what makes him so dangerous. He thinks he knows what he's doing, but he doesn't."

Pearl's shoulders sagged, and he let out an exasperated breath. Jon's promises had seemed too good to be true, and for good reason. The poor man was off his rocker.

"I see. Well, I appreciate you taking the time to come by and tell me."

"We thought it was best you know. Goodbye, Dr. Pearl," Vargas said.

Pearl escorted them outside to where a gray Buick LeSabre was parked in the driveway. Vargas took the keys out of her pocket, then spoke. "Did Lancaster discharge his firearm when he was on your boat? Please be honest with us."

Pearl's mouth tightened. The detectives wanted to take Jon down, and Pearl's admission that Jon had shot his gun would be enough evidence for them to do that. But he wasn't going to rat him out. Jon might be a fake, but that didn't change the magnitude of his courage that afternoon, nor lessen the debt that Pearl owed him for saving Nicki.

"No, he did not," he said firmly. "By the way, has the sheriff's office made any progress in my daughter's case?"

"The department's working on it. We'll be in touch."

- - -

Pearl watched the detectives drive away before going inside. Melanie awaited him in the foyer with Nicki by her side.

"I was right, there is something wrong with him," his wife said.

Pearl wanted to have this conversation alone with his wife. Only the fear had returned to Nicki's eyes, and he couldn't bring himself to tell her to go to her room.

"Daddy, is Jon a bad man?" his daughter asked.

"If those detectives are to believed, he's mentally ill," Pearl said.

"You don't sound convinced," his wife said.

Pearl bolted the door before heading toward the rear of the house with his wife and daughter on his heels. "I'm not. They seem more intent on hurting Jon than helping us."

"They came here to warn us. Jon's not right in the head. He fired a gun while you were racing your boat and could have killed an innocent person. It was reckless."

Pearl was tired, and he was confused. He dropped onto the couch in the den and rubbed his face. "He saved Nicki's life. Doesn't that count for something?"

"Of course it does. But that doesn't change the fact that this man is not mentally stable. I sensed it the moment I met him. Surely you thought the same thing."

Pearl didn't know what to think. Jon had seemed like a loser until Nicki was abducted. Then he'd sprung into action and made things right. It had been inspiring to watch. But Melanie didn't know that; she hadn't been there to experience it.

His wife stood in front of him. "I want you to fire him."

"Right now?" he asked tiredly.

"Yes, right now. We need to hire someone else."

"Jon's in Melbourne working a job. I'll do it tomorrow morning, first thing."

They never fought in front of their daughter. Melanie's eyes narrowed.

"You've got to get rid of him," she said.

"Yes, dear," he said.

"Hey—don't I get a say in this?" Nicki said.

His daughter stood by the fireplace with the shepherd protectively by her side. Her hands were balled into fists, and her cheeks had turned bright red. It had been years since she'd thrown a tantrum, and Pearl had almost forgotten what they looked like.

"Go ahead," Pearl said.

"I don't want you to fire him," his daughter said.

"But he's dangerous," her mother said. "He could harm you."

"Don't believe those detectives. There's nothing wrong with him," Nicki said.

The CSI class had made his daughter adept at reading situations, and Pearl sat straight up. "Do you think the detectives were lying?"

She nodded vigorously. "Yes, Daddy. I do."

"Why do you think that?"

"I did some sleuthing and googled him. He was mentioned in an article about a rescue of a little girl in Jacksonville. The article said Jon worked for Team Adam. My CSI teacher said Team Adam was the best retired law enforcement agents around. They wouldn't take someone who was mentally ill, would they?"

Her reasoning was sound, and her father nodded in agreement.

"Those detectives made up that story. Jon's the real deal. Please don't fire him."

"Your mother and I need to discuss this some more. We won't make any decisions without consulting with you. Does that sound fair?"

Nicki chewed her lower lip in thought. "Okay."

"Good. Now let's watch that movie."

Nicki went into the kitchen to get the popcorn. Melanie dropped onto the couch beside her husband, and laid her hand atop his.

"Are you okay?" Pearl asked.

"I don't know what I am. Angry, frustrated, mostly confused."

He took the remote off the coffee table and powered up the TV.

"Welcome to the club," he said.

CHAPTER 7
DOMINO'S DELIVERS

"Not all superheroes wear capes." That had been the tagline for a Domino's Pizza advertising campaign that Lancaster had always liked. He'd liked it so much that he'd purchased a Domino's deliveryman's uniform, cap, and thermal insulated pizza bag from a seller on eBay and kept them in the trunk of his car for jobs where he needed a disguise. The uniform was a bad fit, and made his belly look more pronounced than it actually was.

Melbourne was a town of quiet streets and modest houses. Nimbs's place was small and unassuming, and Lancaster parked in front and left the engine running and the headlights on, just like a regular Domino's driver would do. Before getting out, he texted the FDLE agents helping him, and got an immediate reply. The cavalry was ready. He texted back:

Give me two minutes

Getting out of the car, he straightened the cap that didn't want to stay put on his head, then took the pizza bag off the back seat and balanced it on his upturned palm as he headed up the front path. A quick glance told him everything he needed to know about their suspect's state of mind. Weeds instead of grass, litter in the bushes, a mailbox stuffed with yellowing flyers. Nimbs was a loser.

But that didn't mean Nimbs didn't have street smarts. Underestimating a suspect's cunning had cost more than one law enforcement officer his life. Reaching the front stoop, he removed a slip of paper from his pocket and held it up to his face, as if checking the address. Just in case there was a hidden surveillance camera under an eave.

The front porch light came on before he could knock. The door opened a foot, and Nimbs stuck his ugly puss out. He'd lost his upper front teeth since his mug shot and looked like a gargoyle. His breath reeked of beer and reefer.

"Hi. Thanks for ordering Domino's Pizza," he said with a smile.

"I didn't order a fucking pizza," Nimbs said.

He squinted at the piece of paper in his hand. "Is this 1249 Rachel?"

"Yeah. Like I said, I didn't order no fucking pizza."

"I'm sorry, sir. We got an order for a large meat lover's and an order of garlic knots for this address. I guess one of your neighbors was playing a prank."

"My neighbors are assholes. Aren't you a little old to be delivering pizzas?"

"It pays the bills. Look, if you don't take it, I'll have to throw it out. It just came out of the oven ten minutes ago. You want it?"

"Free?"

"I'll charge you half."

"Up yours."

"All right, you can have it for free. I'm not going to eat it."

"Why—is there something wrong with it?"

"If you smelled pizza all day long, you'd get sick of it too." He unzipped the pouch and pulled out an empty box. Nimbs dropped his guard and swung open the door. A clear view of the inside presented itself, and Lancaster spied a tactical shotgun leaning against the wall plus several pistols lying on different tables around the room.

The sound of the back door being hit with a battering ram shattered the silence. Not being a cop had its advantages. He didn't have to identify himself, nor did he have to give any warning. Reaching behind his back, he drew the Sig Sauer from where it was tucked in his pants, and aimed it at Nimbs's chest.

"Hands behind your head."

Nimbs did as told. "Aren't you going to read me my rights?"

No one was paying him to follow the law or obey its rules, and he drove his foot into his suspect's groin. Nimbs yelped and sank to his knees.

"Good boy."

Nimbs wore a wife-beater T-shirt, and his arms were covered with tattoos. The one proclaiming him to be a member of the American Foundation caught Lancaster's eye. American Foundation was a notorious sovereign-citizen group, which didn't believe in the government or the rule of law. He pressed the Sig's barrel against Nimbs's nose.

"Is the back of your house booby-trapped?"

Nimbs's eyes flashed, but he said nothing.

"Tell me, or I'll decorate the walls with your brains."

"There's a trip wire in the kitchen," Nimbs said.

"What's it attached to?"

"A hand grenade."

He pistol-whipped Nimbs and sent him sprawling on his back. Then he ran down a hallway to the kitchen to see FDLE Special Agent Tim Byrne and his SWAT team taking down the fortified back door and coming toward him.

"Kitchen's booby-trapped," he shouted.

Byrne and company beat a hasty retreat. He ran back to the front of the house to find Nimbs crawling on his belly down the front path like a slug. Instead of grabbing one of his guns and shooting it out, he'd fled like a coward.

"I'm back."

Nimbs stopped crawling and covered his head with his arms. "Don't shoot me."

"Where is she?"

"I don't know what—"

A sharp kick to the kidney silenced him. "I won't ask you again. I want to know where Janey MacKenzie is, and if the room where you're hiding her is booby-trapped." When an answer was not forthcoming, he knelt down and shoved the Sig's barrel into the crack of his suspect's ass. It was an old SEAL trick that produced immediate results.

"I'm going to count to three. One. Two."

"There's a secret sliding wall in the bedroom closet," Nimbs said, his voice trembling with fear. "She's behind it. It's not wired."

"Are there any other booby traps in the house?" he asked.

"No."

The barrel was shoved in another inch. "Don't lie to me."

"So help me God it's the truth."

"God isn't helping you."

"There ain't any more."

The SWAT team surrounded them, and Lancaster climbed off Nimbs and hurried inside. The house had a shotgun layout, and he found the lone bedroom off the hallway and switched on an overhead light. Piles of dirty clothes littered the floor. His eyes searched for another booby trap, and he only entered after determining it was safe.

The closet door was ajar. He entered and rapped on the walls until he found one that was hollow. By pressing on the wall with his palms, he made it slide to one side. He moved down a corridor to a small space with a bare bulb dangling from the ceiling.

"Sweet Jesus," he whispered.

Janey lay on her side on a cot, naked. Her eyes were closed, and she wasn't breathing. Nimbs had grown tired of her, and tied a noose around her neck and threaded the rope down her back, binding her wrists and ankles. As her muscles had cramped, her legs had straightened to relieve themselves of the pain, leading to self-strangulation.

His eyes burning, he cut the ropes away with his pocket knife. The image of Mrs. Dotson waiting on her couch flashed through his mind. How was he going to break the news to her? He didn't know. As he pulled the rope away, a soft gurgling sound escaped from Janey's throat. He grabbed her shoulders and gave them a gentle shake. Her eyes snapped open, and she looked fearfully around the room, then at him. He removed his cap and placed it on the floor.

"Hi, Janey. My name is Jon, and I'm a private investigator. Your grandmother hired me to find you. How do you feel?"

"He hurt me," she whispered.

"I'm sorry, Janey. He's not going to hurt you anymore."

The SWAT team had entered the bedroom, and Byrne was calling his name. He didn't want them to see Janey like this, so he unbuttoned his shirt and draped it over her. She curled up beneath its protection, her eyes fixed on his belly. She slowly lifted her arm and he let her fingers touch his hairless stomach.

"Feels like rocks," she whispered.

- - -

He followed the ambulance to the Holmes Regional Medical Center and hung around the ER until a silver-haired doctor came out to the waiting room and spoke to him. Janey had been physically and sexually abused. But she had a strong will and would come out of this intact, the doctor said, thinking Lancaster was a relative. They shook hands and he left.

Shelia Dotson lived in a cinder-block house with a light burning brightly in the front window. Parking at the curb, he got out. It was late, and a neighbor's dog barked because it had nothing better to do. He walked across the lawn to the front window and peeked inside. His client was asleep in a wingback chair while *Christian Worship Hour* saved souls on the TV. He didn't want to startle her, so he called her number. Through the window he saw the cell phone in her lap light up. She snapped out of a deep slumber and raised the cell phone to stare at the caller ID. A look of shock registered on her face.

"Jon, is that you?" she answered.

"It sure is," he said.

"Oh my God, there's a man at my front window."

"It's me, Mrs. Dotson. I'm standing outside your house."

The elderly woman sprang out of her chair and approached the window. A pair of bifocals hung around her neck, and she fitted them on her nose.

"You have news about my granddaughter," she said.

"I do indeed."

A split second later she was outside, huddled beside him. She was small and brittle, the top of her head barely reaching his chest. In a trembling voice she said, "You're smiling. My sweet Janey is alive, isn't she?"

"Alive and kicking. I just left her at the hospital."

Her hands were balled into fists, and she brought them to her mouth. "Is she hurt? Please don't lie to me."

"She's been through hell and back, but the doctor I spoke to says she's strong and should heal. Now go put some clothes on. Your granddaughter needs you."

"I'll do that. Wait. I'm not allowed to drive at night."

"I'll give you a lift. You can Uber it home in the morning."

"I feel like I should pinch myself. Do you know what happened earlier tonight? I was watching a sermon on *The 700 Club*. The preacher was reading the gospel of Matthew, and he said, 'If you believe, you will receive whatever you ask for in prayer.' The words gave me strength, so I got down on my knees and prayed to the Lord Jesus that you would find Janey and that she'd be alive. To help things along, I went online to Walmart.com and picked out new utensils and dinnerware for your kitchen."

"You already bought them?"

"I most certainly did. They'll be delivered in a few days."

He struggled for something to say. Janey had nearly died tonight. What would he have done if that had happened? Send the utensils and dinnerware back?

"I guess your prayers were answered," he said.

"They most certainly were. Let me go throw some clothes on." She went to the door, then came back. A confused look spread across her face.

"What's an Uber?" she asked.

"I'll explain during the ride," he said.

CHAPTER 8

SUMMERTIME JOB

His job in Melbourne finished, he drove home listening to a boot-leg Jimmy Buffett concert he'd recorded at the New Orleans Jazz & Heritage Festival on the Acura stage, the recording equipment taped beneath his shirt. He'd had enough wires strapped to his body to be a suicide bomber, and would have gotten thrown in jail if caught, not that he cared. He was devoted to Buffett's music and would do it again if the opportunity presented itself.

The sky was lightening as he parked outside his condo. He lived in Venice Isles in a two-bedroom with a panoramic view of the Intracoastal. The unit had been well above his pay grade until Hollywood had offered to buy the rights to the story behind the YouTube video. His friends had urged him to hold out for a part in the film, and he'd told them to get lost, and bought into the building while it was still under construction.

At first, his neighbors had turned up their noses at his bad fashion statement. Then they'd learned he was an ex-cop and decided he was cool. A day didn't go by without a text questioning a suspicious character lurking about.

He slept a few hours, showered, but didn't shave. While the stubble wouldn't pass for a beard, it gave his face character. Standing at the mirror, he thought back to Janey touching his belly and her surprise. Not all fat men were created equal.

He thought about the Pearls as he dressed. Strange men were trying to abduct their daughter, and no one knew why. Or perhaps someone did know, but wasn't letting on. He liked puzzles, and felt confident that he could solve this one.

– – –

Melanie greeted him at the front door. "Good morning, Jon. While we were having breakfast, we saw a story on the news about Janey MacKenzie being rescued in Melbourne last night. You must be very proud. Congratulations."

Good news traveled fast. He entered and she shut the door behind him.

"We had visitors yesterday after you left," she said. "A pair of detectives appeared on our doorstep wanting to know if you'd discharged your gun while rescuing Nicki. They had very unpleasant things to say about you."

"Detectives Vargas and Gibbons," he said.

The words caught her by surprise. "How did you know?"

"It's not the first time they've spread dirt about me. What did you tell them?"

"Nolan covered for you, and said you hadn't shot your gun. I want to be up front with you. I wanted to fire you after they left, but my husband and daughter were against it. They felt the detectives weren't being honest. I thought it over, and decided they were right. But I need to ask you a question. Why did those detectives lie?"

"We have a history," he said. "A Hollywood studio paid me a lot of money for the rights to make a movie about my rescuing a little girl.

54

Vargas and Gibbons were on duty that day, and felt they deserved a cut because they assisted in the rescue. I thought about it, and decided no. Hollywood wants to tell my story, not theirs. They didn't like it, and have been causing me problems ever since."

"What kind of problems?"

"They sued me, but it got thrown out of court. Then they started harassing me and trying to ruin my business."

"That explains it. I have one more question, if you don't mind. Were you really a Navy SEAL? The detectives said that you weren't."

"I was. You act surprised."

"You aren't what I envision a SEAL would look like. Even an ex-one."

"Did my belly throw you off?"

She blushed. "It did."

"I was born with a condition called gastroschisis, which gave me a big stomach. The doctors fixed the problem, but for some reason my protruding stomach remained. People think I'm fat, but I'm not. Give me your hand."

She lifted her hand, and he placed it against his belly. Her face registered surprise.

"My God, you're as hard as a rock. You must take a lot of grief for it."

"I'm used to it," he said, letting her hand go. "How's Nicki doing?"

"We pulled her out of school, like you suggested. She's upstairs studying."

"I told you last night that your daughter wasn't to leave your sight," he said, raising his voice. "Please get her downstairs."

"We thought you meant when we went outside."

Melanie was challenging him. He'd let it go once, but not a second time. "Don't think these people won't break into your house. Go get her."

"Of course." She went to the foot of the stairway and called for her daughter.

"Nicki, please come downstairs. Bring your laptop with you." There was no response, and her face filled with apprehension. "Nicki, are you there? Answer me this instant." She turned to Lancaster. "She must be plugged into a device."

"Or she's gone," he said.

"You're scaring me, Jon."

Melanie was living in a bubble. So were most wealthy people, who believed that money could stop evil from entering their lives. Brushing past her, he bolted upstairs to the second floor and ran down the hallway. The doorway at the end had a drawing of a chestnut horse Scotch-taped to it, and he pounded on the door.

"Nicki?"

Melanie was right behind him. She twisted the knob and they entered together. Nicki lay on her bed, plugged into her iPhone. The teenager jumped up with a start.

"What's wrong?" she said.

"Nothing, honey. Everything's fine," Melanie said. "I thought you were doing homework. When you didn't answer me, I got worried."

"I was taking a break. I didn't mean to scare you."

"That's okay. Now grab your laptop, and come downstairs with us."

"Sure, Mom."

Nicki scooped up her laptop from a desk and followed her mother into the hallway. Lancaster did a quick sweep before leaving. The bedroom was a shrine to horses, the walls covered with posters of equestrian events held during the last Summer Olympics. The room had a single window facing the front of the house. Gazing out, he spied a white van parked across the street with a retractable aluminum ladder strapped to its roof and two men sitting inside. The van hadn't been there when he'd parked in the driveway a few minutes ago. Melanie edged up beside him.

"Is something the matter?" she asked.

"Any idea what that van is doing parked across the street?" he asked.

"My neighbors must be having their house painted."

"Are you friends with them?"

"We are. The Hartmans were the first people we met when we moved in."

"Call them, and see if you're right."

"You think I'm not?"

"I painted houses one summer when I was a teenager. We showed up at eight in the morning and finished up at four. If the two guys in that van are painters, they should be painting your neighbor's house instead of casing yours."

"How can you see that far away?"

"It's called visual accommodation. My eyes can adjust to distances and make out objects with total clarity. It comes in real handy sometimes. Please call the Hartmans."

Melanie placed a call to her neighbors on her cell phone. It ended with a frown. "They're not having any painting done. Do you think—"

She was asking too many questions, and he cut her short. "Take Nicki downstairs to where your husband is. I'm going outside to talk with these guys."

"Whatever you say, Jon. Should I call 911?"

The average 911 call in a residential neighborhood was worthless when dealing with a real emergency. But Melanie was in distress, and trashing the cops wouldn't help her frame of mind.

"It can't hurt," he said.

- - -

He came out the front door holding his car keys like he was preparing to leave. He went to the driver's door of his vehicle and pushed the unlock button. The car's headlights blinked, and so did its brake lights. Instead of getting in, he sprinted to the street, hoping to get a good look at the pair inside the van, which had its engine running. He was successful. Both had copper-tan skin and wore shades. He tried to determine if it was the same pair he'd seen in the cigarette boat, and decided it was.

"Hey! I need to talk to you!"

The van started moving. With tires squealing, it retreated down the street in reverse, making it impossible for him to read the license plate. Still in reverse, it whipped around a corner and disappeared. There was a science to not getting caught, and these guys were pros.

Frustrated, he went back inside. Melanie was in the foyer, cell phone in hand.

"I'm on hold with the dispatcher," she said.

"You might as well hang up. They took off. It was the same pair from yesterday."

She brought her hand to her mouth. "They're not afraid of anything."

"Oh yes, they are. They're afraid of me. They wouldn't have run like cowards if they weren't. Is Nicki with your husband?"

"They're in the study. How about a cup of coffee? You look like you could use one."

"I never say no to coffee."

She fixed him a cup of coffee in the kitchen. Her cell phone chirped, and she tugged it from her pocket. "My husband just texted me. He has something to show you. This house is so big that we have to text each other, if you can believe that."

"Do you feel safe here?"

"I did when we first moved in. Now, not so much."

"We need to fix that."

"I'm open to any suggestions."

"I know three ex-SEALs who will protect you when I'm not here."

"That sounds like a wonderful idea."

He followed her across the downstairs holding his steaming mug.

"One of our neighbors has a surveillance camera with a partial street view," she said. "He shared a tape from last night with us. It's very alarming. The neighborhood appears to be overrun with men stalking my daughter."

58

They entered the study. The blinds were drawn, and it was dark. South Florida was all about bright-blue skies and sunshine, and the room felt like a cave. Pearl sat on a couch facing a wall-mounted TV, Nicki cross-legged on the floor, doing homework. On the TV's screen the neighbor's grainy surveillance video played. Each time a vehicle drove down the street, Pearl made a mark on a yellow legal pad. He glanced up.

"Hello, Jon. Congratulations. I saw the story about your rescue on the news. My wife said there was a suspicious van parked outside."

"It was the same pair from yesterday. They bolted when I approached them."

"But you shot one of them."

"He was wearing a bulletproof vest. It was them, I'm sure of it."

"Do you think they'll be back?"

"Normally, I'd say no. But this situation isn't normal. These guys don't seem to care if they get spotted. May I ask what you're doing?"

"I'm counting the vehicles that drove down our street last night. My neighbor leads the neighborhood watch group and said we normally get six cars per hour after midnight. Last night, it was triple that."

"Eighteen cars per hour."

"Correct."

"Are there any road closures that you know about?"

"None that I'm aware of. The increase in traffic was caused by five vehicles."

"Let me make sure I'm getting this right. Five different vehicles kept passing your house late last night. How long did this last?"

"From midnight until five a.m. Then it stopped."

Pearl passed him the legal pad. Written on it were the names of five vehicles. There was a Chevy Malibu, a BMW Roadster, a Dodge Charger, a Ford pickup, and a Mini Cooper. Each car had a row of check marks beside it. The list didn't look right, and he quickly realized what the problem was. The white van with the two kidnappers wasn't on it.

CHAPTER 9

KING TIDES

"May I keep this?" Lancaster asked.

"Of course," Pearl said.

Tearing the sheet off the pad, he turned it into a square, and slipped it into his shirt pocket. The more he learned, the less he understood. If the white van hadn't been casing the house last night, then who were the drivers of the other five vehicles? How did they fit into the puzzle? He didn't know, and supposed they would have to wait for one of them to show his face again. In his experience, waiting for a bad guy to act was dangerous. The better choice would be to draw one of them out.

"Would you be up for a field trip?" he asked.

Pearl and his wife exchanged troubled looks. The house was their sanctuary, while the outside world was a frightening and unpredictable place.

"Nicki was nearly kidnapped the last time we went out," Pearl reminded him.

"She was actually kidnapped in your backyard," he replied. "We can't just sit here and wait for another attempt to be made. I want to grab the bull by the horns and confront one of these guys."

Nicki lay on the carpeted floor beside the dog. The conversation was upsetting her, and she pulled the dog closer and gave him a protective hug.

"Where do you have in mind?" Pearl asked.

"I was thinking of a little shopping excursion on Las Olas, followed by lunch. I'm going to tail you, and see if I can catch one of these creeps."

"You want to use our daughter as bait," Pearl said.

"In a manner of speaking, yes. If I can get my hands on one of these jokers, I should be able to make him talk."

"Do you plan to hurt him?" Melanie asked, sounding alarmed.

"I want to put the fear of God into him," he said. "The law doesn't look kindly on adult males who stalk teenage girls. Most guys who do this stuff know this. If I catch one of them, I'll threaten to have him locked up, which should scare the daylights out of him. Then I'll offer to make a deal. I'll let him go, provided he tells me why he's stalking your daughter."

The Pearls again traded looks. They were gambling, and the stakes were high if things went wrong. They needed more convincing, so he said, "My goal is to find out why Nicki is being targeted. There has to be a thread that links these creeps together. If I can discover what that thread is, I can get to the bottom of what's going on here, and keep your daughter out of harm's way."

Nicki rose from the floor and took her parents' hands. She gave them a smile that was best described as courageous. "I want to do it. I want this to stop. Please."

Melanie let out a deep breath. "You sure about this, honey?"

"Positive, Mom. Jon won't let these men hurt me, will you, Jon?"

"No one's going to hurt you, Nicki," he said.

"I'm okay with it, if your father is," Melanie said.

Pearl frowned. As a doctor, he knew that there were no good choices in bad situations. Leaving the house was a scary proposition, but staying inside was equally nerve-racking. The time had come to take action and deal with the situation head-on. "I'm in," Pearl said.

- - -

Each fall, the King Tides swept across South Florida, turning coastal roads into rivers as the full moon swung closer to the Earth than normal. This year's flooding was particularly harsh and had pushed water onto lawns while threatening coastal businesses.

The hand-painted signs were in nearly every yard: No Wake Zone! At least people had a sense of humor about it. If the meteorologists were to be believed, this would one day be a regular event, as gravity and rising sea levels ravaged the coastline. So far no one was screaming too loudly, so the natives just figured out a way to cope.

Lancaster coasted down the flooded streets as he followed the Pearls to Las Olas. On the corner he spied a kid in swimming trunks with a bamboo fishing pole. He lowered his window and stuck his head out. "Catch anything?"

"I caught a shark, but my mom made me throw it back," the kid said.

He waved and drove away. That was the cool thing about living in Fort Lauderdale. The locals had a sense of humor. Except for the occasional evil soul, the natives were friendly, and easy to get along with.

The Pearls drove a white Infiniti SUV that gleamed like a freshly minted coin. It occurred to him that everything in their lives was brand-new. New life, new home, new car. They'd probably thought they'd died and gone to heaven when they'd moved here. Then the problems with Nicki had started, and it had all gone to hell.

The Infiniti braked at a stop sign. Pearl glanced in his mirror at his tail. The good doctor looked scared, and Lancaster wondered if his original assessment was wrong. Abductions were about money, and Pearl obviously had plenty of it. Was Pearl the real target and Nicki just leverage? He had a feeling that he was about to find out.

They drove past palatial Mediterranean-style homes so tightly squeezed together that it was impossible to see the ocean. The streets were quiet, and he used the Pandora app on his cell phone to play a Jimmy Buffett song, "Cuban Crime of Passion." During his first trip to Key West, Lancaster had crashed on the couch of the song's composer, a genial barkeep named Tom Corcoran. Lancaster had been right out of the military, and Corcoran's hospitality had gone a long way to help him get adjusted.

In his mirror he spied a black Ford pickup filled with lawn equipment riding his bumper, the driver a burly Hispanic with a handlebar mustache and borderline crazy eyes.

He called Pearl on his cell phone. "See the black pickup behind me?"

"Yes, I see him," Pearl said.

"I think the driver's following you. There was a black pickup on your list. Did it have lawn equipment in the bed?"

"I believe it did."

"Must be the same guy. I want you to speed up. I've got your back, so don't get scared if he tries anything stupid."

"Got it."

Pearl hit the gas and sent waves onto several manicured front yards. Within moments, a block separated their two cars. The crazy Hispanic punched his horn. Lancaster looked into his mirror and raised his hand as if to say *What do you want?* The Hispanic shook his fist, then passed Lancaster on the left and raced down the street.

His cell phone rang. Pearl calling.

"He's chasing us!" Pearl said. "What should I do?"

"Nothing. Leave the heroics to me."

"What are *you* going to do?"

"Run him down and have a talk with him."

"How are you going to do that?"

"You and your wife ask too many questions. Just drive."

Lancaster ended the call. The Hispanic had caught up to the Pearls and was riding their bumper. The situation was teetering out of control, so he got in the opposing lane, pulling up alongside the pickup. The Hispanic was watching a video on his cell phone while he drove. Lancaster strained to see and made out a girl's face.

"Pull over!" he yelled.

The Hispanic ignored him. Lancaster ripped out his wallet and flashed the badge the department had given him in a shadow box when he'd resigned.

"You heard me, pull over!" he yelled.

Still nothing. He spun his wheel and made their bumpers kiss. The Hispanic started to freak out. Men who stalked children knew the harsh reality of life in prison. Regular beatings, and when that got old, the other inmates often killed them. Desperate to escape, the Hispanic jumped the curb and drove across a heavily landscaped front lawn.

Pearl called him. "He's getting away! Are you going to run him down?"

"No. I'm going to let him go," Lancaster said.

"But he's stalking Nicki!"

"We can't prove that. He hasn't broken any laws besides being a bad driver. If the police get involved, I could get in trouble. Get out of here. I'll meet you in town."

"Whatever you say."

Pearl hung a left at the next intersection and took off. The pickup was still riding on lawns and tearing up irrigation systems, and Lancaster continued to follow. At the block's end, the pickup returned to the street. Lancaster memorized the license plate before watching it drive away.

There was nothing like a car chase to get the heart pounding. He parked in front of a house being tented for termites and caught his breath. His old partner, Devon, was now employed at the Department of Motor Vehicles, and he texted him the pickup's license and a message:

I need to know who owns this vehicle

What's it worth? Devon replied.

I'll take you out drinking

Try harder

Drinks and dinner

Call me tomorrow

How about lap dances at the Cheetah?

Now you're talking. I'll get back to you

He was making progress. He had a license plate and soon would have a name and an address, and that would lead to all sorts of interesting information about their stalker. No sooner had he pulled away from the curb than his cell phone rang.

"There's another guy after my daughter," Pearl said.

CHAPTER 10

The Canadian

Las Olas was where the beautiful people hung out, its immaculate main drag filled with sidewalk cafés and trendy bars. Lancaster rarely went there, preferring beachfront dives where shirts were optional and no one was trying to make a fucking statement.

The Pearls had taken refuge in the public parking lot on the north side of the boulevard, huddled inside their SUV with the windows shut. Pearl nearly jumped out of his skin when Lancaster rapped his knuckles on the driver's window. It lowered.

"You scared me. I never saw you," Pearl said.

There was an art to stealth and concealment, and it had nothing to do with hiding in the shadows. It was all about blending in and not drawing attention to yourself. He glanced into the front seat and saw Nicki sandwiched protectively between her parents, her eyes moist. Part of his job was to make people feel safe; if he didn't succeed, his clients fired him. He stepped away and did a quick inspection of the cars in the next row. He'd checked the vehicles moments ago, but repeated the drill to make the Pearls feel safe.

"Tell me what happened," he said upon returning.

"We drove here and parked in the public lot south of the boulevard," Pearl said. "We got out of the car and started to walk toward Alex and Ani to do some shopping. That's when my wife spotted him."

Melanie leaned forward in her seat and made eye contact. "He came out of nowhere, about thirty-five, wearing jeans and a pale-blue dress shirt. He looked normal, only he wasn't. He was stalking Nicki."

"What tipped you off?"

"I heard him muttering under his breath like a pervert."

"Did you catch what he was saying?"

"Not all of it. But I did hear him say, 'There she is.' He sounded very excited, and was staring at Nicki with a horrible look in his eyes and then glancing at his cell phone. It was all I could do not to take out my can of Mace and spray him. Then Nolan got in his face, and he took off."

"I got a photograph of him." Nicki handed over her cell phone. "Maybe you can send it to the FBI and they can use their facial recognition software to make a match."

"Did you learn about that in your CSI class?" he asked.

"Yes. My teacher said the FBI was the best at catching criminals."

The FBI was run by arrogant assholes who took credit when cases got solved and pointed the finger when they broke bad. Lancaster hoped he never had to work another case with them again, only he wasn't going to tell Nicki that and burst her bubble. Her cell phone's pink case was an inappropriate frame for the photo of the creep that had been following her. The creep wore a diamond stud earring and had a pampered look.

He handed the phone back. "Have you ever seen this man before today?"

"Never," Nicki said.

"How about you?" he asked her parents.

"I've never seen him before," Melanie said.

"He was a stranger," Pearl said.

Their answers sounded honest. Which made the creep a question mark, just like the rest of the men who were stalking Nicki.

"Do you want me to send the photo to you?" Nicki asked.

"Do it later," he said. "Right now, I want to take a walk with you and your parents down Las Olas and do some shopping. Then we can grab some lunch."

"Do you think that's wise?" Pearl asked. "He might still be hanging around."

"That's what I'm hoping," he said.

It was not unusual to see water running down Las Olas after a late-afternoon downpour, the streets being prone to overflowing after heavy rains. But today's flooding was different, the water ankle-deep and rushing past with a biblical force. Standing on the curb, Nicki and her parents looked at him as if to say, what now?

Lancaster kicked off his Topsiders, pulled up the legs of his jeans, and waded in. A school of minnows raced past, tickling his calves. The photograph captured on Nicki's cell phone might help him identify the creep, but that wasn't going to tell him what the man's motivation was. To do that, he needed to get the creep cornered, and put the fear of God into him. Las Olas was filled with alleys, and he planned to drag the guy down one, and make him start talking. As a cop, he was prohibited from doing that; as a civilian, he did it all the time, often with spectacular results.

He reached the median and turned around. The Pearls were taking their time crossing. Traffic was light, and they paid scant attention to passing cars. It wouldn't have been hard for a car to stop, and a bad guy to jump out and grab their daughter.

They joined him on the median.

"Here's the deal," he said. "First, you need to start paying better attention to your surroundings. The driver of one of the cars that just passed was leering at your daughter. It could have been nothing, or he could have had bad intentions."

"I didn't even see him," Pearl said.

"I know you didn't. You need to keep your heads up when you're in public with Nicki. If someone's following you, your peripheral vision will catch him. Understood?"

Nicki's parents looked ashamed, and they both nodded. Nicki was a good kid, and she grabbed both their hands and gave them a squeeze. It brought a smile to their faces.

"Now, here's the plan," he said. "We're going to cross to the other side so you can do some window shopping. Take your time and keep Nicki sandwiched between you. That way, no one can jump out and make a move for her. I'll stay twenty feet back and tail you. If I see the guy from earlier, I'll pull him down an alleyway and make him talk to me. If that happens, I want you to go inside the nearest store, and stay there until I come and get you. We all clear?"

The Pearls said yes. Nicki bit her lower lip and said, "What if someone tries to kidnap me like those horrible men yesterday? Will you shoot them?"

"If I have to," he said.

- - -

They put the plan in motion. The Pearls crossed to the south side of Las Olas and started window gazing. Lancaster remained behind and studied the street for any suspicious characters. Seeing nothing out of the ordinary, he crossed as well.

The block between Eighth and Ninth Avenues was filled with art galleries that sold expensive paintings and blown glass, the storefronts painted in bright pastels with each having its own colorful canopy. The

Pearls strolled down the sidewalk, stopping to point and admire. They were acting like nothing was wrong, and he gave them credit for pulling it off. Most people were not so brave, especially when their kid's welfare was at stake.

Reaching the block's end, they crossed the street. From out of nowhere, a black BMW pulled up to the curb, and a man jumped out holding a garment box. The guy wore alligator cowboy boots and designer threads and seemed intent on making a fashion statement. Either he was going into a store to return an item, or he was a threat to Nicki.

Training for his first deployment to become a SEAL had given him lightning reflexes that were now hardwired into his DNA. He barreled into the man and sent him sprawling to the sidewalk. The garment box hit the ground, and the lid flew off. A purple Lacoste shirt lay inside. Acting embarrassed, he helped the man to his feet.

"I'm sorry, I never saw you. Are you okay?"

The man scowled. "You should be more careful. I could have been hurt."

"Do you need to go to a hospital?"

"No, I'll live. Just watch where you're going."

"I will. Sorry again. Have a nice day."

Lancaster caught up with the Pearls. They had stopped in front of New River Fine Art, one of the street's more prestigious galleries. "I need for you to wait inside the gallery for a few minutes," he said. "I want to make sure that guy doesn't call the police."

Pearl frowned. "But he wasn't hurt. I heard him tell you that."

"He might change his mind and press charges. Have you seen all the billboards on I-95 for personal injury attorneys? People like to sue."

"As a doctor, I'm well aware of how much people like to sue." Pearl looked at his wife and daughter. "Are you okay with going inside for a few minutes?"

Nicki and Melanie both said they'd be fine inside the gallery.

"Don't worry, I'll be right across the street," Lancaster said.

The Pearls entered New River and were greeted by the owner. Nicki turned around and waved to him through the glass front door.

- - -

He crossed to the north side of Las Olas and stood in front of a coffee shop while looking for any sign of the police. As a cop he'd been sued several times, the cases all bull. Yet each one had been settled out of court because the department didn't want to waste money going to trial. The attorneys who'd sued him were bottom-feeders who'd never tried a case. It was a lousy system, yet no one was in a hurry to fix it.

If the man he'd knocked down decided to sue, he'd first have to press charges, and get the cops to believe his version of things. Every store on Las Olas had surveillance cameras fixed on the street, and the odds were good there was a high-resolution video of the altercation that the police would want to see.

Ten minutes slipped away without any sign of the law. He sent Pearl a text, asking him if things were good inside the gallery.

All is well, Pearl replied. Need to go soon. Melanie wants to buy a painting!

Pearl was managing to keep his sense of humor. That was a good sign, since there was a chance the situation with Nicki would get worse before it got better. Across the street, the man in the alligator boots came out of a clothing store talking into his cell phone. The BMW appeared at the curb, and he hopped in and departed.

Lancaster was happy to have that behind him. He didn't like hurting innocent people, but sometimes he had no choice. His cell phone vibrated. Pearl calling.

"What's up?" he answered.

"A guy is staring at Nicki through the front window," Pearl said.

He gazed across the street at New River's storefront. A small group of people was clustered in front of the store, and he couldn't tell which was the offending party.

"Describe him."

"He's wearing chinos and a porkpie hat," Pearl said. "Slender build, milky white skin. There's an airline ticket sticking out of his shirt pocket with an Air Canada logo. He's got a cell phone in his hand that he stares at when he's not looking at my daughter."

Lancaster picked the guy out of the crowd. The Canadian was several inches taller than the group he was standing with and skinny to the point of being unhealthy. "I see him. Stay inside the gallery. I'll be right there."

"Melanie is starting to get scared. Where are they coming from?"

"I don't know," he replied.

He got his shoes soaking wet crossing the street. It was starting to feel like a game of Whac-A-Mole. Every time he got rid of a creep, another one popped up and started stalking Nicki. He hopped a bush in the median and got splashed by a passing car. The navy had conditioned him to being wet, and he pushed it out of his mind. The crowd in front of New River had thinned, and the Canadian stood alone by the front window.

The traffic gone, he started to cross. The Canadian was fixated on Nicki and kept staring at the images playing on his cell phone. The Hispanic in the pickup had also been staring at images on his cell phone. This was the link that tied Nicki's stalkers together. If he could get his hand on the Canadian's cell phone, he'd be one step closer to figuring out what was going on. As his foot touched the curb, the Canadian spied him in the window's reflection and started to walk away.

"Excuse me," Lancaster said. "Don't I know you?"

It was a line that he'd often used as a cop. The Canadian wasn't buying it and beat a hasty retreat down the sidewalk.

"Stop," he said, trotting after him.

"Leave me alone," the Canadian said.

"I don't mean any harm. I just want to talk to you."

"I'll be the judge of that. Go away."

"I'm not a cop."

"Then what are you?"

"A friend of the girl you're stalking."

The Canadian's mouth dropped open, revealing two rows of bad teeth. Darting into the street, he danced around several cars before reaching the median and plowing through the bushes. Lancaster gave chase and ran through the same bushes.

"I just want to talk!"

The Canadian crossed to the other side and ducked into a coffee shop. Lancaster entered a moment later but saw no sign of him. The manager stood at the register holding a napkin to her mouth.

"Where did the skinny guy go?" he asked.

The manager lowered the napkin. "You a cop?"

"Private investigator. What happened?"

"That crazy bastard wanted to use the back entrance. When I said it was off limits, he hit me. If you catch him, kick the crap out of him."

"Will do. Show me where he went."

The manager led him to the storage room. The Canadian had trashed it, and torn bags of coffee beans littered the floor. The door leading to the alley was ajar, and Lancaster stepped outside. The alley was lined with overflowing garbage pails, and the sound of a weeping man filled the air.

"Did he hurt someone else?" the manager asked.

"I'm about to find out."

He walked to the end of the alley, where it intersected with Tenth Avenue. A UPS truck was parked in the street, its uniformed driver standing beside his vehicle. The Canadian lay on his back, his right leg twisted at an unnatural angle and the side of his face bloodied from kissing the pavement. A broken cell phone lay a few feet away, its screen shattered. Lancaster tried to power it up and saw that it was ruined.

The Canadian stopped his weeping. "You win," he said weakly.

"I just wanted to talk," he said.

"So talk. I'm not going anywhere."

He placed the cell phone on the ground, and knelt beside the injured man. To satisfy his curiosity, he removed the protruding airline ticket and studied it. The Canadian had arrived on a flight from Toronto that morning. Why the hell was a Canadian tourist stalking Nicki? It was another piece to a puzzle that got more confusing by the hour.

"Why are you stalking the girl?" he asked.

"You don't know about the videos, do you?" the Canadian said, sounding surprised.

"No. Why don't you tell me about them?"

"Come closer, and I'll explain."

Cozying up with the enemy was a risk, but Lancaster didn't see that he had another choice. Without the cell phone, he had no clue as to what was going on. He lowered his head so his ear was next to the injured man's lips.

That's when the Canadian bit him.

CHAPTER 11
The Call

He walked to the New River gallery holding a paper napkin he'd borrowed from the coffee shop to his wounded ear. Just as the Canadian had started to bite him, he'd instinctively yanked his head and managed to avoid serious injury. His body was adorned with bullet scars from his military days, and losing a piece of his ear wouldn't have been the worst thing to happen to him.

New River sold museum-quality artwork that found its way into many wealthy homes. The Pearls stood in the rear of the gallery by a group of new age sculptures made of acrylic. There were a half dozen in all, and each resembled a horse. Nicki was mesmerized and stared at the sculptures longingly while clasping her parents' hands.

The family turned as he approached, their faces hopeful. His plan to use Nicki as bait had failed miserably, and he decided it would be best to tell them so.

"I struck out," he said.

Pearl said, "What happened to the side of your head? Did he attack you?"

He removed the napkin and saw a tiny spot of blood. "He ran into the street and got hit by a UPS truck. I attempted to have a talk with him while he was lying on the ground, and he tried to bite me."

Pearl recoiled in horror. "He bit you? What kind of animal does such a thing?"

He'd seen worse behavior from suspects, only talking about it wouldn't add anything to the conversation. "According to the airline ticket in his pocket, he flew into Fort Lauderdale from Toronto this morning. Does that mean anything?"

Pearl shook his head. "I don't know anyone from Toronto."

"Neither do I," Melanie said.

He shifted his attention to Nicki. She had grown unusually quiet, and he sensed that she was holding back. "How about you, young lady?"

Nicki released her parents' hands and stared at the floor. "A strange man called the house from Toronto last week. I spoke to him. We didn't talk very long."

Her parents looked shocked. Melanie said, "You spoke to a stranger? Why didn't you tell us?"

"I thought you'd be mad at me," she said.

"And you were right," her mother said.

Lancaster gently touched Nicki's shoulder, and she lifted her gaze.

"Tell me what you said to him," he said.

"I'd just gotten home from school and was in the kitchen making a snack when the phone rang," she explained. "I didn't recognize the number on caller ID, so I ignored it. Then it rang again. Same number. I was curious, so I checked the area code on my iPad using Google, and saw the call was from Toronto. I don't know why, but I answered it. The caller was a man, and he was very excited. He called me this weird name, and I told him that he had the wrong number. He asked me what I was wearing and some other stuff, and I hung up."

Lancaster spent a moment processing this information. There was no doubt in his mind that the caller was the creep who'd just bitten him. But why had he called? And why would he have spent the time and money to fly here if Nicki had hung up on him?

"Did he call back?" he asked.

"Yeah, a couple of times," Nicki said, sounding ashamed.

"Did you take his calls?"

"No, I was freaked out. I just wanted him to go away."

"You said he called you a weird name. Do you remember what it was?"

"No," she said, shaking her head.

It was not uncommon for victims to block out details from bad experiences. This was especially true when the victims were young and vulnerable. He crouched down so he was eye-level with Nicki and said, "I think you do remember, but shoved the name into the recesses of your memory. I want you to help me drag it out. Can you do that?"

"Sure," she said. "Is this an interrogation trick?"

"Yes, it is."

"Will you teach it to me, so I can show my class at school?"

"I'd be happy to. I want you to close your eyes and imagine you've just gotten home from school. You're standing in the kitchen fixing a snack." Nicki closed her eyes and wrinkled her forehead in concentration. "Good. Now imagine you hear the phone ring. You check the caller ID and see it's from Toronto. You hesitate, but decide to answer it. You say hello, and it's a strange man. He calls you a name."

Nicki's eyes snapped open. "Got it!"

"You remember the name?"

"He called me Cassandra."

"Cassandra. That's great, Nicki. Is there anything else you remember?"

"He was breathing hard, like he'd just run a race."

"Very good. Anything else?"

"There was a movie playing in the background."

"How could you tell?"

"I could hear a woman talking, only I couldn't understand what she was saying. She kept talking while the man was speaking to me, so I knew it was a movie."

"Did you make out what the woman in the movie was saying?"

"No. She was talking in a quiet voice, real seductive. I thought he might be watching a porno."

Melanie let out a tiny gasp. She'd come to the same conclusion that Lancaster had, which was that the caller from Toronto was masturbating while talking to Nicki.

"Okay, so you think the man from Toronto was watching a porno movie, and that he was out of breath. You said that he asked you what you were wearing, and some other stuff. Do you remember what that other stuff was?"

"He wanted to meet me. He asked me if I was okay with that."

"What did you tell him?"

"Nothing. I hung up."

"Is there anything else you remember? Think hard."

Nicki gave it some thought and shook her head. "No, that's it. I guess I should have told my parents. I'm sorry."

"Don't apologize," he said. "The call was from another country. You thought he was a weirdo and hung up, and then you forgot about it. Those are natural reactions when dealing with a situation like that. You did nothing wrong."

Nicki hugged her mother and then her father, and everything was good between them again. Lancaster walked to the front of the gallery and stared out onto the street. There were no suspicious-acting males lurking about, and he spent a moment adding the things Nicki had told him to what he already knew. It still didn't make any sense, unless there was a piece to the puzzle that he wasn't seeing. Pearl appeared by his side.

"We're hungry. Do you think it's safe to get lunch?"

"What did you have in mind?"

"The Cheesecake Factory down the street. It's Nicki's favorite restaurant."

"Okay, but you need to let me pick the table."

"Of course, Jon. Whatever you think is best."

"Let me ask you something. This guy from Toronto called the landline in your house. Is that number listed in the phone book?"

"The house line is unlisted. I don't know how he got it."

Nicki's stalkers were determined, and they were resourceful. In his experience, that made them the worst kind of adversary.

"Let's get some lunch," he said.

CHAPTER 12
GEL HEAD

The Cheesecake Factory on East Las Olas was popular with the lunch-time crowd, and there was a fifteen-minute wait to be seated. Lancaster slipped the hostess a folded twenty-dollar bill and said, "I need a secluded table in your restaurant, please."

The hostess hesitated. "Define *secluded*."

"In a corner, backed up to a wall."

"Let me see what I can do."

The waiting area was next to the hostess stand. Nicki sat on a bench with her parents to either side and Lancaster standing guard in front of her, facing the entrance. No one was going to get close to her without first going through him.

The hostess appeared holding menus. "You're in luck. Right this way."

The Pearls rose from the bench and followed the hostess. Lancaster came up from behind, looking for any sign of trouble. The restaurant was packed, the tables positioned so closely together that it reminded him of a mess hall. Their destination was a corner table across from the noisy bar that ran the length of the wall. When everyone was seated, the hostess passed out the menus and said a waitress would be over shortly.

So far, everything looked normal. But he was not going to let his guard down. While the Pearls read their menus, he studied the other diners. Two groups of people made up the lunch crowd. Families and business people. He didn't spot any suspicious-acting males—the profile of Nicki's stalkers.

A waitress appeared. The echo coming off the tile floors made normal conversation impossible, and the Pearls shouted their orders.

"Coffee," he said when his turn came.

Water and bread were brought to the table. Nicki chose a sesame roll and tore it into small pieces before buttering it. She hadn't uttered a word since the art gallery and acted withdrawn. Her parents tried to engage her in conversation and got nowhere.

"Am I ever going to be able to go back to school?" she asked. The question caught her parents off guard. To Lancaster she said, "Am I?"

Nicki was looking into the future and not liking what she saw. Projecting was never healthy, and he tried to allay her fears.

"I don't see why not," he said.

"When?" she asked.

"As soon as I get to the bottom of this."

"But what if you don't figure out what these men want? What then? Do I have to go into hiding like someone in witness protection? I want my life back."

Helping people in distress was like taking a trip, and it always took time. He tried to find an answer that would calm her down, but came up short. There was no answer that wasn't an exaggeration or outright lie, and he wasn't in the habit of telling those.

"I'll figure out what these men want. That's a promise," he said.

"Oh no," Melanie said under her breath. "I just spotted a creep at the bar watching Nicki in the mirror. He won't take his eyes off her. What should we do?"

If Nicki's stalkers shared a common trait, it was a deep fear of being caught, and they were quick to run the moment they sniffed trouble.

"Stop staring at him," he said. "I don't want you to scare him off."

"Whatever you say."

He glanced at the bar. The creep sat on a stool with his back to them. He wore a dress shirt and blue neck tie, nice slacks, and a pair of expensive shoes. He had a weight lifter's broad shoulders and tiny waist, and his short blond hair was slicked back with gel. He alternated watching Nicki in the backbar mirror and looking at his cell phone. A plate of untouched pasta alfredo sat in front of him. Gel Head had lost his appetite.

Nicki kicked him beneath the table. "I'm scared."

"To be forewarned is to be forearmed," he said.

"What does that mean?"

"It means that we're going to protect you." To Melanie, he said, "You said before that you have a can of Mace. Please pull it out of your purse and pass it to your daughter beneath the table."

Melanie passed her Mace to Nicki.

"If he gets near you, spray him in the face," Lancaster said.

"Got it," Nicki said.

He addressed her parents. "Has either of you ever fired a handgun before?"

"I have," Pearl said.

"I'm going to pass you one of my handguns beneath the table. I want you to stick it in your pocket. It's loaded and doesn't have a safety, so you need to be careful."

Pearl's face lost its color. "What exactly are you planning to do?"

"I'm going outside the restaurant. Once I'm gone, I want you and your wife to put the fear of God into this sicko. Hopefully he'll run out the door, which will give me the opportunity to confront him. Sound good?"

Some men caved in the face of uncertainty and danger, while others rose to the challenge. Pearl squared his shoulders. "I'm good if Melanie and Nicki are," he said.

"I'm good," his wife said. "How about you, honey?"

Nicki held the canister of Mace in her lap. Making her part of the attack plan let her stop feeling like a victim, and she no longer seemed scared.

"Let's get him," she said.

- - -

Lancaster laid out his plan of attack and explained each of their roles. There were no questions, and he rose from the table and placed his napkin on his spot.

"Is Team Pearl ready?" he asked.

They said yes. He slid away from the table and headed toward the lavatories on the other side of the dining room. His journey took him past Gel Head, who still hadn't touched his food. A cell phone lay on the bar playing a video. As he passed, Gel Head flipped the cell phone facedown, hiding the screen.

There was no stronger instinct than survival. Nicki's stalkers' attraction to their prey was only surpassed by their desire not to get caught. He turned a corner and came to the restrooms. He waited for a customer to come out, and used him as a shield to walk to the front of the restaurant. Reaching the hostess stand, he spun around. Gel Head was still at the bar, his eyes focused on Nicki in the mirror.

The Pearls were watching him. He made the "okay" sign with his fingers.

Melanie and her husband rose from their chairs. Nolan moved in front of the table, creating a shield in front of Nicki. His hand was in his pocket, touching the handle of the gun. He looked ready for trouble.

Melanie brushed past him and came up behind Gel Head. She forcefully tapped his shoulder, and Gel Head turned to stone and stared at the reflection in the mirror. Melanie tore into him, her voice angry enough to cut through the other diners' conversations.

"You sick bastard! You've been staring at my daughter for the last ten minutes. Don't pretend we didn't see you!"

Gel Head picked up his cell phone and made it disappear into his pocket. He threw money on the bar for his food and hopped off his stool.

"Running away, are you? You coward!"

Gel Head had been confronted before and knew the drill. Walk away and don't say a word. Feeling empowered, Melanie wagged a finger in his face. "My husband took a photo of you on his cell phone. We're going to show it to the police, and file a complaint."

Conversation in the restaurant had stopped. Every diner was watching the scene unfold. Gel Head turned his back and headed for the exit. Melanie kept the barbs coming. "You're a pervert! She's only fifteen years old."

Gel Head picked up his pace, desperate to get away.

"Did you hear what I said? She's fifteen years old!"

Lancaster went outside to wait on the sidewalk. Melanie's threats were nothing more than an angry mother venting. Gel Head hadn't done anything that warranted the police arresting him, and Lancaster needed to be careful in how he handled this.

Gel Head exited the restaurant. Lancaster tried to block his path, and their bodies collided. Gel Head was rock solid, and Lancaster fell backward into the gutter. So much for the nice guy approach. He jumped to his feet and gave chase.

"Wait! I need to talk to you!"

Gel Head was running hard. Reaching the public lot on the south side of Las Olas, he jumped into a black Lexus and was backing out when Lancaster caught up.

"I just want to talk!"

The Lexus nearly ran him over. It was an LC 500, which ran a hundred grand with all the bells and whistles. He memorized the license plate and hobbled back to the restaurant. He called Devon at DMV and caught his friend at his desk, eating lunch.

"Hey, Jon, what's shaking?" Devon asked.

"Any luck on the license plate I sent you?"

"It belonged to a dead guy."

"Crap. I need you to check another plate for me. Same terms as before."

"I'm game. Fire away."

He recited the Lexus's license plate to Devon. His phone vibrated, and he checked the screen. Pearl was calling to check up on him. He switched calls and said, "Eat your lunch, I'll be right in. Tell your wife she's a star." He hung up and resumed speaking to Devon. "Any hits?"

"You're in luck this time," Devon said. "The car is registered to a dude named Zack Kenny from Lauderdale. I've got his address, date of birth, and social security number, in case you're interested."

"Lay it on me," he said.

CHAPTER 13

RESTRAINING ORDER

The Pearls awaited him at their table. Their lunches had been served and were untouched. He pulled up a chair and sipped his cold coffee. The profile of Nicki's stalkers had just expanded to include a man who made enough money to drive a luxury sports car that 99 percent of the population couldn't afford. It was in sharp contrast to the Hispanic in the pickup and the Canadian tourist with bad teeth.

"Please eat," he said.

"Did you get him?" Melanie asked.

"In a manner of speaking, yes. I know who he is, which is enough to get me started. You guys did a great job getting him out of the restaurant."

"Thanks," Melanie said. "The manager came over afterward, and asked us if everything was all right. Nolan explained the situation, so we're good."

"Is that blood on your knuckle?" Nicki asked.

"It's just a scrape," he said.

"Did you fight him?"

"Not really. He knocked me to the sidewalk and ran to his car."

"Why didn't you punch his lights out? He's a sicko."

"I can't prove that, Nicki. If I hit him, it would be grounds for the police to arrest me, and we don't want that happening. But I have his name and some other personal information courtesy of my friend at the Department of Motor Vehicles. Would you like to help me track him down?"

Nicki's face lit up. "You bet I would. When can we start?"

"Right now."

Her parents weren't as excited. Pearl said, "Jon, we're not keen on using Nicki as bait again. It's too risky."

"I just want Nicki to help me do some cybersleuthing and get a bead on this guy. She won't be put in harm's way."

"Maybe if we find him I can get extra credit with my CSI class," Nicki said.

Pearl and his wife exchanged glances. Melanie nodded she was okay with this.

"Very well, go ahead," Pearl said.

"Okay, Nicki, pick your weapon. Cell phone or iPad," he said.

"iPad," Nicki said.

"Pull it out, and let's get started."

Nicki's purse was slung over the back of her chair. She pulled out her iPad and made a space on the table in front of her. It was an iPad mini and the size of a paperback book with a hot pink cover. She tried to get on the internet and frowned.

"I need a password to get on the restaurant's Wi-Fi," she said.

He waved down a waitress and got the password. Nicki connected her device to the internet and said, "Where do you want me to go?"

"Broward County Clerk of Courts. Just type it into Google. When it comes up, you'll have a list of options. Click on 'case search.'" While Nicki typed away, he explained to her parents how he planned to track down Zack Kenny. "About ten years ago, the Florida Supreme Court directed every county in the state to provide electronic viewing for most court records. I'm going to have Nicki find how many court cases Kenny has, which should give us some insights into his motive."

"How do you know for certain that Kenny has a record?" Pearl asked.

"I've never met a deviant that didn't have brushes with the law," he replied. "They're damaged people who can't avoid trouble."

"I'm on the county clerk's page. It's asking me for last name and first name," Nicki said.

"Type in the name 'Zack Kenny,' and make sure you click on the box that says you're not a robot," he said.

"Done. It's loading. Boy, this site is slow."

Slow was in the eye of the beholder. In the old days, he would have paid a visit to the courthouse and spent an entire afternoon pulling up records. Now, he just went to the site and typed in a few commands to get what he wanted.

Nicki's face crashed. "Crap. It says no files match your records."

"If at first you don't succeed, try again. Type in the name 'Zackary Kenny' this time, and see what pops up."

Nicki did so and waited expectantly. "Wow. There he is. Look at all the court cases against him. There must be twenty in all. He must really be a bad guy."

"Are you sure the cases are for the same person?" he asked. "There might be more than one Zackary Kenny living in Broward County."

Nicki visually scrolled down the iPad's screen. "I'm seeing four different birth dates associated with these cases. Do you know when he was born?"

The kid was a natural. He took out his cell phone and punched the "Message" icon. He'd written down the information that Devon had given him, and texted it to himself. This included Kenny's date of birth, which was on his license.

"The Zack Kenny we want was born on May 5, 1983," he said.

Nicki checked the cases. "I've got a match."

"Let me see."

She turned the iPad so the screen faced him. "It's the fifth case from the top."

He found the case and clicked on it. A new page came up with links to the charge filed against Kenny and the various court proceedings. He hit the link that would let him see the charge. A new page appeared, and he read it.

"What did you find?" Nicki asked.

"Four months ago, a lady named Karissa Clement from Delray Beach placed a restraining order against him. Kenny isn't allowed to see her or call her on the phone. Do you think if I called Clement and told her that he was stalking you, she'd talk to me?"

Nicki nodded excitedly. So did her parents. He pushed the iPad back to Nicki.

"Find her for me," he said.

Nicki giggled and started her search. In his experience, teenage girls were not easy company, their mood swings and raging hormones the definition of bad chemistry. Nicki was different and a real delight to be with.

"What can this Clement woman tell you?" Melanie asked.

"Maybe nothing or maybe everything," he said. "I'll find out when I talk to her."

"So you don't know for sure," Melanie said.

"There are no crystal balls in investigations. You go where the leads take you."

"I think I found her," Nicki said. "Karissa Clement of Delray Beach has a résumé posted on LinkedIn and works as a registered nurse at Delray Medical Center. There's some background information and a contact phone number."

"Let me see," he said.

Nicki slid the iPad in front of him, and he had a look. LinkedIn was a popular site for business people looking to network or find a new job. Clement's page contained a brief work history along with favorable postings from people she'd worked with. She hadn't posted a photograph of herself, so there was no way of telling how old she was. But it wasn't a common name, and he had to think this was the same woman who'd put a restraining order on Kenny. He gave Nicki her device back and rose from his chair.

"I'm going to go find a quiet spot, and give her a call," he said.

"Do you really think she'll help you?" Melanie asked.

Most people didn't want to get involved in other people's problems. That was different with people who'd been victimized, especially women, who did not wish the bad fortune that had happened to them to strike someone else.

"Yes, I do," he said. "Let's hope I'm right."

CHAPTER 14

DARK TERRITORY

Boston's in Delray Beach was Lancaster's idea of a bar. Fifty different draft beers on tap, clams on the half shell, and a clear view of the ocean. The four-lane road in front was ankle deep in water from the King Tides, and he parked several blocks away.

It was nearly three o'clock. Karissa Clement had agreed to meet up at the bar and answer his questions concerning Zack Kenny. Over the phone she'd sounded willing to talk about her ex-boyfriend, which he took as an encouraging sign. Getting victims of abuse to relive difficult memories was never easy.

He was running late and started to hurry. First impressions were important when interviewing victims, and he didn't want Karissa not to like him. Kicking off his Topsiders, he crossed the flooded street and hustled down the sidewalk toward Boston's.

At the front door, he put his shoes back on and entered. The interior walls were covered in framed memorabilia of all the good things that Beantown had to offer. Happy hour didn't start until four o'clock, and the place was quiet.

He took a chair at the bar and cased the room. Two seats away, a drunk sipped rum and chatted to a cockatiel perched on his shoulder picking at his beard. Three seats from him, a teenager in cutoffs drank a Coke, her feet barely touching the floor. There was no sign of Karissa, and he wondered if she'd gotten cold feet.

"Looking for someone?" the female bartender asked.

"I'm supposed to be meeting a woman at three," he said. "She's named Karissa, lives in town. Has she been in?"

"That depends. Who are you?"

"I'm a private investigator."

"Were you once a cop?"

"I was. Don't tell me I once ran you in."

"Hardly. I knew from the way you scanned the bar when you sat down. Most customers stare at the TV first. You didn't. That was a tell."

"You're very observant."

"I see a lot. If a person walks into a room and there's a TV on, their eyes will go to it first. I read that ninety-nine percent of the population does that."

"What does the other one percent do?"

"Nothing. They're blind. What's your pleasure?"

"Give me a Corona, no fruit."

"You got it."

While she poured his beer, he checked his cell phone for messages and found none. He'd hit a dead end, and he decided not to let the trip go to waste.

"What's the best thing on the menu?" he asked.

"I'm partial to the lobster bisque," she said, serving him.

"Give me a bowl and some crackers."

"Coming right up."

He sipped beer and watched the soccer match on the TV. The best part of living in Florida was that it didn't take very long to feel like you were on vacation. Out of the corner of his eye, he spied the bartender talking with the teenager in a hushed voice. The teenager hopped off her stool and came toward him.

"You must be Jon," she said.

He hated to be wrong. This girl was too young to be Karissa. Then he noticed the crow's-feet around her eyes and realized she was much older than he'd thought.

"I'm sorry, I didn't mean to ignore you," he said, unable to hide his surprise.

"It's not the first time it's happened," she said. "Let's get a table in the restaurant so we can have some privacy."

He threw down money for the bisque and the beer, and they went into the adjacent restaurant, which had old black-and-white photographs of commercial fishermen and the Red Sox adorning the walls. They picked a table in the rear of the otherwise empty room.

"I realize it's none of my business, but how old are you?" he asked.

"I'm thirty-one, soon to turn thirty-two," she said. "I know, I don't look it. You said over the phone that you wanted to talk about Zack. Is he up to his old tricks?"

She had turned the conversation to her ex-boyfriend without prompting. That was unusual, and it made him wonder if she had an ax to grind.

"Your ex-boyfriend is stalking my client, who happens to be fifteen years old," he said. "I did a background search, and saw that you slapped a restraining order on him. I was hoping you might tell me why you did that."

"I was afraid he was going to hurt me."

"Was he violent?"

"Our relationship was moving in that direction. He was texting me every half hour, and when I didn't answer him right away, he'd call me. I work in a hospital ER as a nurse, and we're not allowed to keep our cell phones powered up. Zack started showing up when he didn't hear from me, demanding that I stop what I was doing so he could see me. He got escorted off the hospital grounds a few times."

"Were the police called?"

"No. The hospital handled it internally."

"Is that normal procedure where you work?"

"I asked them to."

She frowned at the memory, and he could tell that the conversation was starting to hurt. She eyed his glass of beer sitting on the table. He pushed it toward her, and she picked it up and took a long swallow. It left a foam mustache on her upper lip. She wiped it away and then took a deep breath to get her courage up.

"I would have bought you a beer, but I didn't think you were old enough," he said.

"Don't worry about it. I used to like Zack. A lot. I asked the hospital not to call the cops because I didn't want him getting in trouble."

"So the relationship was good at the beginning. Do you still care for him?"

"Hell no. If I saw him, I'd take off running."

"How did you meet?"

"eHarmony. At first, we exchanged emails, and later we talked on the phone. He seemed nice, and he had a great job. Most of the guys on the dating sites are losers. Zack was different, and had class. Our first date was amazing. Can I have the rest?"

He said sure, and she downed the rest of his beer.

"Zack showed up at my apartment complex in a chauffeured limousine stocked with champagne and caviar," she said. "We had this amazing meal at Monkitail and then went to the Hard Rock and saw Usher. We had front-row seats that cost a small fortune."

"That's some first date."

"It was way over the top. He swept me off my feet and made me feel like a princess. We started seeing each other, and he didn't let up.

It felt too good to be true. After a month, the bubble burst, and things turned to shit. Do you mind if I vape?"

"Not at all."

She pulled out a vape and began sucking on it. It had a hypnotic smell that he realized was dope. It calmed her down, and she said, "That's better. Where was I?"

"You were about to tell me how things went sour."

"It was a Saturday night. He came to pick me up, and I met him at the front door. I'd bought this leather outfit that was really sharp, and he looked at me and said, 'No.' I said, 'What do you mean?' and he said no again, only louder. I said, 'You don't like my new outfit?' and he says, 'It's horrible. It makes you look old. Take it off.' I thought he was kidding, so I said, 'Should I wear something else?' and he takes out his cell phone and pulls up a photo of me wearing a sundress and says, 'Wear this. I love this outfit. And put a ribbon in your hair.' I asked him if he was serious, and he said yes, so I changed. But it bothered me. I've never had a guy ask me to change my clothes before. We went to eat at the Capital Grille, and Zack went to the restroom and forgot to take his cell phone. I wasn't feeling good about things, so I picked up his phone and saw that the screen was on and hadn't timed out. I searched the photo gallery and found hundreds of photographs of me, including a bunch that he'd taken when I was asleep after we had sex. In one of the photos, he'd put a pair of handcuffs on the pillow next to my head. It was nasty."

"Did he ever put the handcuffs on you?"

"That came later."

"Did he do it against your will?"

"Uh-huh. We were in his condo having sex, and I dozed off. When I opened my eyes, one of my wrists was handcuffed to the headboard. I started screaming, and Zack picked up a pillow like he was going to smother me. He got too close, and I kicked him in the nuts. That woke him up, and he let me go."

"What do you mean that woke him up?"

"Zack got weird during sex. His eyes would gloss over, and he'd make all sorts of demands. He'd never done anything violent, until the handcuffs."

"Is that when you had the restraining order put on him?"

She stared at the floor, ashamed. "I wish."

"You didn't break it off?"

"No. Zack begged for another chance, so I gave it to him. Stupid me. I guess I liked the fancy restaurants and concerts too much."

They took a break so Karissa could suck on her vape. Lancaster went back into the bar and got his glass refilled and bought a beer for Karissa. The bisque sat on the bar, growing cold. The drunk was eyeing it, and he pushed the bowl toward him. Back inside the restaurant, he handed the beer to her. She thanked him and took a long swallow.

"Feeling better?" he asked.

"That's a relative term," she said. "I never feel good talking about Zack. I'm talking to you because I hope you can get him locked up."

"Would that make you feel better?"

"No, just safer."

"Got it. What led to the restraining order?"

"A month after the handcuffs, Zack went crazy on me. We were having dinner at Coconuts and I showed him the drawing of a rose tattoo I wanted to get on my wrist. It's hard being a nurse when you look as young as I do. Some patients think I'm a candy striper and won't let me treat them. One of the other nurses suggested the tattoo to make me look older. I thought it was a good idea. Zack didn't."

She became quiet and stared at the floor. They were entering dark territory, and he treaded cautiously. "I'm sorry. What happened?"

"He kept saying, 'No, no, no, you can't do that.' I asked him, 'What's the big deal?' and he said that a tattoo would ruin his image of me. I said, 'What image is that?' Zack said he wanted me to stay a little girl. I said, 'Is that all you care about?' And he said yes. I got so pissed off I threw a glass of water in his face and ran out. There was a couple getting out of a cab, and I jumped in and went home. That night Zack sent me a threatening text, so I went to the police and got the restraining order."

"They should have locked him up," he said.

"The detective in charge wanted to. Problem was, I stayed with him after he handcuffed me to the bed, which made the whole thing look consensual. My bad."

The retelling had emotionally drained her, and she shut her eyes.

"Want me to get you something?" he asked.

"A shot of tequila," she said.

His chair scraped the floor as he started to rise.

"I'm kidding," she said. "Just give me a minute, okay?"

"Sure."

A minute turned to two before Lancaster spoke again. "I appreciate your telling me these things. I know it's tough."

Her eyes slowly opened. "I think about Zack every day. I think about going into my apartment and finding him there. Or getting in my car and having him jump me. I can't scrub him from my memory no matter how hard I try." Her open purse lay on the floor between her feet. She picked it up and showed him its contents. Inside was a can of Mace, a pair of brass knuckles, and a handgun. She was carrying around a small arsenal, and it still hadn't made her feel safe. Only locking Zack up would do that.

"I went and got a concealed-weapon permit," she said. "I go to the range three times a week. It's expensive, but what other choice do I have?"

"None," he said. "I'm sorry he hurt you."

"I know you are. So were the cops when I spoke to them. Everyone's sorry, and no one does anything. You told me that he's stalking your client. Want some advice?"

"Sure."

"Zack took hundreds of photographs of me and kept them on his cell phone. He was obsessed with me, and looking at those photographs fueled his obsession. That's the opinion of a psychiatrist at the hospital where I work. If Zack hadn't had those photographs to look at, he wouldn't have gotten so crazy on me."

"Was that the psychiatrist's opinion?"

"Yes. She said that Zack was a sexual deviant, and that deviants fantasize over images and become slaves to them. When I told Zack about the tattoo, he saw the image of me changing, and his twisted psyche couldn't handle it."

"What's your advice?"

"Don't let him photograph your client."

Her words gave him pause. The thread that connected the Hispanic in the pickup and the Canadian tourist on Los Olas and Zack Kenny was that each man had alternated looking at his cell phone and staring at Nicki. Were there images of Nicki on their phones that were fueling their obsession? And if so, where had they come from?

"Thank you," he said. "Thank you very much."

CHAPTER 15

ONCE UPON A MATTRESS

Interstate 95 was rush-hour madness, so Lancaster took State Road A1A back to Fort Lauderdale. What was normally a forty-minute drive took an hour twenty, and it was dinnertime when he pulled into the Pearls' driveway and parked. Instead of getting out, he remained in his car and silently counted to himself. One one thousand, two one thousand. Before he reached three one thousand, a physical specimen named Carlo emerged from the bushes and approached his car. He lowered his window and said, "How's it going?"

"Everything's quiet. Mike is watching the backyard, Karl's on the roof."

He looked up to see Karl next to the chimney holding a pair of binoculars and watching the Intracoastal for trouble. He hadn't seen Karl when he'd pulled in, but that was no surprise. Karl, Mike, and Carlo were ex-SEALs and were adept at blending in to whatever environment they inhabited. Their main business was protecting celebrities and politicians who came to town. Lancaster had served with them and now had an arrangement where they'd help him out if they had downtime, and vice versa.

He got out of the car. "I'm not going to be long. Are you guys still good with staying the night and watching the place?"

"Absolutely. Our calendar's wide open right now," Carlo said. "Can I ask you something? The wife invited us in earlier and served us iced tea. The husband and kid were there. The family seems totally normal and down to earth. Who's after them?"

"Someone's after the kid. A whole bunch of people, actually."

"What did she do?"

"I don't know. And neither do her parents."

"She's innocent?"

That was a good question. Deep down in his heart he wanted to believe that Nicki was as pure as a freshly fallen snow, only there was a nagging feeling in his gut that wouldn't go away. Her stalkers were obsessed with images on their cell phones, which he'd come to realize were of her. It was the only logical answer to what was going on. But what did the images show, and where had they come from? Carlo's cell phone vibrated, saving him from replying.

Carlo had a brief conversation and put his phone away. "Mike just spotted a suspicious-looking boat trolling past the house. I need to go have a look."

"Talk to you later," Lancaster said. As Carlo disappeared into the hedge, Lancaster walked up to the front door to ring the chime. The door opened, and Nolan Pearl ushered him in with an expectant air.

"Hello, Jon. How did your trip to Delray go?" Pearl asked.

"It was a home run," he said. "I talked to the ex-girlfriend of our stalker from the Cheesecake Factory. She gave me the link that ties Nicki's stalkers together."

"That's good news. Can you tell me what the link is?"

"Nicki's stalkers are sexual deviants who fantasize about young girls. Part of their fantasy is looking at images of girls on their cell phones. I need to ask Nicki some questions. I'd like you and your wife to be in the room when I do."

Pearl blinked. The words sunk in, and he took a moment to compose himself. "Do you think there are images of Nicki on these men's phones?"

"I'm afraid the answer is yes."

"But where did they come from?"

"Your guess is as good as mine."

"You don't think Nicki is posting photographs online, do you?"

"I don't know who's behind it. It could be one of her friends or a classmate at school. Or it could be a stranger who's fixated on her. I only know one thing for sure: there are photographs of Nicki that are being circulated on the web, and her stalkers are fantasizing over them when they're pursuing her. That's the link."

"Oh my God," Pearl said.

- - -

Nicki was at her father's desk on her laptop when they entered the study. Melanie sat on the couch, engrossed in her cell phone. The German shepherd sprang to life from the floor, and in atonement for past mistakes, curled its upper lip.

"Jon needs to speak with us," Pearl said.

Nicki closed her laptop, came around the desk, and quieted the dog. "You made a breakthrough, didn't you? I can see it in your face."

Nicki was a smart kid, there was no question about that. But was she as innocent as she acted? Or was she hiding a dark secret from her parents? He didn't know her well enough to know the right answer. He sat on the free end of the couch so he faced her.

Pearl pulled up a chair while Nicki remained standing.

"I did make a breakthrough this afternoon," he said. "I'm going to tell you and your parents what I learned. In return for my doing that, you need to answer some questions for me, and be totally honest with your answers. Do we have a deal?"

"Sure," the teenager said.

"Good. Here's what I learned. Your stalkers share one thing in common. Each is holding a cell phone when they're following you. That's because the stalker is fantasizing over photographs of you that are stored on his phone. I want to know where those photographs came from and who posted them on the internet. Do you know?"

Nicki's mouth dropped open but no words came out.

"Honey?" her mother said.

Still nothing. A long, excruciating moment passed.

"Nicki, answer Jon's question," her father said.

"It must have been Tyler Steeves," the teenager said quietly.

The parents exchanged worried looks. The name was new to them. Lancaster put his hands on his knees and leaned forward. "Is Tyler your boyfriend?"

"Not really. We haven't gone on a date or anything."

"Do you like him?"

"I guess. He's pretty cute."

"How did you meet him?"

"Tyler goes to Pine Crest, he's a grade ahead of me. We met during the school musical. It was called *Once Upon a Mattress*. I played Princess Winnifred."

"Was Tyler also in the play?"

"Tyler was a cameraman with the AV crew. Our school's drama coach, Mr. Rossi, filmed our rehearsals so he could critique us."

Tyler had a video camera, and Nicki appeared to have a crush on him. That was a recipe for disaster. He thought he knew what had happened, but needed to hear it in Nicki's own words.

"Did Tyler film you in private?" he asked.

"Just once," she said.

Her parents turned to stone. This was bad. He lowered his voice and pretended they weren't in the room. "Was this Tyler's idea?"

"Yeah. He thought it would be fun."

"Tell me what he filmed."

"There's a scene in the play where I sing a song while lying on a bunch of mattresses in my pajamas. One night after everyone else had left, Tyler talked me into singing the song wearing a bra and my underwear so he could video it. We watched it later and both giggled. He promised to erase it, but he didn't."

"He posted the film on the internet, didn't he?"

"Yeah."

"Which site?"

"YouTube."

YouTube was the largest site in the world for video consumption. This was getting worse, and he said, "How did you find out what Tyler had done?"

"One day in the cafeteria, he showed me the video on his cell phone. He said he'd gotten ten thousand hits. I freaked out and begged him to take it down."

"Did he?"

"Not right away."

"How long before he took it down?"

"It took him a couple of days."

"Why didn't Tyler do it right away?"

"Tyler wants to direct movies. He's got his own channel on YouTube where he posts videos that he makes. Something like a dozen movie producers contacted him after seeing my video, and offered him work. Tyler was afraid that if he took the video down, he wouldn't get any more offers."

"But he did take it down."

"Yeah, finally."

"Do you know if Tyler had any further contact with these movie people?"

"He exchanged emails with a man named Sydney who worked at a big studio and also talked to him on the phone. Sydney said he could get Tyler a job on a movie he was making this summer. Sydney also wanted to contact me and offer me a part."

"Did you talk to Sydney?"

"He sent me an email. I didn't reply."

"Did Tyler give Sydney your email address?"

"I guess he must have."

"Do you think Tyler gave Sydney other information about you?"

"Probably. Sydney knew a lot about me, like where I went to school, and what grade I was in. It was icky. Tyler must have told him."

The puzzle no longer had as many missing pieces. An alluring video of Nicki on the internet had attracted the wrong kind of attention from the wrong kind of people.

"You said Tyler and Sydney talked to each other over the phone," he said. "Do you know if they ever met?"

"The meeting never happened," Nicki said. "Tyler told me that Sydney wanted to fly to Fort Lauderdale and take us out to lunch. When Tyler told him that I wasn't interested, Sydney backed out. Tyler wasn't happy."

"Did Tyler pressure you to meet with Sydney after that?"

"He asked me a few times, but I said no."

"That was very smart of you. It sounds like Sydney was more interested in meeting you than Tyler."

"You're probably right. I thought the whole thing was a put-on."

"Why did you think that?"

"Because Tyler's videos aren't very good. You should see the comments that viewers post on YouTube. Most of them are awful."

"But your video got ten thousand hits. How do you explain that?"

"I can't." She shrugged her shoulders.

Something wasn't adding up. A rank high school kid didn't get ten thousand hits on YouTube unless he had talent or was posting porn. Nicki claimed she was wearing underwear in the video, but Lancaster knew that could be a lie because her parents were in the room. Maybe she'd been naked.

"Do you have a copy of the video that we can see?"

Embarrassed, Nicki nodded. "It's pretty bad."

"I'd still like to see it. This is for your benefit, Nicki. I'm pretty sure that video is tied to these men who are stalking you. Seeing it will help me confirm that."

She looked to her mother and father. "Do you want to see it too?"

"Yes," Melanie said. "Now go get it, honey."

Nicki retrieved her laptop and sat on the couch sandwiched between her parents. She typed in a command, Windows Media Player appeared, and a video started to play. She placed the laptop on the glass coffee table so everyone could watch.

"Don't laugh," the teenager said.

The three adults in the room watched intently. On the small screen, Nicki lay atop a pile of mattresses wearing a white bra and pink panties. It could have been a sexy pose, only she looked terribly self-conscious. The look on her face suggested that she knew this was a bad decision but had gone along with it anyway. She started to sing, and it didn't get any better. Her voice was pleasant but nothing to write home about. The image of the uncomfortable teenager did not change.

The song ended, and the screen went dark. On a scale of one to ten, Lancaster gave it a two for effort. It had little to recommend it, yet somehow it had garnered a large audience. But of who? What type of viewer wanted to watch an embarrassed teenage girl mangle an old song in her underwear?

Nicki climbed into her father's lap and buried her head into his chest.

"I'm sorry," she said. "I should have told you."

- - -

Pearl walked him outside to his car. "Please tell me what you're thinking."

"Your daughter's no sex kitten," he said.

"Excuse me?"

"She's not sexy in that video. So why so many hits? And why did some pervert pretending to be a movie producer contact Tyler and try to arrange a lunch so he could meet her?"

"You think that man used Tyler to try to get to Nicki?"

"He sure did. Perverts stalk teenage girls on the internet all the time. The stories they invent to get close to their victims boggle the imagination. The problem is, Nicki is anything but sexy in that video. So why all the attention?"

"Maybe it was a fluke."

"YouTube doesn't work like that. If a video doesn't hook a viewer in a few seconds, they click away. I should know, there's a video of me that's gotten half a million hits. I did some research on why videos go viral. It's never a fluke."

Pearl looked confused. "Then what are you saying?"

"I'm asking you, is this the tip of the iceberg? Has Nicki done other videos with Tyler Steeves that she won't tell us about? Is that in her makeup?"

"No. Nicki wouldn't do that," Pearl said, raising his voice.

"You're sure about this," Lancaster said.

"I'm one hundred percent sure," Pearl said. "Nicki has never caused a problem. We couldn't have asked for a better child to raise, and that's saying a lot these days."

"You've had no issues with her?"

"None."

"How about disagreements?"

"What do you mean?"

"I'm looking for a reason why Nicki might become angry with you, and do something stupid that would lead to the situation we have right now."

Pearl gave it some thought. "Well, she did ask us if she could take horseback riding lessons. I said no, and she got angry. I've seen too many young girls become paralyzed after taking nasty spills. It's a dangerous sport."

"How long was she upset at you?"

"A few days. She got over it."

Or maybe Pearl had misread the situation and Nicki hadn't gotten over it. Her bedroom walls were covered with horse photos. Did they act as reminders of her father's refusal to let her sit on a horse? He took out his car keys.

"You and your wife need to sit down and talk to her about it," he said. "I'm going to pay Zack Kenny a visit. I'll call you if I learn anything."

"Do you think I'm wrong about my daughter?" Pearl asked.

"Maybe," he said.

CHAPTER 16
PROMISED LAND

The DMV information that Devon had provided to Lancaster included the address of the luxury apartment building where Zack Kenny lived. It was called Sunrise Harbor and was located in the community of Coral Ridge, a few short blocks from the ocean.

Sunrise Harbor was on the high end of the rental experience and had its own parking area with a small guardhouse equipped with multiple surveillance cameras. Lancaster flashed his old cop badge to the uniformed guard when asked for ID.

"Is there a problem?" the guard asked.

Telling the guard his business was a risk. If he was chummy with Kenny, he might alert him that there was trouble brewing. Or, the guard might be helpful, and share valuable information. His uniform was wrinkle-free and proudly worn. It made Lancaster think he was ex-military and could be trusted.

"A tenant named Zack Kenny," he said.

The guard let out a whistle. "Can't say I'm surprised."

"Is he a troublemaker?"

The guard put his hand on the roof of Lancaster's car and lowered his voice. "Zack had a runaway living with him. Girl couldn't have been more than fifteen years old. His neighbor blew the whistle, and it caused a real stink."

"Did the police get involved?"

"It didn't get that far. The renters' association runs the building with an iron fist. They had a meeting in the community room and a hundred and fifty people showed up. Zack came with his attorney and claimed that he was helping the kid out. Nobody believed him. He was told to get rid of the girl or face eviction. He put up a fight but finally agreed, and the runaway moved out."

"Has he caused any other problems?"

"No, but it's only a matter of time. I know his kind."

"Which is what?"

"He's a perv."

"You were a cop once, weren't you?"

"Military Police."

"What makes you think he wasn't helping the kid out?"

"This place is loaded with beautiful unmarried women. You should see the pool on the weekends. It's enough to make you drool. Zack could have his pick, only he doesn't want that. He's into little girls, the sick bastard."

"Is he here now?"

"Hasn't come home yet. You going to arrest him?"

"I just want to talk to him. Do you mind if I wait inside?"

"Be my guest. Park in one of the visitor spots or someone will raise a stink."

"Will do. Thanks for the help."

The guard went inside the guardhouse and made the guardrail rise. Lancaster drove inside the complex, parked, and kept the engine running and basked in the AC. Back during his cop days he'd been offered a desk in the sex crimes unit but had declined out of fear of what he'd do if he caught a suspect harming a kid. Zack Kenny was bringing out the same kind of raw emotions, and he tried to stay focused on the job he'd been hired to do. He needed to get his hands on Kenny's cell phone and look at the images of Nicki Pearl stored in its memory. His gut was telling him there was more than the video of Nicki singing while lying atop a pile of mattresses.

To pass the time, he did a Google search on his cell phone and was soon reading Kenny's work profile on LinkedIn. He'd been employed as a securities broker with the same firm for eight years and recently been promoted to vice president. He had a solid work history and a decent education. He didn't think Kenny's employer knew about the restraining order or the problems with his apartment association, which told him that Kenny was doing a good job of keeping his personal life hidden. During the day he was a respectable businessman, but at night he was a creep.

A familiar black Lexus parked three spaces down. Lancaster killed his engine and hopped out of his vehicle. He was going to confront Kenny and take his cell phone once Kenny got out of his expensive sports car. Nicki's stalkers were slaves to their phones, and he was determined to find out why.

But Kenny didn't get out of his car. Instead, he remained behind the wheel with his head bowed. Either he was taking a nap, or he was looking at his phone. Lancaster silently came up behind the Lexus and stared through the driver's window at the cell phone in Kenny's lap. A video was playing with fuzzy images dancing on the screen.

Kenny's head turned. He flipped the cell phone over, hiding the screen. Lancaster placed his cop badge against the glass.

"Get out of the car."

Kenny shook his head.

"Get out of the car before I drag you out."

Kenny blinked. Decision time. He lifted the cell phone off his lap and ripped off its rubber protective cover. Then he slammed the cell phone's screen violently against the dashboard with all his might. He did this so many times that it must have made his arm hurt. But he wasn't done. Throwing open his door, he leaped out of the car and threw the cell phone against the pavement, picked it up, and gave it a mighty heave over a hedge that separated the complex from its neighbor. A triumphant look spread across his face, and he turned around and walked away. Lancaster followed him.

"Do the people at your brokerage firm know about the restraining order Karissa Clement slapped against you? Or that you shacked up with a fifteen-year-old girl?"

Kenny slowed but did not stop. The words were having an effect.

"I can tell them. Or you can stop and talk with me. It's your call."

Reaching the entrance to the apartment building, Kenny stopped and spun around. His mouth was as thin as a paper cut, his breathing short. His clothes were expensive and so was his haircut, and he had a perfect bronze tan, courtesy of a tanning salon.

"How much do you want?" Kenny asked.

"I don't know what you're talking about," he said.

"You want money, right? That's why you're here."

"This isn't a shakedown."

"It sure feels like one."

"Have you been shaken down before?"

Kenny said nothing. People with sordid backgrounds who made a decent buck were vulnerable to blackmail, and he guessed Kenny had paid for people's silence before.

"Then what is it?" Kenny said.

"I want to know why you're stalking Nicki Pearl."

"Never heard of her."

"You were watching her at the Cheesecake Factory today. You're obsessed with her. I want to know why."

Kenny shook his head. "I'm afraid you've got the wrong person."

"You have images of her on your cell phone. That's why you threw it away."

"You're grasping at straws."

"Then what were you just looking at?"

"Baseball. I'm a big Marlins fan."

"Do you always throw your phones away?"

"What I do with my cell phone is none of your business."

This wasn't working, and he decided to take a different tack.

"Would you like me to send a copy of the restraining order to your boss? Or tell him about the fifteen-year-old runaway you kept in your apartment?"

"My boss is a she, and she doesn't care what I do in my free time. I make millions for my firm every year. I'm entitled to have a little fun after work."

"A little fun? Sleeping with minors is a crime."

"I have no idea what you're talking about. By the way, how did you get in here? This is a private parking lot, and you're trespassing. If you don't leave, I'll go inside and call the police. I mean it."

He *was* trespassing and could get himself and the guard at the front gate in real trouble if Kenny made good on his threat. He started to retreat.

"Stay away from Nicki Pearl," he said.

"I told you, I don't know her. Now get out of here and don't come back."

Kenny used a key card to enter the building, where he boarded an elevator in the lobby. Lancaster waited until the elevator doors were shut before venturing over to the concrete dividing wall that Kenny had tossed his cell phone over. It was a foot taller than he was, and he put his hands on the ledge and pulled himself up to have a look.

Sunrise Harbor's neighbor was another luxury apartment building. It had all the trimmings, including an Olympic-size swimming pool with reclining lounge chairs. A uniformed janitor was picking up cushions and towels. A whistle snapped his head.

"Want to make yourself a quick buck?"

The janitor hustled over to the wall. He was Hispanic with a face older than his years. South Florida was filled with boat people who'd fled Cuba looking for a better life, only to discover the best they could do was menial jobs in the service industry. Lancaster pulled himself up so he was sitting on the wall.

"My name's Jon. What's yours?"

"Jorge," the janitor said.

"Hey, Jorge, nice to meet you. My girlfriend and I just had a fight, and she tossed my cell phone over the wall. That will teach me to forget our anniversary. I'll make it worth your while if you'll look around the grounds and find it for me."

"You want me to find your cell phone," Jorge said, sounding pissed.

"It won't take five minutes. Come on, I'll make it worth your while."

"Sure you will."

"You're not going to help me?"

"No. I need to finish up."

"What if I come over and look myself?"

"You can't do that."

His anger was palpable. Had Jorge been a doctor or professional person back in Cuba? Lancaster had met Cubans with degrees who weren't allowed to practice in the States, and it had hardened them. Pulling out his wallet, he removed a handful of cash.

"Fifty bucks for your trouble. How does that sound, Jorge?"

Jorge stared at the money, and his eyes took on a faraway expression. Lancaster imagined him climbing aboard a makeshift boat made of tires and making the treacherous passage to Key West only to discover the promised land wasn't so great after all.

"Make it a hundred," Jorge said.

"You first have to find my cell phone."

Jorge removed a cell phone with a broken screen from his pants pocket.

"I already did," the unhappy Cuban said.

CHAPTER 17
THE SKIN CANVAS

Back in his car, Lancaster attempted to power up Kenny's cell phone and got a dark screen for his trouble. Under the hope it was a power issue, he plugged the cell phone into the charger connected to his car's cigarette lighter. Nothing happened. Kenny's smashing it on the pavement had been the kiss of death.

He was getting pissed. Nicki's stalkers were good at covering their tracks, and he still didn't have a solid reason why they were pursuing her. Did they share a crazy fetish about teenagers belting out songs from old Broadway musicals? It was a stretch, and he had to believe something darker was lurking below the surface.

Lancaster's cell phone beeped. The battery was dying, and he replaced Kenny's phone in the charger with his own. His phone was new, courtesy of his ex-girlfriend tossing the old one out of a moving car. Replacing it had been a snap. A quick trip to the Verizon store and forty-five minutes later he'd walked out with a new Droid, his contacts and apps restored. Kenny's phone was also a Droid, and he wondered if Kenny had bought it from Verizon, which had more locations than a hamburger chain. If he had, then all his data was stored in the cloud and could be easily restored. It gave him an idea, and thirty seconds later he was talking to a Haitian named Croix Tedesco.

"How's the forgery business?" he asked.

"Those days are behind me," Croix said in his lilting Caribbean accent. "I run a tattoo parlor these days."

"That's not what I hear. I hear you're banging out fake visas for immigrants who've overstayed their welcome. I hear these visas are so good that they even fool ICE agents."

Croix coughed into the phone. "What do you want, Jon?"

"I need a fake driver's license and matching credit card," he said.

"I see. Come by tomorrow and I'll make one for you. My tattoo parlor is called the Skin Canvas and is on Sunrise Boulevard across the street from the Family Dollar store. My office is in the back."

"Let me rephrase that. I need a fake driver's license right now."

"I'm afraid that's impossible. I'm heading out to dinner."

"Stay right there. Understood?"

"It's my wedding anniversary. My wife will not be happy with me."

"Listen, my friend, I'm not asking you, I'm telling you. If I get there, and you're gone, I'll turn your life upside down. Am I making myself clear?"

The line went quiet. Lancaster waited him out. He'd been working undercover for the sheriff's office when he'd inadvertently stumbled across Croix running a false passport operation. Some criminals were more useful not behind bars, and he'd used Croix to create false identities to help him catch some very bad people. Their relationship was a solid one, but at the end of the day, Croix was still breaking the law, and could be taken down with a single phone call.

"Loud and painfully clear," the forger said. "I'll be here."

- - -

The Skin Canvas was doing a brisk business, and he drove behind the building to park. Back when he was a teen, the only people with tattoos were military or worked in carnival sideshows. Now everybody and his sister was getting inked.

He approached the back door. A Mercedes 500SL was parked in a spot marked Reserved. Croix had done well for a guy who'd come to the States with just the shirt on his back. On the Mercedes's rear bumper was a Pine Crest School sticker. He knocked, and when the door swung in Croix pretended to be happy to see him. Croix was a small man, delicate boned, and favored silk shirts with colorful patterns and fine gold jewelry.

"You mad at me?" he asked.

"Yes," the forger said. "My wife is pissed."

"I'll pay you back someday. This is important."

Croix ushered him inside, and he entered a windowless room filled with the finest 3-D printing equipment money could buy. The room's AC was kept ice cold to ensure the humidity did not harm the equipment. From the front of the building came the steady hum of mechanical needles puncturing human skin.

"How do you put up with that noise?" he asked.

"You get used to it. Have a seat so I can take your picture."

He sat on a stool in front of a blue screen while Croix spent a minute adjusting the room's light. The forger was usually talkative; not so tonight. Lancaster didn't want to ruin the relationship and decided to level with him. "Let me explain what's going on. I've been hired by a family to protect their teenage girl, who's being stalked by a group of perverts. The girl is clean. Not selling drugs or posting dirty pictures of herself on the internet. She goes to Pine Crest School. Doesn't one of your kids go there?"

Croix's jaw tightened. "Who told you that?"

"I saw the bumper sticker on your car. Which one?"

"Brie, my oldest. She really likes it. What did this girl do to draw this unwanted attention to herself?"

"She didn't do anything."

"What you're implying is that this could be my daughter."

"Or one of her classmates."

"This is disturbing. What is this girl's name?"

"Nicki Pearl."

"That name sounds familiar. Don't move." Croix snapped a head shot with a camera mounted on a tripod, then removed a thumb drive from the back of the camera and transferred the image to a computer sitting on a desk. Using a software program, he mounted the photo onto the template of a Florida driver's license while Lancaster looked over his shoulder.

"What grade is she in?" Croix asked.

"Nicki's fifteen, so I guess she's in the tenth grade. You may have seen her in a musical the school put on, *Once Upon a Mattress*. She was one of the leads."

"Ah, yes, now I remember her. A lovely child. But what you've said makes no sense. Why are these men stalking her? What has she done to make them want her?"

"Nothing. Look, I'm sorry I ruined your dinner plans, but I've got to get to the bottom of this. Nicki's life is in danger."

"I understand. What name should I put on your driver's license?"

"Zackary Kenny. I've got his address, DOB, and Florida driver's license number."

"Give them to me."

He gave Croix the information. Five minutes later, he was holding a laminated driver's license with a shimmering security hologram that looked every bit as good as the real thing. "I also need a credit card with Zackary Kenny's name on it."

"Visa or American Express?"

"Whatever's easiest."

"Visa is easiest." Croix pulled up another software program and went to work on creating a fake Visa card with Zack Kenny's name. "What you plan to do with this card? A charge won't go through. Visa makes vendors run checks on all purchases."

"I know that. I'm betting Zack Kenny is a Verizon customer, so I'm going to visit their store and buy a new cell phone and get them to download his information onto it. He's looking at images of Nicki, and I need to see them. I plan to use cash to make the purchase. The credit card and driver's license are just for show."

"Images? What kind of images?"

"I don't know."

"But you said this girl wasn't posting images of herself on the internet. Then what is this fellow looking at?"

That was the $64,000 question. What was fueling Zack Kenny's obsession, as well as those of the other sickos who were relentlessly pursuing Nicki? He'd come up with a theory and decided to test it out on Croix.

"Do you ever look at porn on the internet?" he asked.

"When I'm bored," Croix admitted.

"Then I'm sure you've seen head shots of female actresses photoshopped onto images of women engaged in group fellatio and gang bangs. The images are phony, but they can still turn you on. I think that may be the situation here."

"You think Nicki's face has been photoshopped onto other girls' naked bodies?"

"Yes. It's the only explanation I can come up with."

Croix shook his head. "If what you're saying is true, then it could be any teenage girl who's being victimized by these men. Even my own daughter."

"Yes, it could."

A fake Visa card spat out of the 3-D printer. Croix trimmed it to the proper size and laminated it with an ultrathin layer of plastic coating. Handing it to Lancaster, he said, "If you do get this man's information, how do you plan to access it?"

Lancaster didn't pretend to know everything. He said, "What do you mean?"

"If this man is a deviant, then I'm sure his cell phone is encrypted. Unless you know the password, you won't be able to find what you're looking for," Croix said.

His shoulders sagged. He didn't use a password for his own cell phone, and had not considered that Kenny would use one to keep his images of Nicki hidden.

"I don't know the password. Any suggestions?"

"You will need to hack the phone. I know a man who can help you. He's Russian and owns a strip club. His dancers get customers drunk and take them to VIP rooms, then pass their cell phones through a hole in the wall. While they're giving blow jobs, the Russian hacks their phones and gets their banking information. The next day, he transfers a few thousand from their checking accounts to his bank. If the customer raises a stink, he threatens to blackmail them."

"He videotapes the VIP room?"

"Correct. Do you know him?"

"I know his kind. Would he hack Zack Kenny's cell phone if you asked him?"

"Normally, I would say no. He is a mobster and very secretive. But he has a problem that you can help him fix with your connections in the police department. In return, I believe he will hack the pervert's cell phone for you."

"What kind of problem are we talking about?"

"He's being shaken down by a pair of detectives and pays thousands of dollars each month in protection money to keep his club open. Now, the detectives are pressuring him to give them a piece of the action."

"They want to be silent partners in the club?"

"A straight fifty-fifty split. In return, the detectives will supply the dancers with cocaine, which they will peddle to their customers."

"Are these detectives vice cops?"

"I don't think so. I believe they work in homicide."

"Then how are they getting their hands on the blow?"

"The cocaine is supposed to be incinerated, but the detectives have a way of siphoning off a few pounds before it's taken away to be burned. If you can get them off the Russian's back, I believe he will hack the pervert's cell phone for you."

"Can't I just pay him to do this?"

"He won't take your money. But if you do him a favor, he will respond in kind."

The two pieces of fake ID were clutched in his hand. He stared at them long and hard. He believed in following a case down whatever road it took him. But that didn't mean getting in bed with a mobster, and there was no doubt in his mind that this Russian was nothing less than a devil with a thick accent.

But what if he decided not to pay the Russian a visit? Then he was back to square one and would have to start over. Normally, that wouldn't be a problem, only he was running out of time. By the grace of God and a lot of luck, Nicki had managed to thwart her stalkers, but that wouldn't last forever. Eventually, a stalker would get his hands on Nicki and steal her away, and her parents would never see her again.

"What is this Russian's name?" he asked.

"Sergey."

"Call him and set up a meeting."

"Consider it done," the forger said.

CHAPTER 18

BOOTY CALL

He left the tattoo parlor with his new identity in hand and drove to the closest Verizon Wireless store. It was fifteen minutes before closing when he walked through the front doors and was approached by a fresh-faced young woman wearing a name tag that identified her as Meg. He used the story of his ex-girlfriend tossing his cell phone out of a moving car because it was funny and also true. To help sell the story, he took Zack Kenny's broken cell phone out of his back pocket and showed it to her.

"Wow, she really did a number on it," Meg said.

"I need to buy a new one," he said. "Call it the price of love."

Meg went behind the counter and got on a store computer. He handed her the fake driver's license and Visa card and gave her Kenny's social security number, which he'd committed to memory in case she asked for it. He held his breath as she searched for Zackary Kenny.

"Okay, I found your account," Meg said. "Your phone is the Motorola Z2 Droid. We have a special going on. I can upgrade you to a Z Force Droid for thirty bucks."

"Is it worth it?"

"Absolutely. I got one myself. It's the best phone I've ever owned."

"Sold," he said. "Can I download my apps and contacts to it?"

"Of course. You're on the Unlimited Plan, which offers unlimited data, text, and calls plus HD streaming and a mobile hotspot. Want to keep it?"

"Yes, ma'am."

"You're in luck. You bought insurance the last time you purchased a phone, so this new one's covered. The only charge is for the upgrade."

"This is getting better all the time." Taking out his wallet, he pulled out a pair of twenties. "I'll pay cash. My credit card is nearly tapped out this month. I have a favor to ask. Will you help me download my apps and data? I'm not good with that stuff."

"You bet," Meg said.

- - -

He walked out of the store holding a new Z Force Droid with Zack Kenny's personal information stored on it. So far, his plan had gone without a hitch. If he was lucky, Zack Kenny didn't encrypt his personal information, and he'd be able to see what Kenny was looking at without having to jump in bed with a Russian mobster.

No such luck. The phone was locked and needed a password. He backed out of the space and was soon on Sunrise Boulevard heading west. Taking out his own phone, he pulled up Google and tapped the tiny microphone embedded in the search bar. The word "Listening" appeared on his screen, and he spoke into his phone.

"Directions to the Booty Call, Fort Lauderdale."

"Here are your directions to the Booty Call, Fort Lauderdale," an automated female voice said. "Continue to drive west on Sunrise Boulevard for five point two miles. You are on the fastest possible route and should reach your destination by 8:20 p.m."

He arrived right on time. The club was a concrete building painted hot pink with royal palm trees framing the entrance. A valet with fresh stitches on his chin took his keys. Inside, a woman showing heavy cleavage said the cover was twenty bucks.

"I'm here to see Sergey," he said. "Croix Tedesco sent me."

"I don't know any Sergey," the woman said.

"My name's Jon Lancaster. I'll be inside waiting for him."

"You haven't paid me."

"Nor do I plan to."

He passed through a beaded curtain into the club. The bar was shaped like a horseshoe with the dance floor in its center. A young lady wearing a piece of dental floss gyrated on a brass pole to the beat of deafening electronic dance music. He found an empty chair at the bar and ordered a Bud. It set him back twelve bucks.

A man built like a bodybuilder and wearing a black suit caught his eye. The man was checking out the patrons, intent on finding someone. Lancaster took a swig of beer and hopped out of his chair. He'd spent thirty months training to be a SEAL and never once lifted a weight. Big muscles only slowed you down. The man in the suit pointed a finger at him.

"You Lancaster?"

"My friends call me Jon."

"My boss wants to see you. Let's go."

The man in the suit slapped his hand on Lancaster's shoulder. A split second later, the man was kneeling on the floor, writhing in agony. Pain being the great equalizer, Lancaster gave him enough juice to drain the blood from his face. When the man in the suit had taken enough torture, he released him. The man rose rubbing his thumb.

"Touch me again, and I'll break your arm," Lancaster said.

The dancer had stopped her routine and was watching. So was everyone else in the joint. Watching a fat guy take down a strong guy was not a dynamic they were used to seeing. He took his change off the bar and slipped it under the dancer's G-string.

"Just a little misunderstanding," he said.

- - -

Sergey's office was more of a living room, with a leather couch and a glass coffee table. Three walls were taken up by flat screen TVs. A feed from the club played on one; a feed from a VIP room where a patron was getting a friction dance showed on the second; the YouTube video of him popping the kidnappers was on the third.

Sergey was sprawled on the couch. His unbuttoned shirt revealed a hairless chest covered in bright tattoos. He was going bald and wore an elaborate comb-over. He pointed at a chair leaning against a wall. Lancaster grabbed it and sat down.

"You have more hits than the latest Justin Bieber video," the Russian said. "Do you enjoy being famous?"

"It isn't the worst thing that ever happened to me."

"Does the video help you get women?"

"It's a good icebreaker. They usually ask how the little girl that I rescued is doing."

"Do you know?"

"Kid's fine. Her parents sent me a Christmas card last year."

"How touching."

"Glad you think so. Croix told me about your problem. I have a solution."

In Lancaster's experience, Russians were difficult to read. Something resembling a smile crossed Sergey's face. Without getting up, he fetched two beers from a small fridge, and placed one on the coffee table in front of his guest.

"Tell me," Sergey said.

"When cops shake down businesses, they choose ones that are breaking the law. The owners don't go to the police because they're afraid of being arrested. Your problem is worse because you're breaking a lot of laws. Your dancers are blowing customers, you're videotaping the sex and using it for blackmail, and you're hacking cell phones and draining bank accounts. That's enough to get you put away for fifteen years."

The Russian mobster sipped his beer. "Not good."

"Not good at all. Here's my solution. These detectives want your dancers to move coke that they plan to steal from the police stockade. I have friends on the force that I'll tip off. These detectives will get busted, and your problem goes away."

"Will my name be left out of this?"

"Yes. The detectives won't know you set them up. Now let me ask you a question. How are these detectives stealing the coke? The stockade is tightly run. It's hard to steal drugs without it getting noticed and reported."

"I asked the detectives, and they explained the deal," Sergey said. "The police have drug-sniffing dogs that they use on busts. One of the handlers uses cocaine to train the dogs on a course. Before the handler returns the cocaine, he switches the drugs for flour. The handler is a veteran officer, so no one suspects."

"How much is he stealing?"

"A kilo every other week."

"A kilo has a street value of twenty-five grand. Fifty grand a month is a nice haul. Give me these detectives' names, and I'll get it taken care of."

"I don't know their names," the Russian said. "They flashed their badges the first time they visited the club but did not present me with their identification. However, I do have a video that I secretly took of them stored on my computer. Will that help?"

Lancaster knew most of the detectives with the department and said yes. Sergey put his beer down and powered up the thin laptop on the coffee table. In the Broward County Sheriff's Office, 98 percent of the cops were brave, honorable women and men who risked their lives every day to keep the public safe. The 2 percent that were bad had reputations, but managed to keep their jobs because other cops were loath to turn them in.

Sergey flipped the laptop around. A video played on the small screen. It had been taken inside the same office they were now in. On the video, a Hispanic woman and her partner stood with Sergey in the room's center. The woman was doing the talking while wagging her finger in Sergey's face, doing the old shakedown. He stared and realized it was Detectives Vargas and Gibbons. He leaned back and shook his head.

"You know them?" Sergey asked.

"I sure do," he said. "They're bad cops, and plenty of their colleagues on the force know it. No one will shed a tear when they go down. But I have to ask you again. I'm familiar with the stockade procedures for handling drugs, and they're strict. Did you learn *exactly* how the dog handler is getting the cocaine out of the building?"

"He uses his cowboy boots," the Russian explained. "He comes to work with plastic bags filled with flour stuffed in each boot. Each bag weighs half a kilo. He gets a kilo of cocaine from the stockade and works the dogs on a course. The course has places where the cocaine can be switched, including a small shed. He picks a moment and hides in the shed and makes the exchange."

Lancaster nodded. It was everything he needed to make a call and get an investigation started. "This is going to take a few weeks. In the meantime, continue to deal with them like nothing's changed."

Sergey closed his laptop. The Russian had gotten what he wanted and looked pleased. Lancaster handed him the Droid with Zack Kenny's information.

"Your turn," he said.

CHAPTER 19
BRUTE FORCE

Hacking a cell phone was virgin territory for Lancaster. He didn't have a clue as to how a hacker got his hands on personal information stored inside a phone. Was it skill or luck or a combination of both? To his surprise, it was none of the above.

It was called brute force. Using a sophisticated software program, a hacker could systematically try many passwords or pass phrases until the correct one was found. The method was fast when used to check short passwords, but grew longer when the password consisted of a combination of numbers, letters, and symbols.

To aid his search, Sergey needed personal information about Zack Kenny. This included names of pets, favorite foods, names of schools he'd attended, girlfriends, and any other easily remembered things that might be turned into a password.

Using his Droid, Lancaster got on the internet and pulled up Kenny's LinkedIn page, which contained the names of Kenny's previous workplaces. He recited this information to Sergey, then found Kenny's profile on Facebook, and read off the names of schools Kenny had attended and his favorite musicians and movies.

"This isn't very much," Sergey said. "What about hobbies or pets?"

"I don't have any of that," he said.

"What else can you tell me about him?"

"He's a sexual demon who's attracted to young girls."

Sergey frowned. "Then we're probably looking at a long password."

"That would be a good assumption."

"Then this could take a while."

"How long are we talking about?"

"Days," the Russian hacker said. "My software program will test hundreds of thousands or even millions of words and eventually get a hit. But it's a long process."

"Is there a way to speed it along?" he asked.

"Get me more information. That usually does the trick."

He thought back to his meeting with Karissa Clement. She'd been happy to share what she knew about Zack, and with a little prodding might provide him with a piece of information that would unlock her ex-boyfriend's cell phone.

"Where's a quiet place I can make a phone call?" he asked.

"You can use a VIP room," Sergey said. "If a girl comes in, kick her out."

"Tell me the way, would you?"

– – –

Sergey gave him instructions, and he soon found himself in an empty VIP room with mirrors on the walls and ceiling and a red leather couch with a gaping tear in it. He took a spot on the couch and gave Karissa a call. She answered with a cheery voice.

"Hey there. I was thinking about you. How's your investigation going?"

"I've hit a wall," he said. "I was hoping you could help me."

"I'd be happy to try. By the way, you didn't tell me you were a celebrity. I googled you when I got home and read up on you. I also watched the video on YouTube. Where did you learn to shoot like that?"

"I was in the military."

"Five hundred thousand hits. You must have women swarming all over you. It said online you were a Navy SEAL. Is that true?"

"Guilty as charged."

"You're the bashful type, aren't you?"

Karissa was more assertive and self-assured over the phone than she'd been in person, and the conversation was starting to sound like a date. Either she liked to flirt or there was real interest, and he decided to tread cautiously. "I don't like to talk about the past. There's an expression in police work. You're only as good as your last case. Right now, I'm striking out and need your help in a big way."

"I'm more than happy to help. Can I ask you a question?"

"Sure."

"You don't wear a ring. Are you single?"

"I am."

"So am I. And I think you're cute. Fire away."

He didn't remember a woman ever calling him cute before. Maybe his mother had when he was a baby, but that was a long time ago. It made him feel strange, and he glanced at his reflection in one of the room's mirrors. His face was bright red.

"I confronted Zack in the parking lot of his apartment building," he said. "He knew I wanted his cell phone and smashed it on the ground. I went to a Verizon store and conned them into believing that I was Zack. A salesperson sold me a new phone and downloaded all of his personal information onto it. I want to look at his data, but it's password protected. I was hoping you could help me hack it."

"Wow. What do I have to do?"

"I need the names of Zack's pets and his hobbies and stuff like that. People use familiar names for passwords."

"Let me think for a second."

"I'm going to put you on speaker so I can type your answers into my phone. Is that okay?"

"Sure thing."

He balanced his cell phone on his lap and put it on speaker. Then he minimized the screen and opened up an app called InkPad. On the screen appeared a yellow legal pad and a keypad. He'd started using InkPad when he was a detective and had found it invaluable when questioning subjects during investigations. Everything he wrote down was stored in the cloud and could be accessed on his desktop computer, on his mobile device, or by going on the internet and logging in to his personal account. There was never a chance of him losing important information by forgetting to empty his pockets before he put his clothes in the wash.

"Ready when you are," he said.

The door to the VIP room opened. A black dancer wearing a string bikini strolled in with a drunk customer. She had the customer by the tie and dragged him like a horse.

"This room's taken," he said.

The dancer frowned. "You in here by yourself?"

"It would appear so."

"Want me to come back when I'm done?"

"No, thanks."

"You sure? They don't call this place the Booty Call for nothing."

"I'm sure. Have a nice day."

He rose from the couch and showed her out. She wiggled her ass as she left, just to let him know the invitation was still good. He returned to his spot on the couch, picked up his cell phone, and took Karissa off speaker. "You still there?"

"I'm here. Where are you? Who was that?" Karissa asked suspiciously.

He normally didn't discuss the details of his cases with strangers. Only Karissa had heard everything and was probably thinking he was a real sleaze. If he wasn't straight with her, she'd hang up, and a good source of information would be lost.

"I'm in a strip club called the Booty Call," he said. "The owner is a Russian hoodlum who's also a hacker. He's helping me get information off Zack's cell phone. I'm sitting in a VIP room, and a dancer just came in by mistake."

"That sounds crazy enough to be true," she said.

"I wouldn't lie to you. It's all true. I'm going to put you back on speaker. Ready?"

"Fire away."

- - -

Ten minutes later they were done. As they exchanged goodbyes, Karissa asked him to keep her apprised of how things played out with Zack, and he agreed to call her once his job was done. He walked back to Sergey's office feeling like he was making progress.

He rapped on the door, and a familiar voice invited him in. He entered to find Sergey lying on the couch talking on a cell phone. The Russian mobster motioned for him to sit and ended the call.

"That was my bouncer. He's at the hospital getting X-rayed. You hurt him."

"I hardly touched him," he said.

"Your touch is a deadly one. You ruptured the tendon in his hand. He's no good to me now."

"Sorry."

Sergey pulled himself up to a sitting position so he faced his guest. "I've read about the SEALs. You're the world's most elite warriors but have problems adjusting to the real world when you leave the military. Would you say that is a true assessment?"

"Maybe for some of us. I think I've done okay."

"Once a warrior, always a warrior. I think that would describe you."

Lancaster shrugged and did not reply. He didn't like when people tried to analyze him. In his experience, the only people who truly understood SEALs were other SEALs. The only reward for being a SEAL came from within, and that was a difficult thing for outsiders to appreciate, let alone comprehend.

"How would you like to come work for me?" Sergey said, breaking the silence. "I will make it worth your while."

"Doing what?"

"Running security at my clubs."

"No, thanks. I like the gig I have now."

"I will leave the offer open in case you change your mind."

Lancaster opened up the InkPad app on his phone. "I just got off the phone with Zack Kenny's ex-girlfriend. She gave me the names of his pets, his college fraternity, his hobbies, and the nickname of his high school football team. Hopefully, it's enough information for you to hack the password on his cell phone."

"Let's find out," Sergey said.

The thin laptop sat on the coffee table, still connected to the recently purchased Droid using a USB connector cord. This allowed the laptop's hacking software to test passwords without them having to manually type them into the Droid. Sergey picked up the laptop and the Droid and balanced the two devices on his lap. Lancaster read off the information that Karissa had given him, and Sergey entered it into the laptop.

"Excuse my ignorance, but how does this work?" he asked.

"It's fairly simple," the Russian said. "The software program on my laptop will test hundreds of variations of each word you give me. The program will try the word in all lower case, then the same word in upper case, and all sorts of variations. If none of those work, the program will try the same words with the number one in back of it, which is common when people are creating passwords. If that doesn't work, the program will try the word with the numbers one and two in back of it, which is also common. This will be done with every word. If none of those combinations produces the password, the program will connect the various words and start the process over."

"How long will it take?"

"It could take five minutes or it could take several hours; there's no way to know. I hope you are not in a hurry. There's no way to rush this."

"I'm here for the duration. I'm running over to Lester's Diner to grab some dinner. You want anything?"

Sergey grunted no. His fingers danced across the keyboard like a pianist.

"Call me if you crack the password," he said.

"You will be the first to know," the Russian replied.

CHAPTER 20

CASSANDRA

There were two twenty-four-hour restaurants in Fort Lauderdale where cops went to eat. The first was Lester's Diner on State Road 84, which was known for its big coffee pours; the second was the Primanti Brothers by the beach, which had made its reputation serving mouthwatering sandwiches piled high with coleslaw and french fries. Because Lancaster had worked the beach area as a cop, he'd done his eating at Primanti, but had never tried Lester's Diner. But he'd heard that the food was good.

Lester's was doing a brisk business, and he stood in line to place his order. The diner was over fifty years old and a reminder of a bygone era, with a long stainless-steel counter with stools that faced a row of booths. Every seat in the place was taken. There were no TVs hanging on the walls, and not a single patron was looking at a cell phone. It was all about good food and good conversation.

At the counter sat a pair of uniformed cops. Lancaster had made a lot of friends during his time on the force, but this duo was unfamiliar. Both were pushing forty and had receding hairlines and sun damage on the back of their necks. They were engaged in a silent game of tug of war, with neither willing to pick up the check, which their server had slapped down between them several minutes ago.

. His turn came. He ordered a tuna melt for himself and a corned beef sandwich for Sergey. The Russian claimed he wasn't hungry, but there was no harm in bringing him a sandwich anyway. He paid and was given a receipt with a number.

There was a small alcove by the entrance where he stood to wait for his order. He had a clear view of the two cops and the unpaid check on the counter. Back when he'd had a partner, it was standard procedure to alternate paying for meals. It beat the hassle of splitting the cost and trying to calculate how much each owed on the tip.

The server walked by and eyed the unpaid check. She asked the cops if either wanted a refill on their drinks. Both of the cops declined.

He was starting to smell a rat. The sheriff's office had clamped down on cops asking for free meals from local restaurants, but the practice still went on. Another minute passed with neither of the cops reaching for his wallet.

A cook came out from the kitchen and spoke to the cops. The cook had graying hair and a droopy mustache. A picture of the original Lester hung in the alcove, and the cook had the same jawline—either one of his kids or a younger brother.

The conversation was brief between the three men. The cook slid the check off the counter and made it disappear. The cops smiled and hopped off their stools. As they walked out, Lancaster read the names on their name tags and memorized them.

His number was called. He went up to the register to claim his food. The cook stood next to the cashier, talking under his breath.

"Excuse me," Lancaster said. "I used to be a cop. What those two officers just did was wrong. I'm happy to make a phone call, and get them straightened out."

The cook shifted his attention to Lancaster and scowled.

"That won't change anything," the cook said.

"Are you the owner?" Lancaster asked.

"I am. Do you know how many times I've had to pay for cops eating in my place? Over fifty in the past year alone. I'm not running a food kitchen here. It's no different than if one of them stuck his hand in the till and robbed me."

"I got their names as they were walking out. I can get them in trouble."

"No, you can't. We've complained before."

"What happened?"

"Nothing. They were back a week later acting like nothing happened. The cops stick together."

"This time will be different."

"No, it won't. Enjoy your food."

The owner turned his back and returned to his kitchen. Lancaster told himself he'd tried, and he went out to his car and ate his melt and the juicy pickle that came with it. The food was tasty, and he licked his fingers when it was gone. The conversation with the owner bothered him, probably because what the owner had said was true. The sheriff's office internalized problems instead of airing them out in public. Cops broke the law on a regular basis and most of the time didn't get properly punished for it. It made him wonder what would happen after he reported Vargas and Gibbons for pushing cocaine at the Booty Call. Would the department bust them, or would they limit the arrest to the canine instructor who was doing the actual stealing? By doing that, the PR department could issue a statement saying that it was an isolated incident, and not reflective of the upstanding men and women who protected Broward County.

He had to rethink this. His cell phone vibrated, and he tugged it from his pocket. The number was unfamiliar, but he answered it anyway.

"Hi, Jon, this is Karissa," the caller said. "Can you talk?"

Her voice sounded different, less playful.

"Sure. Is everything okay?" he asked.

"Everything's fine. Thanks for asking. I'm at work. Cell phones aren't permitted in the ER, so I'm calling you from a pay phone in the lobby."

"I didn't know they still had pay phones," he said.

"They do inside of hospitals. I remembered something about Zack that might be helpful. I don't know why I didn't remember before when we talked."

Because victims of abuse often suppressed memories of their abusers, he thought he knew the answer, but he knew better than to say this.

"That's great. What is it?" he asked.

"Zack was obsessed with a woman named Cassandra," she said. "That might be useful when your hacker is trying to gain access to Zack's cell phone."

Cassandra was the name the Canadian had called Nicki on the phone. He'd found another link, even if he wasn't quite sure what it meant.

"That's very helpful. How did you find out? Did Zack tell you?"

"It was nothing like that. One night, Zack was staying over and I caught him mumbling her name in his sleep. He said it over and over. Cassandra, Cassandra, Cassandra, like he was longing for her. The next morning, I asked him and he flat out denied it. I wasn't happy about it, you know?"

"I wouldn't think so," he said.

"The next time we slept together, I happened to wake up in the middle of the night. I don't know why, but I started whispering in his ear. I said, 'Zack, this is Cassandra. This is Cassandra.' Hold on a second."

"Sure," he said.

Karissa had a brief conversation with another nurse who was walking by. She came back moments later. "Sorry, but I need to run. We just had a group of schoolkids in a bus crash brought in."

"Wait. Don't leave me hanging like that," he said. "What happened when you whispered in Zack's ear?"

"He got aroused, big time."

"He had a thing for this woman."

"In the worst way. I woke him up, and asked him who Cassandra was. I told him if he lied to me, I'd kick him out. He fessed up and said she was an English professor he'd had when he was in college that he'd fallen for and never forgotten."

"Did you believe him?"

"I believed that part about him being in love with her. There was no mistaking that. The rest of it was a fib."

"Why do you think that?"

"Zack was obsessed with teenage girls. That was why he lusted after me. I have to think Cassandra was a young girl that he wanted, but couldn't have. Shit, I'm being paged. Let me run. I hope this helps."

"It helps a lot. Thank you for reaching out to me."

"Anytime, Jon. Goodbye."

The line went dead. He pulled out of his space and drove back to the Booty Call wondering how Cassandra played into this. Was she a youthful porn star that Kenny had become enamored with? Perhaps Nicki Pearl resembled Cassandra, which would explain Kenny's obsession with Nicki. Or was Nicki connected to Cassandra and secretly doing porn? The secret to solving a case was to dig a hole and not stop digging until you found what you were looking for. It was a laborious process, but in the end, it usually paid off.

He entered Sergey's office to find the Russian engaged in conversation with one of his dancers. The dancer wore next to nothing, and was distinguished by a long blonde ponytail hanging down her back. Every dancer had a gimmick that set her apart from the other naked ladies she shared the stage with. The ponytail was unusually long, and he found himself wondering if it was real.

The cell phone with Zack Kenny's data sat on the coffee table, its screen showing. Sergey had hacked the password with his software program. Lancaster grew excited; he was nearing the finish line, and would soon know why these creeps were stalking Nicki.

"I thought you were going to call me," he said.

"I have a business to run," Sergey said, his eyes on the upset dancer.

Lancaster slipped the cell phone into his pocket. Before he left, he needed to talk with his benefactor. He pointed a finger at the dancer and then pointed at the office door. Sergey understood, and a minute later the dancer was gone.

"I want to know how the deal with Vargas and her partner works," he said. "Do they give you advance notice before they bring the coke to the club? Or do they just show up unannounced and drop a bag into your lap?"

"They call me in the morning, and bring the coke by in the afternoon," Sergey said.

"Is the deal always the same?"

"Yes."

"Any idea why?"

"Vargas told me that the dog trainer steals the coke in the morning, and passes the drugs to them in a Mexican restaurant near police headquarters where they meet for lunch. Vargas and her partner then come straight here and deliver the coke."

"Is it done that way every time?"

"Yes. They are amateurs."

"What do you mean?"

"Amateurs follow a script and never deviate from it. The drugs are stolen, they meet at a restaurant near where they work, the transfer is made, and Vargas and her partner drive straight here. Professionals would never be so obvious."

The closest Mexican joint to police headquarters was called Zona Fresca. It had a spacious dining room that was often full, and he envisioned Vargas and her partner picking up the coke without other patrons in the restaurant being the wiser.

"Give me a few weeks to get this nailed down," he said. "In the meantime, continue to play ball with Vargas and her partner. Don't say anything out of line and make them suspicious. And don't talk to anyone else about this. Are we clear?"

"My lips are sealed. Are you going to screw them?"

"Yes. And the police will not be involved."

"No police?"

"Nope. I'm going to the Florida Department of Law Enforcement. They enjoy busting dirty cops. Rest assured, your name will be left out of it."

"No blowback?"

"No blowback. On that you have my word."

Sergey sprang off the couch, and they shook hands. It was the first time his host had stood up. He was barely five feet tall. Short men had a hard time in the criminal world, yet the vertically challenged Russian had managed to survive. His host was a smart operator, and someone Lancaster might call upon in the future.

"One last thing," Lancaster said. "What password opened the phone?"

"Fendi123," Sergey said.

Fendi was Kenny's favorite cat. Karissa had given him this piece of information, and he reminded himself to thank her the next time they spoke. As he started to leave the office, Sergey stopped him.

"Let me give you advice," the Russian hacker said. "In my country there is an expression. Sometimes, the cards play you. Be careful with Vargas and her partner. They are dangerous."

"I'll do that. Thanks for the warning," he said.

CHAPTER 21

VideoVault

Lancaster went home and fixed a pot of coffee. He was starting to drag and needed a caffeine jolt to get the pistons firing. Holding a steaming mug in one hand and the new cell phone in the other, he went onto his condo's balcony and parked himself on a cheap folding chair that he'd bought online. He blocked out the sounds of moths banging against the overhead light and sipped his drink.

He slowly snapped to. The caffeine would wear off in an hour, and then he'd have to decide whether to fix another cup or hit the sack. He didn't like working when he wasn't 100 percent. It produced mistakes with bad consequences.

The cell phone had timed out, and he typed in "Fendi123" to open it up. Icons for dozens of apps appeared on the screen, many of which were foreign to him. He needed to look through each one and review the information stored upon it. The reason why Nicki Pearl was being stalked was stored on this device. Once he found out what that reason was, he'd be one step closer to giving Nicki and her family their lives back.

He drained his mug. He liked the Pearls and hoped he found nothing that would shed a bad light on Nicki. But his gut told him that wasn't the case. Strange men didn't stalk young girls for no reason. Nicki was somehow connected to these men.

He clicked on the first app. It was called Android Pay, and it let users buy things from online merchants or from physical stores. Zack Kenny had an account, and as Lancaster scrolled through his most recent purchases, he saw nothing out of the ordinary.

The next app was called Arcus and was a real-time weather app. He spent a minute looking at the features before exiting out. Then came an app called Calculator, which performed simple mathematical equations. Next up was an app called Calendar that contained Kenny's important dates and appointments, including days he worked out at a gym with a personal trainer, got his weekly pedicure, and had his biweekly haircut. The guy was a real narcissist, and Lancaster wondered if that went with being a pervert.

The next app was called Contacts and contained Kenny's many personal and professional contacts. He scrolled through them and saw a page devoted to Karissa Clement. Zack had done a real number on Karissa, and he didn't want him hurting her again. He erased her contact page with a few strokes on the keypad.

He got lost in the phone. The lights on neighboring buildings had gone out, as had the lights on the boats on the Intracoastal. The city had gone to sleep, and he'd hardly noticed. He decided not to quit and fixed a second cup of coffee.

An hour later found him studying a collection of photos on the Gallery app. Most were work related and showed Kenny and his coworkers engaged in company celebrations, while the rest were from a Carnival cruise that Kenny had taken to the Bahamas. None were sexual in nature or contained images of Nicki.

The apps were in alphabetical order. He smothered a yawn and came to the very end. An app called VideoVault stared back at him. He clicked on it, and a landing page appeared. It was a service to store videos on the cloud. Zack Kenny had an account, and it was password protected.

He sat up straight in his chair. He had looked at everything on the Droid except what was stored on this app. By process of elimination, that meant that VideoVault had what he was looking for. But what exactly was he going to find? Were there videos of Nicki besides the one of her singing in her underwear? If that was the case, then the innocent young teenager wasn't so innocent after all.

He clicked on the password box. A keyboard appeared on the bottom of the screen. He typed in "Fendi123" and hit "Enter." The message INCORRECT PASSWORD appeared. Kenny used a different password to protect his VideoVault account. On a hunch he typed in "Cassandra123" and hit "Enter." The default message again appeared.

He spent a moment gathering his thoughts. Most password-protected apps only allowed a person three tries to gain access. If he typed in a third incorrect password and failed, the app would shut down, and he would be forced to go to the VideoVault website and create a new password. This would require him to answer questions Kenny had completed when he'd set up his account. He might get lucky and be able to correctly answer those questions with the information he had about Kenny, or more than likely, he'd encounter a question he didn't know the answer to, and fail. If that happened, the videos stored in Kenny's account would not be accessible to him.

He had one more chance. If he blew it, he was back to square one. He pulled out his own phone and used Google to find the phone number for the Booty Call. A minute later he was talking to Sergey, hoping the Russian could help.

"You have made my life miserable," the hacker said.

"What did I do now?"

"Nothing. It's what you did before. Try running a strip club without a bouncer. My customers are all over the dancers, touching them in the wrong places. I've already had two of the girls quit."

"Want me to send someone over?"

"Is he big and muscular?"

"No, he's actually average size, but he's good in a fight."

"I don't want a fight! Fights are bad for business. A bouncer must be menacing. The customer looks at him and thinks, 'I don't want him messing with me,' so the customer behaves himself. If the bouncer isn't here, the customer turns into an animal. Does that make sense?"

"A guy with a baseball bat will do the same thing."

"A baseball bat."

"Have a guy sit on a stool with a baseball bat leaning against the wall. I knew a bar where they did that. There were never any fights."

"That is not bad advice. What do you want?"

He explained the situation, hoping Sergey would have a solution. The Russian did not disappoint him.

"This should not be too hard," Sergey said. "We know the password for the phone was Fendi123, which is a combination of letters and numbers. The letters are the name of a pet, and the numbers are sequential. More than likely, the password for the VideoVault app is also a combination of letters and numbers, most likely a name and a sequence of numbers which are easily remembered. You have already tried Fendi123 and also Cassandra123, and neither worked. What is the significance of the name Cassandra? Do you know?"

"It's the name of a woman the owner of the phone has a thing for."

"So you believe her name is probably the name in the password."

"That's a good assumption."

"I would agree. When men use names in passwords, the names are either of a favorite pet or a woman. That leaves us with figuring out the numbers that follow the name. Usually, people use their birth dates because these numbers are easily recalled. This is not the case with criminals, who tend to use combinations of numbers that are known only to them. If you can get that number, you will have an excellent chance of hacking this app. Now, if you will excuse me, I have another dancer who wants to quit."

Sergey said something that sounded like a curse, and the call ended. He told himself the Russian would get over it and called Karissa. He got voice mail and left a message saying that it was urgent. A half hour later, she called him back.

"Hope I'm not interrupting anything," he said.

"I'm still at work and just took a break. What's up?" she asked.

"I found an app on Zack's cell phone where videos are stored, but it's password protected and I can't get in. Zack likes to use a combination of names and numbers in his passwords. I think the name is Cassandra, but I can't figure out the number. Did Zack ever share with you any special numbers?"

"Try six, eight, seven, nine."

"What's the significance?"

"Zack's older brother perished in a car accident. They were close. His brother's birthday was June 8, 1979. Zack used to drive a Lincoln Continental that had a keypad entry system. That was the password he used, six, eight, seven, nine."

"You're sure those were the numbers?"

"Positive. I saw him punch it in enough times. What kind of videos do you think he has stored on his phone?"

"I'm guessing they're pornographic videos of young girls."

"Will he get in trouble if you're right?"

"If the videos are sexual in nature and the girls are underage, I'll turn the phone over to the sheriff's office and they'll have him arrested. I'll keep your name out of it."

"I know you will. Call me if you have any more questions."

"I will. Thanks for the assist. You've been a great help."

"Goodnight, Jon. Be safe."

He ended the call. He put his own cell phone into his pocket, then picked up the new cell phone that lay at his feet. It had timed out, and he typed in "Fendi123" to bring the screen to life. He scrolled through the apps until he found the VideoVault icon and clicked on it. The landing page filled the small screen. He clicked on the password box, and a keypad appeared on the lower portion of the screen. He typed in "Cassandra6879" and hesitated before hitting the "Sign On" button.

He took a deep breath. It was late, with hardly a light in the sky or down below. It was just him and the darkness. If he'd learned anything in the military and later as a cop, it was that evil was real and darkness was its playground. He needed to be careful when he stepped into the darkness, because if he wasn't, evil would envelop him, and he'd never be the same.

He hit the button and gained entry to Zack Kenny's account. He was one step closer to learning the truth. There were a dozen videos stored in the secure area. Each one had a title, and they all began with the name "Cassandra" and ended with an exclamation mark. Cassandra says hi! Cassandra learns to dance! Cassandra takes a shower! Cassandra discovers love! Just reading the titles made his skin crawl, and he clicked on the first video. It was called Cassandra plays coy! A few moments later, the video began to play. The lighting was muted, and he strained to see a young girl lying naked in bed. Her face looked terribly familiar.

"Jesus Christ," he muttered.

CHAPTER 22
CASSANDRA PLAYS COY!

A naked teenage girl of no more than fifteen years of age lay beneath a filmy sheet, fondling herself while talking to the camera, inviting the viewer to come visit her. Sensual music played in the background like a siren's song, the setting a cheap hotel room. The furniture gave it away. Queen-size bed, flat screen TV, coffeepot on a shelf above the minifridge—all of life's essentials crammed into four hundred square feet of living space.

The video had been shot in the early morning. Rays of sunlight fought their way through the blinds. On the TV, *Family Guy* was playing, the baby cartoon character named Stewie spouting politically incorrect things to the screen. The teenage girl pulled down the filmy sheet and exposed her breasts. She pinched one of her nipples and let out a little laugh. Her skin was olive-colored, and her eyes were big and innocent. It was hard not to get aroused, and he turned away.

"Jesus Christ," he said again.

The girl in the video was Nicki Pearl.

She didn't look exactly the same as the teenager he knew. The girl in the video wore makeup and heavy eyeliner and had her hair styled. But there was no doubt it was her. Same wide eyes, same high cheekbones, same bee-stung lips. It was Nicki.

Her hand dropped, and she started to masturbate. Her moans were low and harsh.

Leaving the cell phone on the arm of his chair, he went to the balcony, and stared into the darkness. He heard her reach orgasm, and he shook his head. She had pulled the wool over his eyes and her parents' as well. Fooled them into thinking that nothing out of the ordinary was going on when in fact she was making porno videos on the sly.

He didn't think Nicki was involved on her own. He guessed Tyler Steeves, the boy from her school, was a better videographer than he seemed because he didn't want to get caught making and posting pornography. It would have been easy to blame him, but the sad fact was, Nicki appeared to be enjoying herself.

But maybe he was wrong. Maybe Tyler was a Svengali who'd cast a spell over Nicki. It was not uncommon for charming boys to persuade impressionable girls into doing things that they would never consider doing on their own. Maybe Tyler had slipped her drugs at a party and taken control of her.

He told himself that Nicki was a victim. She was a sweet, innocent kid, and would never have gotten involved in making porn on her own.

He went to his chair and retrieved the cell phone. The video was over, the screen dark, and he scrolled to the next entry. He needed to watch all the Cassandra videos, and find evidence of Nicki being drugged or coerced. Then he'd go to see her parents, get them to press charges against Tyler Steeves, and force him to take the videos down from the porno sites where he'd posted them. Tyler was responsible for predators like Zack Kenny stalking Nicki, and he was going to pay for his crimes.

- - -

The greatest lies are the ones we tell ourselves. He was convinced that Nicki was a victim. The facts didn't support it, but sometimes the facts were wrong. He'd been around her enough times to form an opinion, and his opinion was a positive one.

The third video was titled CASSANDRA TAKES A SHOWER! and watching it changed that opinion. To say that he'd been deceived was an understatement. He'd been thoroughly conned. Nicki was a willing participant in the video, and she seemed to be enjoying herself. The video was exactly as the title suggested. It showed the teenager taking a hot shower while recording a video of herself with a cell phone on a selfie stick. While steaming water sprayed her naked body, she sensually rubbed soap suds across her breasts and crotch while talking obscenely to the camera.

"Want to fuck me?" she asked. "I bet you do. I'm waiting here for you."

The shower lasted for a few minutes, and so did the teasing. When she turned off the water and stepped out of the shower stall, her cell phone briefly scanned the bathroom. The door was closed, and she was alone. There was no teenage boy egging her on. It was just Nicki and her cell phone.

Nicki took the cell phone off the stick and propped it against a soap dispenser on the sink. The move was practiced, like she'd done it before. Standing naked in front of the vanity, she dried herself off with a fluffy towel and continued to taunt.

"What's taking you so long? Can't you see how horny I am?"

She was good. Her delivery was smooth, without an ounce of self-consciousness. Like she'd done it a hundred times before. She dried her hair with a blow dryer and brushed it out. Picking up her cell phone, she reattached it to the stick.

"Bedtime," she said. "Are you ready?"

She walked into an adjacent bedroom. She turned the stick and used the phone to lead the way. There was no one else in the picture.

The bedroom was dimly lit, and he stared at the shadows, desperate to find an accomplice. There was none.

A shaded lamp sat on the bedside table. It was the room's only source of light. She turned it on and off a few times with her free hand and finally left it on. The bed was a king with a wooden frame. Attached to the frame was a metal contraption similar to a fishing rod holder on a boat. She slipped the selfie stick into the holder and clamped it into place so the cell phone was pointed at the bed. Pulling back the bedcover, she lay down on the top sheet so her body was exposed to the screen.

She started to play with herself. A door opened, and a dark-skinned man of Middle Eastern descent made his entrance. He was in his midthirties and trim, with the body of a runner. He climbed on top of Nicki and they began to have intercourse. It made Lancaster's stomach churn, but he continued to watch, hoping an accomplice would pop up in the shadows and save him.

No luck. This was a solo effort.

He watched the remaining Cassandra videos. Each video ended with the same Middle Eastern man coming into a hotel room and having sex with Nicki.

He rubbed his face with his hands. He tried to imagine her parents' reaction when he showed these videos to them. It was going to be awful.

He went inside and found his charger. The Droid was running low on juice, so he plugged it into an outlet in the kitchen and then fixed a rum and coke. He rarely drank to get drunk, but this was one of those special occasions. His reality had been shattered, and he needed to calm down. He took a long gulp of his drink and shut his eyes.

This was going to end badly. The Pearls had hired him to save their daughter, when in reality there was no way to save her. The Cassandra videos were out there in cyberspace, and any twisted soul could get his hands on them and fantasize over having sex with Nicki. He supposed the Pearls could sell their house and go into hiding and wait a few years for Nicki to grow up, but what kind of life was that? It would be like being in the witness protection program, only the Pearls wouldn't have the government watching their back. They'd be on their own and always fearful.

He supposed there were other options. The Pearls could pay to change Nicki's appearance through plastic surgery. She could be given a new face and would be able to go out in public and not be stalked. South Florida was a haven for cosmetic surgery, and her parents would have no problem finding a qualified surgeon to do the job.

But what if Nicki said no? What if she refused to go into hiding or let a plastic surgeon cut her? Nicki had a dark side, and there was no telling how she'd react. Confronting her in front of her parents was going to be hard.

He topped his glass off and went into the bathroom and washed his face with hot water. He was no stranger to porn—it was hard to surf the internet and not see a naked woman—but watching the Cassandra videos had made him feel dirty, and he guessed it was because he knew the performer. He cared about Nicki and wanted her problems to go away, but the damage had been done, and there was no going back.

He was startled to see that he'd emptied his glass, and he returned to the kitchen and fixed himself another drink. The cell phone sat on the counter still plugged in. It was 75 percent charged, so he disconnected it and went into his study. He needed to download the videos to his laptop for safekeeping.

He connected the Droid to his laptop with a USB connector. The VideoVault app on the Droid had timed out. He typed in the password, hit "Enter," and was taken to Zack Kenny's account. He decided to start from the top, and download each video in the chronological order that they were stored on the app.

His eyes grew wide. The screen was blank. He used his finger to move around the page, thinking he had been taken to another landing page. No such luck. Kenny's account was empty. The Cassandra videos had been erased.

CHAPTER 23
FIVE DAYS IN PARIS

He cursed.

Without the Cassandra videos, he could neither confront Nicki nor tell her parents what he'd found. Without proof, it would be his word against hers, and he felt sure that she'd deny the whole thing. After all, hadn't she denied any involvement already?

He knew what was going on, only he couldn't prove any of it.

When he was home, he often did things the old-fashioned way. Taking a legal pad and pen out of a drawer, he wrote down everything he could remember about the Cassandra videos. He started with their titles, then next to each title wrote down the specific things he'd seen on the video, such as the furniture in the room, the clothing Nicki was wearing when the video began, if there was music playing in the background or a TV show, and anything else that came to mind. Each of the videos had been dated and were one to six months old. The oldest videos were at the beginning, and he took a stab at their exact dates. The rum wasn't helping his memory, and he forced himself to concentrate.

Finished, he threw the pen on the pad. There was no doubt in his mind what had happened. While checking out the apps on Zack

Kenny's phone, he'd done something suspicious while navigating one that had raised a red flag. The app's manufacturer had sent Kenny an email alerting him to the skullduggery. Kenny had realized he'd been hacked, and used his laptop or iPad to go to his VideoVault account and erase every damaging file as fast as he could.

Lancaster had screwed up. He should have downloaded the Cassandra videos to his laptop instead of watching them first on the newly purchased Droid. But he'd let his curiosity get the better of him, and had paid the price.

He picked up the legal pad and went onto the balcony. He moved his chair up to the railing and sat down. The stiff breeze blowing off the Atlantic felt good against his face, and he stared at his notes. Something was bothering him, and after a long minute the discrepancy hit him. In the CASSANDRA SAYS HI! video he'd spied an episode of *Family Guy* playing on a TV set in the background. That would have been normal in any part of the world except the Middle East. As a SEAL he'd performed covert missions in Yemen, Somalia, Iraq, and Syria. Before entering these places, he'd been indoctrinated in radical Islamic culture. One of the things he'd learned was that books, magazines, and TV shows produced in the West were forbidden in those countries. A Muslim caught watching *The Big Bang Theory* on a cell phone might get his hand cut off.

The Pearls had lived in Dubai for five years. Dubai was more tolerant than most of its neighbors, but *tolerant* was a relative term in the Middle East. He didn't know if Western television was available to expats living there or not.

He took out his cell phone. It was three in the morning and not a good time to be sending text messages. But he needed to know, so he sent Pearl a message. Before he started asking questions, he wanted to be sure that he had his facts straight.

Sorry for the late hour. Are you up?

Pearl was a surgeon and often on call. He was hoping that Pearl kept his cell phone on a bedside table, and that it wasn't muted.

Jon? What's going on? Pearl replied moments later.

I'm working late. I need your help.

Fire away.

When did you move here with your family?

Why is that important?

The story that Pearl had told him about his family's move to the United States wasn't jiving with the dates on the videos. Perhaps he hadn't heard Pearl right the first time. He needed to nail this down.

Let me ask the questions. When did you move here?

Three months ago.

The oldest Cassandra videos had been downloaded to Kenny's VideoVault account six months ago. That meant they'd been made while Nicki was living in Dubai with her family. Or maybe Nicki and her mother had moved here first, before her father.

Did your family move at the same time? he texted.

I don't understand your question, Pearl replied.

Did you all come over together? Or did Nicki and your wife come earlier?

We came at the same time. Will you please tell me what's going on?

He didn't know what was going on. All he could do was keep going and hope the truth presented itself to him.

Your family lived in Dubai, correct?

Correct.

The whole five years?

Yes.

How strict is it there?

Very. They tolerated us, but that was because we had something they wanted.

Were you able to watch American television?

No. It was forbidden.

Could you stream it over the internet?

Not possible. The government censored the internet. Nicki was very upset when we first moved. She couldn't watch her favorite shows.

He had hit a wall. If shows like *Family Guy* weren't available in Dubai, then how had an episode been playing on a TV set in a hotel there six months ago? He wrestled with it and came up with only one solution. The hotel room wasn't in Dubai or any other Middle Eastern country. It was somewhere else.

His phone vibrated in his hand. Pearl was calling him. Lancaster didn't know what to say without devastating his client, and he decided to stonewall him.

"Hello, Dr. Pearl," he said.

"Hello, Jon. I'm lying in bed with Melanie. My cell phone is on speaker so she can hear you. You've found something, haven't you?"

He wasn't going to lie. "Yes."

"You sound troubled."

"I'm very tired, Dr. Pearl, that's all."

"Are you going to tell me what you've found?"

"Not over the phone," he said.

He thought he heard Melanie gasp.

"You want to speak to us in person," Pearl said.

"Yes."

"Would you like to come over now? I can't imagine we're going to get much more sleep tonight."

"I think tomorrow morning would be better."

"Why wait?"

"I want Nicki to be in the room with us. I have questions to ask her."

A pause. Then, "Nicki's involved in this situation, isn't she?"

"I didn't say that," he said.

"But that's where this is heading. You've found evidence linking Nicki to these horrible men, and you're afraid to tell us over the phone. Hold on a second." Melanie was weeping, and her husband spoke soothingly to her before returning to the line. "It's not a total surprise. My wife and I had a long conversation with Nicki after dinner. You were right—Nicki is holding a grudge because we refused to let her take horseback riding lessons when we lived in Dubai. We had no idea how angry she was with us. She's been holding it in for a while."

He'd found a possible motive. Nicki had wanted to get back at her parents, so she'd gone and made a slew of pornographic videos out of spite and posted them on the internet under a false name, never thinking the videos would come back to haunt her.

"That explains a lot," he said.

"So you've figured it out," Pearl said.

"Perhaps. I still need to talk to your daughter. What time can I come by?"

"Why won't you tell me now?"

"Because I'm missing a piece of the puzzle. When you were living in Dubai, did Nicki take any trips out of the country for an extended period of time?"

"We took several family trips."

"I mean by herself."

"Let me think. There was a school-sponsored trip to Paris seven months ago that Nicki went on. She was gone five days with her class."

"Do you know where she stayed in Paris?" he asked.

Melanie spoke up. "She stayed in the Intercontinental Hotel with the rest of her classmates."

"Did she have a private room?"

Hesitation, then, "Yes, she had a private room."

"Did this trip take place before or after you said no to the horses?"

"After. Is that the piece of the puzzle you're looking for?"

Five days in a private room in a Paris hotel was more than enough time to make a bunch of sleazy videos and put them out for the world to see in cyberspace. It all made sense, and he felt ready to confront Nicki and get her to admit what she'd done. That would be the first step toward getting this situation resolved.

"Yes, it is," he said. "What time can I come by?"

"We usually have breakfast around eight."

"See you then."

CHAPTER 24
DOWN THE RABBIT HOLE

In his experience, the best way to break bad news was over a meal. Eating food calmed people down when they were upset. He was sure there was a scientific explanation for it, not that he needed to hear it. Food soothed troubled souls.

He drove to the Pearls' house with the smell of freshly baked bagels filling his car. He'd gotten to the Bagel Snack on Powerline a few minutes before opening and there still had been a line stretching down the sidewalk. According to the owner, the key to making a delicious bagel was the quality of the water. South Florida tap water was not fit for consumption, so the owner imported water from New York. It showed in every bite.

He parked in the Pearls' driveway and took two bags off the seat before getting out. As he neared the front door, Carlo emerged from the hedge. He handed him a bag.

"Good morning. That's for all of you," he said.

Carlo glanced into the bag and grinned. "Thanks, Jon."

"I should be the one thanking you. How have things been in my absence?"

"Karl and I were talking about that earlier. This street has way too much traffic for a residential neighborhood, especially at night. They're after the girl, right?"

"Yes, sir."

"Have you figured out why? She must have done something."

It was an obvious conclusion that he'd been avoiding for days. Call it a state of denial born out of respect for the parents and their child. But that was no more.

"I'll tell you someday over a cold beer," he said. "In the meantime, I need to book you for a few more days until I get this worked out. Are you available?"

"Calendar's wide open. Provided you keep bringing us food."

"Deal."

"Do you ever miss being a SEAL?" Carlo asked. "I was thinking the other night how those missions were probably the best time of my life."

It was the best time of Lancaster's life as well, until he'd spotted a little boy getting too close to his unit in Yemen. The hump beneath the kid's shirt looked suspicious, and Lancaster's quick thinking had saved his unit from getting blown up. He'd been a hero, but it hadn't changed the fact that he'd shot a child, and he'd put in his papers the next week.

"I don't miss it at all," he said.

Pearl greeted him at the front door. The doctor looked upset, and justifiably so. If Nicki had been honest with her parents, a private investigator wouldn't have been needed to figure out what was going on. Instead, the Pearls could have gone to the police, and gotten the Cassandra videos taken off the internet. Nicki's lying had destroyed her parents' faith in her and harmed their family. He handed his client the second bag.

"That's very thoughtful of you," Pearl said. "We haven't told my daughter anything. Before you talk to her, I want to hear what you found."

They stood in the foyer facing each other. They could hear Nicki and Melanie in the kitchen fixing breakfast. *The Today Show* played in the background.

"I found a dozen lewd videos of your daughter on Zack Kenny's cell phone," he said. "She posted them under the name Cassandra. They were made before your family moved here. Based upon things I saw on them, I think they were shot in Paris."

Pearl brought his hand to his mouth. "A dozen?"

He nodded. It was a big, painful number.

"What is she doing on them?"

"Sometimes she's lying in bed, other times she's on a couch or in a chair or she's dancing. In one, she's taking a shower. She's naked and talks dirty to the camera and then masturbates until she reaches orgasm."

"Does she have sex in them?"

"Yes. In the last nine videos, she has sex."

"Another teenager?"

"No, her partner is an adult."

Pearl took a deep breath as if to steady himself. Lancaster placed his hand on the doctor's shoulder and left it there. "We need to get this out in the open. That's the only way we can move forward and come up with a solution."

"I agree, Jon. And so does Melanie."

"Nicki may not react well when I tell her what I've found. I want you and your wife to sit on either side of her, in case she decides to run. Nicki has to hear me out. Understood?"

"Loud and clear."

He lowered his arm. "Good. I'm glad we're on the same page."

They went to the kitchen. It had a small breakfast nook that contained a round table with four place settings and glasses of OJ. There was a basket with muffins, to which Pearl added the bagels. Melanie and Nicki were at the stove scrambling eggs and cooking bacon. The food was ready, and they fixed four plates. Melanie muted the TV, and they moved to the nook with their plates of food. Nicki sat sandwiched between her parents and dug in. She still had sleep in her eyes and wore no makeup. It was a far cry from the creature he'd watched the night before.

"I know why these men are stalking you," he said, looking at the teenager as he spoke. "But before I tell you, I need to ask you a question."

Nicki put down her fork. She could feel her parents' stares, and it made her uncomfortable. She wiped the corners of her mouth with a paper napkin.

"Okay," she said.

"Before you moved to the United States with your parents, you went on a school-sponsored trip to Paris. You did something bad there, didn't you?"

Ashamed, Nicki stared at her plate and did not reply. Melanie leaned toward her daughter and said, "Nicki, answer the question."

"Who told you about Paris?" Nicki asked.

"I figured it out on my own. I'm a private investigator, Nicki. If there's a secret out there, I'm going to uncover it. Now, why don't you tell me what happened."

"I screwed up," the teenager said under her breath.

"I know you did. Start from the beginning, and don't leave anything out."

She took a deep breath. "We got there on a Friday night and checked into the hotel. It was late, so the teachers who were chaperoning us decided to eat in the hotel's restaurant. We ordered our food, and one of the chaperones ordered wine so we could have a toast. I think the waiter liked me, because he kept refilling my glass when it was empty."

"Did you get drunk?" he asked.

"Yeah. I'd never had alcohol before, and I got a little woozy. Some of the other kids were messed up too." She fidgeted uncomfortably in her chair. "We went back to our rooms and got ready for bed. It was after midnight, and I was really sleepy. Just as I was climbing under the covers there was a knock on my door. It was a girl named Mandy Schumacher. We're in the same grade, and she was my friend. Mandy said she was having a party in her room, did I want to come? I didn't see the harm, so I put my clothes back on and followed Mandy down the hall to her room. There were a bunch of other kids from my school there, and they were getting drunk."

Nicki picked up her OJ and took a swallow. Her story made sense. Nicki had gotten drunk and acted out in rebellion against her parents and shot the videos.

"How did Mandy get the liquor?" he said. "Did a chaperone give it to her?"

"The chaperones didn't know about the party. Mandy got the booze from the minibar in her room. The hotel was supposed to empty all the little bottles of booze out of our minibars, but Mandy's room got missed. There was vodka and rum and some stuff that I'd never heard of before. The kids were mixing the booze with Coke to hide the taste, and they were all getting really smashed."

"Did you get smashed?"

Nicki nodded and stared at her plate. Lancaster sensed that they'd reached the truly bad part of the story. He pressed her. "What happened then, Nicki?"

"What does this have to do with these men stalking me?"

"Everything. Now tell us."

The kitchen had grown uncomfortably quiet.

"I passed out and got my stomach pumped," the teenager said.

"What?" her mother shrieked.

"You never told us," her father said, equally aghast.

Nicki lifted her gaze. She avoided her parents' stares, preferring to look at Lancaster instead. "I don't remember much of what happened. Mandy said that I threw up and then my eyes rolled up in my head and

I passed out and hit the floor. I banged my head on the side of a chair, and everyone thought that I'd hurt myself."

"Did you?" he asked.

"Luckily, I didn't break anything," she said. "Mandy went and got the chaperones. One of them called the front desk, and an ambulance came and took me to a hospital. When I came to, there was a rubber tube stuck down my throat and a nurse was pumping my stomach. It was really gross. I stayed in the hospital for a day, and then I was released. I was really weak, and I stayed in my hotel room for the rest of the trip."

And made the videos, he thought. He put his elbows on the table and leaned forward and looked her in the eyes. "How many days were you in your hotel room?"

"Four."

"What did you do during those four days?"

"I slept a lot and read a Stephen King book on my iPad. We also watched a lot of TV."

"We? Was there someone with you?"

"The chaperones alternated staying with me. I was pretty weak. I guess they were also making sure that I didn't get drunk again."

"Did you?" Melanie asked.

Nicki turned to face her mother. "No, Mom. I learned my lesson. I haven't had anything to drink since that trip, and I'm not sure I ever will."

"Good choice," Melanie said.

"So one of the chaperones stayed with you while you recuperated," he said, wanting to get the conversation back on track. "Were they with you all the time?"

Nicki faced him. "Yes. I was pretty weak. They had room service bring up my meals. It got pretty boring."

"Did they sleep in the room with you as well?"

Nicki nodded. "Yeah. The room had a couch, and the chaperones slept on it."

"Every night?"

"Uh-huh. I still don't understand what this has to do with these men stalking me."

She had to be lying. The videos had been made outside of Dubai when Nicki was by herself and not under her parents' watchful eye. The presence of a twenty-four-hour chaperone would have made that impossible. Was this another carefully constructed lie designed to hide a bigger truth? It sure felt that way.

"I'm sorry, Nicki, but this isn't adding up," he said. "If you got drunk and went to the hospital, your parents would have known. It was the chaperones' responsibility to report the incident when they got home, and the school would have notified your parents. They would have also received a bill from the hospital."

"The school didn't know," Nicki said.

"Why not?"

"Because the chaperones didn't tell them."

"And why is that?"

"Because we agreed not to."

"We? Who exactly is we?"

"Everybody who was on the trip. The other kids were afraid the chaperones would get fired because they served us wine the first night at dinner. But that wouldn't have been fair. The chaperones didn't make us drink the wine or the booze out of the minibar. We did that. We made a bad decision, and it was our fault."

"So nobody in your group talked about it."

Nicki nodded.

"Did you agree with this, or were you talked into it?" Melanie asked.

"It was actually my idea," Nicki said. "You and Daddy always said that I have to be responsible for my actions, and not blame other people when things go wrong. I wasn't going to blame the chaperones for my screwup, so I convinced everyone on the trip to keep quiet."

"How did the chaperones feel about that?" Melanie asked.

"They thanked me."

"What about the hospital bill?" Lancaster asked. "How did you hide that?"

"That came after I got home," Nicki said. "I grabbed it out of the mail, and paid it with a money order."

The story was a lie. There could be no other explanation. Because if it wasn't a lie, then his theory about how the videos had gotten made flew out the window.

"Do you have any proof that this happened, Nicki?" he said. "Is there some evidence that you can show me?"

A dark cloud passed over the teenager's face.

"You don't believe me," she said.

"I didn't say that," he said. "I just want to see some proof."

"You think this is all bullshit, that something else happened," she said.

"Nicki!" her mother scolded.

"Jon is trying to help us," her father reminded her.

"He doesn't believe me," Nicki said.

Her parents' silence was deafening. Nicki pushed her plate forward and rose in her spot. Her mother slipped out of the nook, and Nicki came right behind her.

"I'll show you," the teenager said.

Nicki stormed out of the kitchen and down the hallway to the study with Lancaster and her parents hurrying to catch up. An iPad sat on the desk, and Nicki took her father's leather chair and let her fingers play across its keyboard. Lancaster stood behind her, wanting to make sure she didn't erase anything. Nicki went into a folder called "Pictures" and pulled up a series of images that were time-stamped seven months ago.

"See for yourself," the teenager said.

On the iPad's screen was a photograph of Nicki lying in a hospital bed with a nurse attending to her. Her face was white, and her hair was matted down.

"Mandy took that in the hospital," Nicki said. "I was looking a little rough."

The next photo showed Nicki lying in a bed in a hotel room, flashing the peace sign to the camera. Two of her school friends flanked her.

"Mandy took that on the day I came back to the hotel."

Nicki took them through the rest of the photos of her recuperation. They showed each day of Nicki's recovery in which she seemed to regain her strength and facial color and included her friends from school and her chaperones, all of whom were female. Whatever doubts that Lancaster had harbored about Nicki's story were put to rest.

The last photo showed Nicki and her classmates at Charles de Gaulle airport, preparing to board their flight home. Nicki looked better than in the previous photos, but she had yet to fully recover. The booze had done a real number on her, and Lancaster didn't doubt the claim that she hadn't had a drop to drink since.

"Do you believe me now?" Nicki asked.

He was beaten, his theory of what had happened in Paris in flames.

"Yes, Nicki. I believe you," he said.

"Can I go upstairs to my room?" she asked her parents.

Melanie said yes. Nicki exited the collection of photos and left the study. Lancaster could feel the weight of her parents' stares. They wanted to know why he'd put them through this torture. He didn't have a good answer and decided to stall them. An image on the iPad's screen caught his eye. He sat down in the leather chair and clicked on it. The photo was of Nicki taken several years ago, when she was maybe nine or ten years old. With her was a woman who could have been Nicki's identical twin, aged twenty years. The resemblance was uncanny. They were facially the same, right down to their smiles. The older woman wore a black windbreaker with the initials FBI stenciled in white above the breast pocket.

"Who is this?" he asked.

He got no answer, and lifted his head to see that he was alone. He picked up the iPad and went into the foyer. Melanie had gone upstairs to talk to her daughter while Pearl stood at the foot of the stairs wearing a worried expression.

"This is very upsetting," Pearl said. "I'm not sure what we accomplished here."

"We've actually accomplished a great deal." He pointed at the female in the black windbreaker in the photo. "Who is this woman with your daughter?"

"That's my sister-in-law, Beth."

"Is she with the FBI?"

"That's correct. She works out of Quantico."

"Excuse me, but why didn't you ask for her help with this situation? The FBI's resources are unlimited."

"Melanie and Beth don't have much of a relationship. Beth was interning with the FBI when she was a senior in college. She was at the Pentagon on 9/11 and lost several friends. She took exception when I took the job in Dubai."

"Do she and her sister talk?"

"Not in years."

"What's your sister-in-law's full name?"

"Elizabeth Daniels. Everyone calls her Beth."

Melanie appeared at the top of the stairs and beckoned to her husband to join her. Pearl started up the stairs and turned to him. "If Nicki didn't create these pornographic videos, then who did?"

"I don't know, Dr. Pearl. I thought Nicki filmed herself and put them there, but now I'm not so sure."

"Then where did they come from?"

"I don't know."

"Nolan, please," Melanie called from the second floor.

Pearl hurried up the stairs. Lancaster returned the iPad to the study and went outside to his car. He knew that he'd found something important, even if he didn't entirely understand what it was. Sitting behind the wheel, he used his cell phone to get on Google and did a search on Elizabeth Daniels, Federal Bureau of Investigation. Several dozen links came up, mostly of cases that Daniels had worked on that had been covered by the media. She'd had a spectacular career with arrests of serial killers and human-trafficking rings. An article from the *Boston Globe* dated seven years ago caught his eye, and he clicked on it. It featured a photo of Daniels leading a group of FBI agents in a bust of a child-trafficking ring. The article stated that underage girls were being trafficked from Mexico to Boston to be used as prostitutes, the operation generating $1 million a month. Daniels was quoted in the article thanking the Boston police for helping bring the traffickers to justice. Her title was mentioned, and his eyes grew wide. Special Agent Elizabeth Daniels ran the FBI's Violent Crimes Against Children unit, and was responsible for the FBI's ongoing fight against sexual predators.

CHAPTER 25
THE ONE THAT GOT AWAY

He went home and did a deep dive on Beth Daniels.

Outside of the newspaper articles chronicling her FBI busts, there wasn't a lot of information about her. She didn't have a Facebook page, and her name didn't come up on any of the public record search sites. He checked to see if she owned a home in Virginia near Quantico where she worked. That also drew a blank.

He read the many newspaper articles in hopes a nugget of information might turn up, but they weren't much help. He supposed he could have called Melanie and started asking questions, but couldn't make himself do it. He'd been hired to figure this damn thing out, and asking her sister to fill in the blanks was cheating.

Several of the newspaper articles contained dramatic photographs of Daniels standing at a podium fielding reporters' questions. She had a real presence, and it came through in every shot. She was a force to be reckoned with.

Daniels was not the only FBI agent in the photos. She had a team, and they stood behind her in each of the shots. Three men and one female. No names were given. If he could find out who one of them was, perhaps they'd lead him to Daniels.

He went back through the articles to see if any of the agents were quoted. After many hours of looking, he finally found a name. In the *Boston Globe* story about the bust of the child traffickers, Special Agent Heidi Winkler gave a brief statement. He decided that Winkler was the lone female he'd seen in the newspaper photos.

He did an online search on Winkler, hoping she'd lead him to Daniels. She, too, had her information hidden, except on her Facebook page. Winkler had two toddlers, a boy and a girl, and posted cute photos of them at every opportunity. There was no mention on her Facebook page that she worked for the FBI.

Winkler had 120 Facebook friends. The friends section had a search engine, and on a hunch he typed in the name "Beth" and hit "Enter." Winkler had only one friend named Beth, and her name was Beth Skye. Her profile picture was of a sunset. He clicked on it, and, like magic, Beth Skye's page popped up.

He started to read. There was scant personal information on Beth Skye's page. She lived in Virginia and had graduated from Dartmouth and that was it. But there were postings from friends, and by scrolling through them, he learned that she was an avid runner, a reader of mystery and thriller novels, and that she lived with two Doberman pinschers, Max and Danny, who accompanied her on her runs. There was also a posting between Heidi and Beth about going to a pistol range to practice target shooting.

The photos section wasn't much help. Mostly photographs of sunsets and/or her running with her dogs, her face hidden from the camera. In one she was accompanied by a man in running shorts whose face was also hidden. He guessed this was her boyfriend.

He clicked on her favorites pages, and learned that she liked music by Linkin Park and Depeche Mode and her favorite books were *Red Dragon*, *Whoever Fights Monsters*, and *The Hanover Killers*. He knew the first two books. *Red Dragon* was a novel by Thomas Harris that had introduced the character Hannibal Lecter, and *Whoever Fights Monsters* was FBI agent Robert Ressler's chilling account of his tracking the country's most notorious serial killers. The last book, *The Hanover Killers*, was new to him.

There was nothing else on Beth Skye's Facebook page. He exited Facebook, and went to Google, where he did a search of *The Hanover Killers* and discovered that it was a self-published book about the unsolved murders of two female college students that had taken place at Dartmouth College in the winter of 1999. The book had been written by a reporter named Mike Salinero, who'd covered the story for a local paper called the *Valley News*. The book was available on Amazon, Barnes & Noble, and Smashwords in both paperback and e-book editions. Beth Skye's page had said that she'd gone to Dartmouth, and he wondered if she was somehow connected to this case.

On his Kindle, he ordered the e-book edition of *The Hanover Killers*. A message on the page thanked him for his purchase and told him that the book was in the process of downloading.

He tucked his Kindle under his arm and went to the kitchen and poured himself an iced tea. He'd lost track of the time and saw that it was five o'clock. He'd spent the better part of his day trying to figure out how Special Agent Beth Daniels fit into this confusing puzzle, and his instincts told him he was getting close. In the living room, he put his drink on the coffee table, sat down on the couch, and started to read.

- - -

Dartmouth was one of the country's most prestigious research universities and a member of the Ivy League. Tucked away in the sleepy burg of Hanover in New Hampshire's Upper Valley, it was a leader in medicine, engineering, and business, a place of higher learning where nothing exciting ever happened.

That had all changed on a bitterly cold Saturday evening in late January 1999. An eighteen-year-old student named Phoebe Linkletter was working a part-time job at Banana Republic at the local mall, and phoned her roommate to say she'd meet her at a popular watering hole called the Canoe Club after she got off work. When Phoebe didn't show up at the arranged time, her roommate called the police. Three days later, Phoebe's naked, mutilated body was found in a wooded area on the outskirts of town. The Dartmouth police conducted an investigation and hauled in Phoebe's boyfriend, whom she'd broken up with right before the holidays. The boyfriend had a rock-solid alibi for the night of the killing, and was released.

One week later, an eighteen-year-old exchange student named Naseema Agarwai went missing. Naseema had gone to her part-time job at a yoga studio in a strip mall, and never returned to her apartment a half mile away. Two days later, her naked and disfigured body was found in a field behind the Hood Museum of Art. The crime scene was identical to the Linkletter killing, right down to the way Naseema's body was displayed like a snow angel on the frozen ground. Believing they might be dealing with a serial killer, the police contacted the Manchester office of the FBI and asked for their help. The FBI sent two seasoned field agents to work the investigation. While the agents were on campus conducting interviews with friends and classmates of the victims, a third student was abducted. She was a sophomore named Beth Daniels, and her miraculous escape from her kidnappers would earn her the title of "The one that got away."

Daniels was walking from class to her apartment complex when two men wearing black ski masks jumped out from behind a hedge. They began wrestling with her and tried to tie her up. Beth put up a hell of a fight, and she landed some serious blows before being subdued and thrown in the trunk of a dark sedan. In their haste to escape, her abductors did not slam the trunk with enough force, and it did not properly close. It had been a harsh winter with lots of ice, and the roads in Hanover were filled with potholes. Several miles outside of town on a quiet two-lane road, the sedan hit a pothole so hard it popped the trunk open. The jolt also woke Beth up.

"At first, I didn't know where I was. All I could see was bright blue sky, and I started wondering if I'd died and gone to heaven," Daniels later told the newspaper. "Then the trunk started to close and the sky disappeared. It was so scary."

Daniels stuck her foot out and stopped the trunk from closing. The sedan had slowed down, and she decided to take her chance. Her wrists were tied behind her back, so she struggled to pull herself to a sitting position, then managed to get her feet beneath her. With the sedan still moving, she jumped out and rolled across the macadam, dislocating her shoulder and chipping two front teeth. Then she got up and fled into the woods. The sedan had pulled over, and her abductors ran after her.

"They chased me for a while, and I could hear their breathing," Daniels was quoted as saying. "Whenever the breathing got closer, I made myself run faster. The ground was slippery, and I heard one of them fall and his partner fall on top of him. I stopped and turned around. I looked right at them, and I cursed them. Then I took off."

With that, the killings at Dartmouth had ended. No more coeds disappeared, and life returned to normal. The FBI sent a special team to Hanover to take over the case. The team had a profiler who determined that the killers either lived in the area or had spent a great deal of time in town. This conclusion was based upon the killers' use of back roads and geographical knowledge of the campus. Hanover had a population of seventeen thousand, and two strangers would have been noticed. The killers were local.

This revelation had sent a chill through the community. If the killers lived in the area, who were they? Did they work at the campus or in town? Perhaps they were public employees and worked at the post office or sanitation department. Or maybe they were students or teachers. It could have been anyone.

During her tussle with her abductors, Beth had managed to rake her fingernails across one of the men's faces. The police forensics department had gotten a tiny piece of this skin from Beth, and turned it over to the FBI, who had run it against a database of known serial killers. It had turned up nothing, and everyone had forgotten about it. But then an unusual thing happened. Men living in Hanover came to the police department and gave samples of hair or saliva so that their DNA could be run against the abductor's. The men did this to clear themselves so that their friends and family would know they were not one of the monsters that had taken two innocent young lives.

Within a week, over a thousand men were cleared. At the end of two weeks, the number was three thousand. And by week three, every single male in Hanover who wasn't in a nursing home, lying in a hospital bed, or in jail had been tested and cleared. If the killers were locals, they had done a good job of rendering themselves invisible.

And that was how the book ended, with a giant question mark hanging over the town and its people, the case unsolved, the killers never brought to justice. In the epilogue, the author had speculated as to who the killers might be. He'd also interviewed Beth Daniels, who was a senior at Dartmouth at the time of the book's writing. Her life had gone back to normal, except for one thing. She no longer wished to be a research scientist, and had decided to study criminology and enter into law enforcement.

He'd found Special Agent Beth Daniels.

- - -

He placed his Kindle on the coffee table and stared into space. The pieces of the puzzle were swirling around, and he was having a hard time fitting them together. Daniels looked like Nicki, just older, and she also looked like Cassandra on the lewd videos he'd watched. He'd come to the conclusion that Nicki hadn't created the videos because there was no time in her young life to have slipped away from her parents and done so. Someone else had created and posted them on the internet sites visited by perverts.

It felt like a cleverly constructed sting. Put tantalizing videos of a pretty teenager on the internet and draw the scum out from beneath their rocks. The FBI was masterful at setting up stings, and he could see them orchestrating this. If that was true, then Beth Daniels was certainly behind it, since this was her turf. But why had she gone and used her niece as bait? Daniels was in the business of catching sexual predators, and would have surely known the danger she was putting Nicki in.

He didn't know the answer and decided to find out. Soon he was on his laptop searching the internet for a phone number for the FBI's offices at Quantico. The FBI was massive, and Quantico housed several divisions—including the Violent Crimes Against Children/Online Predators unit. He called a general information number, and an automated voice answered. He listened to the directory and punched the number that would allow him to dial by name. There were a lot of agents, and he was happy that Daniels was at the beginning of the alphabet. Her extension was #167. He punched it into his cell phone's keypad and heard the call go through.

"This is Special Agent Elizabeth Daniels. I'm in the field and can't take your call. Leave a message, date, time, and I'll return your call at my first opportunity."

A short buzz filled his ear. He wrestled with how much to say, and decided to keep his message short and sweet.

"Good evening. My name is Jon Lancaster, and I'm a private investigator living in Fort Lauderdale. I would like to speak to you about the Cassandra videos. We can do this over the phone or in person. Please call me when you get this message. I'll be up."

He left his cell phone number and ended the call. Then he got an iced tea and went onto his balcony and sat in a chair and watched the day come to an end. Beth Daniels had become an FBI agent because of her past. She was on a mission, and probably the kind of agent who worked all hours on cases and regularly checked her voice mail.

His eyelids had grown heavy. He hadn't gotten much sleep in the last few days and was exhausted. His bed was calling him, only he didn't want to be asleep when Daniels rang him back. He didn't expect her to be forthcoming with information and would have to word his questions carefully and draw her out. He needed to be sharp to do that.

Sipping his drink, he wondered how long it would be before he got a call back.

CHAPTER 26

DANIELS

The blare of a car horn snapped him awake.

It took him a moment to get his bearings. He was still in a chair on the balcony, and it was pitch black outside. The lack of city lights suggested early morning. His empty glass sat by his feet; beside it, his cell phone. By glancing at the screen, he could tell if he'd gotten any calls while asleep. There were none.

Special Agent Daniels hadn't called him back. He would have bet money that she was going to. His batting average was poor when predicting women's behavior, and he guessed that was why he was still single.

He heard the horn again. His unit faced the front of the building, and he went to the railing and looked down. A car was parked by the guardhouse, trying to get in. The apartment had twenty-four-hour security, but at night the guard often went inside to drink coffee with the cleaning people.

The guard came out of the building and trotted toward the guardhouse. Instead of going inside, he walked around the security gate and greeted the visitor. It was a woman, and she hung out of the open driver's window and flashed her credentials. They had a brief conversation, then the guard punched a code into a keypad and the gate rose. The visitor pulled in and found a parking space and got out. The guard met her at the entrance to the building, and used a key card to gain entry. She went in and the guard started to follow, only to be rebuffed. She didn't want his help. The guard looked uncomfortable with this, but said nothing. The visitor entered, and the front door closed behind her.

The building had two hundred residents, and the visitor could have been here to visit anyone, but his gut told him it was Daniels, come to pay him a visit. He'd worked with the FBI doing jobs for Team Adam, and he knew that they kept a fleet of private jets at an airport in DC that agents could hop on when a case broke wide open.

He went inside and brushed his teeth and ran a washcloth over his face. Then he unlocked the front door to his apartment and went to the kitchen and brewed a pot of coffee. He pulled a carton of half-and-half out of the fridge and saw that it had expired. As he poured it down the drain he heard the front door open.

"Hello. I'm in the kitchen making coffee. Come on back."

No response. He cleared his throat.

"I'd offer you something to eat, but I'm afraid all I've got is cheese and crackers and a couple of slices of cold pizza."

Still no answer. Daniels was definitely not the friendly type. He took a pair of mugs out of the cabinet and set them on the counter.

"How do you like your coffee? I've got sugar and sweetener."

Daniels stepped into the kitchen. She was slight of build and maybe five six in her bare feet. Her resemblance to Nicki was uncanny, right down to the center part in her jet-black hair. She wore a dark-green pantsuit and had a badge pinned to the jacket lapel. Clutched in her hands was a .40-caliber Glock that was pointed at his chest.

"FBI. Put your arms in the air."

"Is that a no on the coffee?"

"Do it!"

He played cool and stuck his arms in the air. She made him walk into the dining room and had him sit in a chair. He'd bought a dining room set to fill out the apartment and didn't think he'd used it once, preferring to eat on the balcony or while watching TV in the living room. The chair creaked under his weight.

"Put your hands behind the chair," she ordered him.

"Is this necessary? I called you, remember? And I unlocked the door."

"It could be a trap."

"If you thought it was a trap, you would have brought backup."

"Stop arguing with me."

She was on edge, her voice high-pitched. Squeezing a trigger was easier when the shooter was under duress. Not wanting to get shot, he stuck his arms behind his back. She handcuffed his wrists and used a plastic tie to secure the cuffs to a rung in the back of the chair. Then she came around the chair and stood in front of him. The Glock was returned to its jacket holster. She crossed her arms and gave him a stern look.

"You can make this hard, or you can make this easy," she said.

"Easy sounds better," he said.

"Tell me where you stored the Cassandra videos."

"They were on a cell phone that I purchased, but they were erased."

"You're saying you don't have them."

"If you don't believe me, you can check. My laptop is in my study. The password is 'jimmybuffett,' all lowercase. My cell phone is on the balcony on the floor. The second cell phone that had the Cassandra videos is next to it."

"Why do you own two cell phones?"

"I'm working a job. I bought the second one using a false identity so I could look at data that a guy had stored on it."

"That's against the law."

"I think I knew that."

She retrieved the laptop and placed it on the dining room table so he could watch her look through it. "What am I going to find on here?" she asked.

"Mostly bootleg concert videos of Jimmy Buffett that I shot on my cell phone," he said. "There's also a video of me fishing with a buddy of mine."

"No kiddie porn?"

"No, ma'am. Would you like me to explain what's going on, or do you prefer stumbling around in the dark?"

She shot him a pair of daggers. "Watch your mouth."

"Just trying to help."

She took her time reviewing the videos stored on his laptop. Finding nothing illegal, she went onto the balcony and got the two cell phones, and reviewed their contents while he watched. It was an old interrogation trick. She was hoping he would twitch when she got close to finding what she was looking for. When the cell phones turned up empty, she marched into his bedroom and began pulling open drawers and dumping their contents onto the floor.

"There's nothing to find," he called out to her.

"I'll be the judge of that," she replied.

She returned to the dining room and opened the drawers on the china cabinet he'd taken from his parents' house after they'd passed away. Each item she pulled out of the cabinet was given a cursory examination before being placed aside. His grandmother's porcelain serving ladle slipped out of her grasp and shattered on the floor.

"Are you trying to provoke me?" he asked. "Because if you are, it won't work."

She did not apologize for the breakage. She was filled with hostility, her rage simmering just below the surface, and he imagined her in the trunk of the Hanover killers' car, facing certain death. It was the kind of experience that most people never got over.

"You're wasting your time," he said. "I don't have any kiddie porn. I'm a private investigator on a job."

"Keep talking, and I'll put a gag in your mouth."

The kitchen was next. He craned his neck and watched her pull out the silverware drawer and turn it upside down. Then she attacked the cabinet stocked with canned goods. She was going to wreck the place if he didn't stop her.

"You're the girl in the Cassandra videos, aren't you?" he said.

The commotion came to a halt. She returned to the dining room and stood in front of his chair. The blood had drained from her face, her cheeks white.

"What did you just say?" she said.

"You're Cassandra," he said.

"I don't know what you're talking about."

"Yes, you do. I just figured it out. The FBI decided to create the Cassandra videos and posted them on the internet to draw out sexual predators. It was a clever idea, except for one thing. You couldn't use a real underage girl to make the videos without breaking the law, so you volunteered, and a company of video magicians age-regressed your face and body and Cassandra was born."

Daniels looked like she wanted to strangle him. She had spent a lot of the FBI's money creating the Cassandra videos and hadn't expected anyone to figure out the deception. He rattled his handcuffs and she glared at him.

"Are you going to let me go? I can help you."

"Not until I finish searching your place."

"What are you expecting to find?"

"Evidence. I'm not buying your story. You're a pedophile, and pedophiles keep libraries. Once I find your library of videos and images, I'm going to arrest you, and throw your sorry ass in jail."

"You're wrong. I'm working a case and found the Cassandra videos stored on a guy's cell phone."

"And then you erased them."

"I didn't erase them. The guy did. He found out what I'd done, so he used a computer to go to his account and erase the videos."

"Your story sounds like bullshit. Sit tight. I won't be long."

He was growing angry. He hadn't done anything wrong, yet she refused to hear him out. It was time to show his hand. "What if I told you that I was working a job for your sister and brother-in-law, and that it led me to you?"

"Nice try. My sister lives on the other side of the world with her family."

She finished wrecking his kitchen and then moved to his study. The wall in the study was covered with framed photographs of him as a SEAL and as a detective, and he wondered if she noticed them or cared that he'd once been a cop.

She came out of his study looking pissed. Her eyes canvassed the dining room, and fell upon the hall clothes closet. It was the one place she hadn't checked, and she marched over to it and yanked open the flimsy door. On the top shelf was a cardboard box containing his collection of bootleg recordings of the Jimmy Buffett concerts he'd attended. She pulled the box down and started to rummage through it. Finding the CDs, she grabbed a handful and waved them in the air.

"Gotcha," she said.

CHAPTER 27

SISTERS

Daniels placed him under arrest and read him his rights. When he asked her to play the CDs on his laptop, she tuned him out. It was a classic case of tunnel vision. She thought he was a pervert, and nothing he said was going to change her mind.

She got a knife from the kitchen and cut him free from the chair. With his wrists still handcuffed behind his back, he stood up. One of his legs had gone to sleep, and he shook it awake. She took it as a hostile action and drew her gun and aimed it at him.

"Don't do that again," she said.

"You think I'm going to jump you?" he said.

"I wouldn't put it past you."

"But I'm handcuffed."

"Trapped animals will try anything."

"Am I an animal?"

"You most certainly are."

The breath caught in his throat. Daniels *wanted* to shoot him. She had decided he was a monster and was looking for a reason to pump a bullet through his heart. If he made another sudden move that she deemed a threat, his life was over.

"I'm not a monster. Call Melanie. She'll tell you."

"Melanie?" she said, not understanding.

"Yes, Melanie Pearl, your sister. Call her."

"I don't have her number."

"How can you not have your sister's number?"

"My sister lives in Dubai. We haven't spoken in years," she said.

Daniels didn't know that her sister had returned to the United States and was living in Fort Lauderdale. He was not going to pass judgment on her about this. He had a brother he hadn't spoken to in years, so he knew how torturous family relations could be.

"I hate to be the messenger, but your sister and her family left Dubai three months ago and resettled in Fort Lauderdale," he said. "Your brother-in-law now runs the neurology department of a local hospital. They're my clients. I was looking through your niece Nicki's laptop computer and saw a photograph of you wearing an FBI windbreaker. That's why I contacted you."

Confusion spread across her face. "What the hell are you talking about? Why did my sister hire you? What's happened to her?"

"I'll tell you, but first stop pointing that gun at me."

"I don't think so."

He slowly sank into the chair. "How about now? I can't attack you sitting down."

Daniels considered it, then decided he wasn't a threat and put her gun away. She picked up the two cell phones off the dining room table. "Which one is yours?"

"The blue one," he said. "Your brother-in-law's number is in my contacts. Tell him that you're with me, and that I asked him to text me a photograph of Nicki."

"Why should he do that?"

"Because then you'll understand why I contacted you."

"You better not be playing games with me."

"I'm not. Call him."

Daniels made the call and placed the phone to her ear. She hadn't seen her niece in over five years. That was a long time when a kid was growing up. She was going to be surprised in the change in Nicki, and not in a pleasant way.

Nolan Pearl answered the call. Lancaster could faintly hear his voice.

"Nolan, this is your sister-in-law, Beth," Daniels said without emotion. "I'm here with a man named Jon Lancaster who claims to be a private investigator. Lancaster says you hired him to do a job. Is that true?"

"Hello, Beth. What a surprise. It's been too long," Pearl said without emotion. "Yes, we did hire Lancaster. Are you here in Fort Lauderdale?"

"Yes, I am. I arrived a few hours ago," she said. "Lancaster tells me that you and Melanie moved back three months ago."

"We did."

"Why didn't you contact me?"

"That was Melanie's decision, Beth, not mine."

"She won't bury the hatchet, will she?"

"You said some horrible things to her."

"Ask him to send you a photograph of Nicki," Lancaster said.

Daniels put the phone against her chest. "Shut your mouth."

"Just do it, will you? I'm getting sick of these handcuffs."

"You think I'm going to take them off?"

"Yes, and then you're going to apologize to me."

The comment rattled her, and she resumed talking to her brother-in-law. "You still should have let me know you were here. Let me tell you why I called. Lancaster wants you to take a photograph of Nicki, and text it to his cell phone. Will you do that for me?"

"Of course, Beth. Are we going to see you while you're in town?"

"If I have the time, yes."

"I'm sure Nicki will be thrilled. Give me a minute to send you the photo. It's been nice talking to you. It's been too long."

"Yes, it has."

Daniels ended the call. Her eyes found Lancaster's face, and they stared at each other for a long moment. They both knew she had made a mistake. But she wasn't going to admit it just yet. It was part of her training. The FBI taught its agents to create theories when conducting investigations, and to shoehorn the evidence they found to make those theories work. That worked most of the time. When it didn't, innocent people often ended up getting hurt.

His cell phone vibrated in her hand. She fumbled opening the Message app.

"It's from Nolan," she said.

"Brace yourself for a surprise," he said.

She opened her brother-in-law's message and stared at the screen. Her other hand came to her mouth and stayed there.

"Oh my God, is that Nicki?" she said in shock.

"It sure is," he said. "Your niece looks just like Cassandra." He let a moment pass, then said, "Do you have any idea how much harm you've caused her?"

She kept staring at the screen. "What are you talking about? What's happened?"

"Well, since you don't believe a word that I say, why don't you call your sister and let her explain the situation to you?"

She moved toward his chair. She still hadn't made a move to free him, and he sensed that she was taking a perverse pleasure in keeping him prisoner.

"I want you to tell me what's going on," she said.

"Call your sister," he said.

"You're not going to tell me?"

"No. Call Melanie. I'm sure she'd enjoy getting caught up."

She snarled at him like a junkyard dog. Moving to the couch, she sat down and made the call. Soon she was engaged in conversation with her sister. The pleasantries were short and awkward. She grew silent as Melanie told her about Nicki's stalkers and the attempted abductions. Her eyes grew moist, and tears raced down her cheeks.

"This is terrible. I'm so sorry, Mel," she said.

They continued to talk. He rose from his chair and entered the kitchen. Silverware and canned goods covered the floor, and it looked like a tornado had hit it. He cleared a space with his feet and leaned his back against a wall. As a kid he'd read a book about Houdini that had included explanations of how the famous escape artist had gotten out of handcuffs without using a key, and he decided to give it a shot. He lowered his handcuffed wrists as far as he could. Kicking off his right shoe, he lifted his right leg, and slipped his foot through the circle created by his arms, all the while hopping on his left leg to stay balanced. It worked, and he repeated the exercise with his left leg.

His wrists were now in front of his body. His arms had started to cramp, and he shook them to make the pain go away. Then he went in search of a ballpoint pen. He found one in a cup beside the fridge and unscrewed it and removed the cartridge. Houdini could open a handcuff with a paper clip, so Lancaster had to believe it wasn't terribly hard. He jammed the cartridge in the tiny space between the ratchet and locking mechanism and, finding a soft spot, pressed it hard. The handcuff came free. He repeated this with the other wrist and again achieved success.

He smelled coffee. The pot was still on. He could be a bastard with Daniels, or he could be nice and pretend like nothing had happened. The second approach was more to his liking, and would give them a fresh start. He poured two mugs and grabbed the sweetener and returned to the living room.

Daniels was still on the phone with her sister. Melanie was doing all the talking, while Daniels listened and wiped away her tears. He placed a mug and sweetener on the coffee table, followed by the handcuffs. Her eyes registered surprise.

"I was wrong," she whispered. "I'm so sorry."

"Did you tell her about the Cassandra videos?" he whispered back. She shook her head.

"You have to," he whispered.

"I don't know how," she whispered back.

CHAPTER 28
SWEET SIXTEEN

The conversation between Daniels and her sister dragged on. Lancaster started to feel like he was intruding and went into the kitchen to tackle the mess Daniels had made. He put the silverware into the dishwasher and set it on wash, then stocked the canned goods back on the pantry shelves. The cans all had sizeable dents in them. He could not remember encountering a law enforcement agent with such anger issues, and he wondered how long it would be before her superiors took notice.

"Do you have any more coffee?" She stood in the doorway wearing a sheepish expression, the empty mug dangling by its handle from her finger.

"For you, anything," he said.

"You're funny. Do you want to kill me?"

"No. You made a mistake and you said you were sorry. We're good."

"My sister said you were a decent guy. She was right."

He refilled her mug while taking a hard look at her. The rage was gone, replaced by disappointment and shame. She'd been ready to make a bust, and it had gone south instead. He'd had the same thing happen to him as a cop and knew the hollow feeling it left.

"How much did you tell your sister?" he asked.

"Not much. Melanie was always the alpha. I just listened. It sounds like she and Nolan have been through real hell. Not to mention what Nicki's been through. How did these sick bastards connect my niece to the Cassandra videos?"

"Nicki was in a high school musical. A boy at her school coaxed her into singing a song from the musical in her underwear, and he posted it on YouTube. The video's pretty bad, yet it got ten thousand hits. Mostly from sickos who saw the Cassandra videos. One of them pretended to be a Hollywood producer and contacted the boy and got Nicki's personal information, which he must have posted online."

"You're a hell of a detective, Jon. I'm impressed."

"That's why I get paid the big bucks. Can I ask you a question?"

"Go ahead."

"I'm assuming you posted the Cassandra videos on a site that the FBI can monitor. That allows the FBI to collect the IP addresses of the men that download the videos, and get them on your radar so you can watch them. Am I right?"

"You're right, we do monitor them. The Cassandra videos aren't illegal to download because it's me the viewer is looking at. But if we catch one of them downloading other child pornography, we nail them."

"That's what I figured. Here's my question. There are a dozen Cassandra videos. Based upon the date stamps, it appears you posted one video each week to keep the bad ones hooked. That tells me you had a big audience for them. How many downloads were there?"

Daniels sipped her coffee. "I don't know the exact number."

She was lying. Websites had cookies that allowed their designers to see how many visitors had come to the site in real time, and he envisioned Daniels checking the site a few times a day to tally the number of perverts she'd ensnared in her trap. She knew the number, but wasn't willing to share it with him.

He went into the bedroom to clean up the mess. She followed him and stood in the doorway holding her mug. "I never would have created those videos had I known I was putting Nicki in jeopardy. The last time I saw her, she was a little kid."

She wasn't willing to take the blame for the harm she'd caused. He'd known cops like her before. It was all about making the bust, and if innocent people got harmed, too bad. Maybe she hadn't realized the videos would hurt her niece, but that didn't mean there wasn't another teenage girl out there who bore a resemblance to Cassandra and whose life would be upended.

He put his socks and underwear back in their respective dresser drawers. His Kindle was at the bottom of the pile of clothes, the copy of *The Hanover Killers* front and center, and he was tempted to shove it in her face, and ask her if the harrowing experience described in the book had driven her to create the Cassandra videos.

He decided against it. Rising from the floor, he placed the Kindle on the bedside table. He turned around and saw her gazing at a framed photograph on the dresser. It was a group photo of his SEAL team taken in Yemen with the team wearing facial hair disguises and head scarves. His protruding belly made it easy to pick him out of the group. She shifted her gaze to him. She did not acknowledge the photo or his presence in it, which he found surprising. Most people who had seen it wanted to know more.

"When do you plan to tell your sister about the videos?" he asked.

"This afternoon," she said. "Melanie and her husband are taking Nicki to a birthday party for one of Nicki's friends. My sister invited me to join them."

"They shouldn't be taking Nicki out," he said.

"I told her the same thing," she said. "Melanie said that three guards you recommended are going to accompany them. Are they any good?"

"They're ex-SEALs," he said.

"That works," she said.

He went to the dining room to clean up the mess around the china cabinet. The sight of his grandmother's ladle lying in pieces on the floor got him angry, but he kept his feelings bottled up. He placed the shards onto the palm of his hand and deposited them into a wastebasket in the kitchen. She was right on his heels.

"That was old, wasn't it?" she asked.

"It was a family heirloom," he said.

"I'm sorry. I'll replace it. It's the least that I can do."

He nodded and returned to the dining room and put the rest of the pieces back into the china cabinet. Replacing a broken ladle was easy; fixing her niece's situation was not. It would require taking the Cassandra videos down from the web and coming up with a strategy to protect Nicki from further harm. So far, Daniels hadn't said that she was going to do any of these things. Maybe she had a plan and didn't want to share it with him. Or maybe the sting was so important to her that she planned to keep it going, and didn't care what happened to Nicki. It sounded cruel, but he'd seen stranger things in law enforcement. Daniels glanced at her watch and frowned.

"Something wrong?" he asked.

"I told Melanie I'd meet her at eleven thirty, and it's already five after eleven," she said. "I don't want to be late and get things off on a bad foot."

"I hope it goes well with your sister."

"If you don't mind, I'd like you to accompany me."

"Why is that?"

"I want you there when I talk to them," she said. "It'll make things easier."

For who? he nearly asked.

"If you think it'll help," he said.

"I do," the FBI agent said.

- - -

The Harbor Beach Surf Club was a members-only yacht club located on Highway A1A that charged more to rent a dock slip than most people paid for their mortgages. Lancaster had driven by its gated entrance many times but never been inside.

Daniels's rental was a silver Dodge Challenger. It was from Hertz and was part of their Adrenaline Collection. She drove like a New York cabbie, her right foot alternating between hitting the gas and slamming on the brakes. It was like riding a bull, and he kept his hand pressed to the dashboard and prayed she didn't rear-end another car.

"How much farther?" she asked.

"It's less than a mile up the road," he said. "Do you always drive so fast?"

"I have a need for speed. Does that bother you?"

"You could get pulled over. A1A has its own patrol."

"I'll bat my eyelashes and talk my way out of it."

She hit her blinker and turned into the club. A security guard found her name on a list and put a pass on her dashboard. They drove a short distance to the pavilion where the birthday party was being held. The club dated back to World War I, and there was nothing fancy about it. Just a marina, a brick pavilion that had restrooms and a covered area with picnic tables, and a private stretch of beach on the other side of A1A.

After parking, they got out and approached the pavilion. It was decorated with silver helium balloons and streamers with the birthday girl's name. About fifteen parents and the same number of kids were eating burgers and dogs and making lots of noise.

The Pearls sat at a picnic table in the shade. Nicki was eating a hot dog and looked like she was having a good time. Her parents sat to either side of her. Neither was eating. Carlo stood nearby, wearing an untucked white shirt to hide the firearm he was carrying. Although Lancaster didn't see Karl or Mike, he knew they were nearby.

The Pearls stood up. Nicki put her dog on a paper plate and rushed her aunt. They hugged, and Daniels got choked up and wiped away a few tears. Nicki's parents stayed in their spots wearing thin smiles. Daniels broke free of her niece and came up to them.

"Hey, Melanie," she said.

"Hey, Beth," her sister replied.

"You haven't changed."

"Neither have you."

"I wish you'd told me you'd moved back."

"I've been busy. You know how it is."

Daniels was a bully, except when around her older sister. Then she was a wimp. Daniels shifted her attention to her brother-in-law.

"Nolan."

"Beth."

"You look good."

"That's funny, I don't feel good," Pearl said. "Melanie tells me that you tore Jon's condo apart before calling us. I can't say it surprises me. You were always one to shoot first and ask questions later."

An awkward silence ensued. There was not enough pavement for Lancaster to stare at. Nicki came over and broke up the party.

"They're going to cross A1A so they can go swimming in the ocean," the teenager said. "Can we go too? I brought my swimsuit with me. It's under my clothes."

"Let's ask Carlo," Melanie said. "Carlo, what do you think?"

"Is this a public or private beach?" Carlo said.

"Private. Only the club's members can use it," Melanie said.

"That should be okay," Carlo said.

"Yay!" Nicki said.

The birthday party was abandoning the pavilion for the beach. The partygoers walked single file down a gravel path through the mangroves. The Pearls were the last to leave, with Carlo behind them talking on his cell phone to his partners. Daniels stayed behind, shamed by the exchange with her brother-in-law. In her hand were the keys to the rental. Did she really think she could just leave?

Lancaster went over and snatched the keys out of her hand.

"You're not wiggling your way out of this one," he said.

CHAPTER 29
A BIGGER MONSTER

The partygoers used the striped walkway to cross A1A. By the time they reached the beach, Nicki had seven adults protecting her. The teenager stripped off her clothes to reveal a pink bikini underneath and joined her friends in the water.

Lancaster stood a dozen yards away, taking everything in. There were perhaps twenty other swimmers enjoying the beautiful day, and a lone lifeguard sitting in a high chair. Daniels stormed over and grabbed his arm.

"Give me back my car keys," she seethed.

"Not until you tell your sister and her husband what you've done," he said.

"If you don't give me my keys, I'll arrest you."

She had been reduced to threats, and he laughed under his breath. "What do you plan to tell the judge? That you ransacked my place without a warrant and held me against my will? Or that you made kiddie porn without considering the consequences?"

"Third time. It wasn't intentional."

"That's a cop-out. I've dealt with perverts. Porn is the fuel that keeps them going. That's especially true with pedophiles."

"I want my keys."

He'd had enough of Daniels and tossed her the keys. A reflection caught his eye. It was coming from the lifeguard chair, and he stepped forward for a better look. The lifeguard had a cell phone in his hand, and alternated looking at its screen and the kids playing in the water. In one of the Cassandra videos, the girl was wearing a hot-pink bikini. Talk about baiting a trap, he thought.

Daniels edged up beside him. "What are you looking at?"

"I thought you'd left," he said.

"Would you like me to go?"

"No, I'd like you to help."

"How so?"

"I found another stalker. I want you to arrest him."

"The lifeguard? Why? Everyone looks at their cell phones."

"Two people drowned last weekend from a rip tide. The lifeguard should be watching the people swimming in the water. Instead, he's looking at the Cassandra videos on his cell phone and thinking the kid in the pink bikini is the same girl."

"You're sure about this?"

"I've already encountered a handful of these guys. They're all the same. Once they spot Nicki, they whip out their cell phone and watch the videos they think are of her. They're obsessed with her. Wait. There he goes."

The lifeguard climbed down from his chair. He had sun-bleached hair and sunblock smeared across his nose, and his legs were nut brown and hairless. He was pushing fifty and very fit. He went toward the water holding his cell phone in front of him so he could look at the screen while he walked. None of the bodyguards nor Nicki's parents noticed. He was a lifeguard, entrusted with keeping people safe, the perfect disguise.

"Care to join me?" Lancaster asked.

"Let me handle him. Watch my back."

"Now you're talking."

They took off down the beach. Daniels had invisible wings on her feet, and he struggled to keep up with her. The lifeguard didn't see them until it was too late. He dropped the cell phone to his side, his thumb nervously punching the screen.

Daniels whipped out a wallet and flipped it open. She shoved her badge into his face. "FBI. Give me your cell phone. Do it nice and slow."

The lifeguard didn't move, his thumb still jabbing the screen.

"I won't tell you again," she said.

His thumb was working overtime trying to exit the app he'd been using. Daniels had seen enough; she drew her gun and pointed it at the lifeguard's chest.

"Get it from him," she said.

Lancaster stepped forward and tried to take the cell phone out of the lifeguard's hand. The lifeguard's leg twitched. Sand flew in the air. Lancaster ducked and it missed him. Daniels wasn't as fortunate and got hit in the eyes. The lifeguard went for the gun, and they wrestled for its possession. It went off, the barrel pointing at the sky. Lancaster jumped in. A man never stopped being a SEAL. His commander at basic training had said that. The lessons a SEAL learned became part of their DNA and could never be erased. He grabbed the lifeguard's wrist and bent it back, the bones ready to break. The gun slipped out of the lifeguard's hand, and he crumpled to the sand.

Lancaster retrieved the gun and the lifeguard's cell phone. Daniels was trying to right the ship and get her vision back. He glanced at the cell phone's screen. A Cassandra video was playing. The app was VideoVault, the same app that Zack Kenny had used to watch the Cassandra videos, and he wondered if that played into the FBI's sting.

He held the cell phone up to Daniels's face so the video was the first thing she saw.

"Guilty as charged," he said.

- - -

Discharging a firearm was a great way to break up a party. Every person on the beach or swimming in the water took off running, including Carlo and his partners, who whisked the Pearls away to safety. That left just Daniels, the lifeguard, and Lancaster.

The lifeguard's cell phone was a treasure trove of sleaze and contained hundreds of videos of underage girls performing lewd acts. If presented at trial, it was enough evidence for a jury to find him guilty and send him away for many years. Daniels snapped the silver bracelets on and led him to the rental parked across the street.

"Do you want to talk to me?" Daniels asked.

The lifeguard stared at the ground and did not reply.

"If you play ball, I'll see about reducing the charges," she said.

The lifeguard's head snapped. "What do you want to know?"

"Tell me about your partner."

"I don't know what you're talking about."

"I think you do. Roll on your partner, and I'll get you sent to a country club prison with a bunch of white-collar criminals where you won't have to be afraid of getting a shiv stuck in your back every time you take a shower."

"Can I think about this?"

"You can think about it all the way to the police station."

She opened the rental and shoved her prisoner in the back seat. She slammed the door and came around to the front of the car. Lancaster joined her. They turned their backs on the lifeguard so he couldn't read their lips while they spoke.

"We make a good team," she said.

"Is that supposed to be an apology?" he asked.

"You still angry with me? Get over it."

"Only if you help me solve Nicki's problem."

"We'll get that fixed. But first I need to put this asshole's feet to the fire and find out what he knows. Care to join me?"

"You haven't said what you're looking for. Why do you think he has a partner?"

Daniels gave him a long look. He thought back to the question he'd posed to her earlier. How many sickos had downloaded the Cassandra videos? Ten thousand? A hundred thousand? The number had to be huge, way too many for the FBI to track down every single person who'd done so. Something else was in play here, and he realized that Daniels was chasing a much bigger monster.

"I'm in," he said.

She flashed a smile. It was the first time she'd done that. It made her look even prettier, and he broke into a grin. It was the wrong thing to do. Her smile vanished, and she turned and got in the car.

CHAPTER 30
CREEPIE

Lancaster told Daniels to drive to the sheriff's office on Eller Drive. He'd worked out of this office for several years and was on a first-name basis with the staff. Business was booming, and there was a wait to get their suspect booked.

Being an FBI agent had its privileges. Daniels found the desk sergeant and got the lifeguard moved to the head of the line, where he was fingerprinted, had a mug shot taken, and had his arrest report filled out. The lifeguard's name was Richard "Rusty" Newman and he was forty-nine years old. Rusty sat in a chair with his wrist handcuffed to its leg and answered the desk sergeant's questions. When asked if he'd like to call a lawyer, he declined. This was significant, for it meant Rusty might be willing to share information with Daniels and perhaps strike a deal.

Interrogations were done in a cramped room on the second floor that reeked of cigarettes. Smoking in the building was forbidden, but suspects were sometimes allowed to light up in the hopes it would lead to their cooperation. His handcuffs removed, Rusty sat with his back to the wall and stared into space. He'd been treated with contempt by every cop he'd encountered, and had to know that it was only going to get worse. Adults who abused children were not treated well by the system. This was especially true in prison, where they were often forced to live in solitary confinement for their own safety.

Daniels and Lancaster stood on the other side of the room. Daniels had reviewed the library of porn stored on Rusty's cell phone and told Lancaster there was enough sick stuff to send the lifeguard away for twenty years.

"Tell me about your partner," Daniels said.

"I don't have a partner," Rusty said.

"Then how about your friend. Tell me about him."

"I have a lot of friends."

"I want to know about one in particular. Tell me about the friend who's into this stuff who you hang out with."

"I run solo. I don't hang out with anybody," Rusty said.

Daniels stepped forward and dropped her voice. "If I check the calls logged on your cell phone and your emails, there won't be one name that keeps popping up?"

"No, ma'am," Rusty said.

"But you know other guys who are into this stuff," she said.

"Sure. But I don't socialize with them. You hang with other people, you inherit their problems. If another guy gets arrested and you're with him, you'll get arrested too."

"You've been good at hiding your tracks, haven't you?"

Rusty chose his words carefully. "I'm not going to apologize about who I am. I know these things are wrong, but I can't stop it. So I try to be careful."

The interrogation was starting out well. Rusty was saying the right things and also being respectful. His willingness to help also felt real.

"You've got hundreds of pornographic photographs and videos stored on your cell phone," she said. "Where did you get them from?"

"Lots of places. I downloaded some, others were sent to me," Rusty said.

"Sent to you by who?"

"Guys I met in chat rooms."

"Do you know their names?"

"No, guys in chat rooms use aliases."

"Really. What's your alias?"

"Captain Rich. Richard's my real name."

"If I showed you particular images I found on your phone, would you remember where they came from?"

"I can try. My memory's pretty good."

Daniels removed her own cell phone from her jacket pocket and powered it up. She had transferred Rusty's library to a file on her cell phone. She found a particular photograph and held the cell phone in Rusty's face. The photo was of a naked teenage Mexican girl tied to a bed. She wore a shiny gold medallion around her neck, and looked like she would have preferred being dead to enduring any more abuse. Her torturers stood beside the bed wearing black leather masks.

"Does this look familiar?" the FBI agent asked.

Rusty's face displayed no emotion. "Yeah, I remember that one."

"Who sent it to you?"

"Guy named Creepie. Spelled with an 'ie' instead of a 'y.' Look, I only looked at that photo once. I'm not into torture."

"No? Then why didn't you erase it?"

"I must have forgotten."

"You're already in enough trouble, Rusty. Don't compound your misery by lying to me. Your situation will only get worse if you do."

Rusty had started to sweat. Looking at the torture photo hadn't bothered him. But the thought of Daniels putting the screws to him did.

"All right, maybe I looked at it a couple of times," he said.

Daniels returned the cell phone to her pocket. She crossed her arms in front of her chest and looked at Rusty like he was a rodent.

"Why are you staring at me like that?" the lifeguard said.

"The girl's body was found in a field on the side of a highway in Houston seven years ago," Daniels said. "She was an illegal immigrant who came across the border to find work. She was raped and strangled to death."

Rusty shook his head in disbelief. "I asked Creepie when he sent the photo to me. I emailed him and said, 'Did you kill her?' Creepie emailed me back and said they'd let the girl go."

"And you believed him."

"Yes, I believed him. Guys into S&M like to boast about it. Creepie didn't do that. He said the girl survived, and I believed him."

"I found three other torture photos in the library on your phone. The FBI has these same photos. Guess what? The girls in all three ended up dead."

Rusty's eyes went wide, and his hands balled into fists.

"Fuck me," he said under his breath.

"Did Creepie also send you these photos?" Daniels asked.

"Yeah. He told me the girls in them survived."

"Do you see where this is headed, Rusty? You could be charged with being an accomplice to four murders if you're not careful."

"I didn't know. You have to believe me."

"I want to believe you, but you need to do more. Did Creepie send you any other images of girls being tortured? Think hard."

Rusty scratched his chin and gave it some thought. "About six months ago, he emailed me a photo of a young black girl he was putting through the paces, and asked me if I wanted to see more. I said yes, so he sent me the rest and I downloaded them."

"How old was this young woman?"

"She was young, maybe fifteen."

"What else do you remember about her?"

"She was hog-tied and had a gag ball in her mouth. It was pretty graphic."

"How many photographs of the black girl were there?"

"Five or six."

"What else do you remember?"

"They were shot inside a house. There was furniture, and the floor was carpeted. The look on the girl's face was pretty horrible. I decided to erase them."

"If I showed you those photographs again, would you remember them?"

"Probably. Was she also killed?"

"Yes, she was killed."

- - -

Daniels decided to take a break. She asked Rusty if he wanted a drink, and he said he'd like a Diet Pepsi. She went to the door and motioned for Lancaster to follow her.

They went into the hallway, and the door to the interrogation room locked itself behind them. The door had a square-shaped two-way mirror. Daniels gazed through it for a moment. When she was satisfied that Rusty wasn't going to do something crazy, she walked to the end of the hallway and fed money into a vending machine.

"You want something?" she asked.

"A water would be good. My phone buzzed in my pocket three times while we were in the room. I'm guessing that's your sister and brother-in-law checking in. What would you like me to tell them?"

Daniels bought two bottled waters and handed him one. They both had a long drink. He sensed that she was struggling for an answer. It was rare for a suspect to open up like Rusty was doing. She needed for him to keep talking for as long as she could.

"Want me to stall them?" he suggested.

"You don't mind doing that?" she asked.

"You've got a head of steam going. No need for distractions."

"Tell them I'll call them tonight and give them the details." She drained the water and tossed the empty in the trash. "I need to make a phone call and make sure that Rusty hasn't turned up on any other databases. Would you mind going out to the rental, and getting my briefcase? It's locked in the trunk."

"Sure."

Daniels handed him the keys, and he walked out of the building. The FBI had recently gotten a black eye courtesy of O. J. Simpson's parole hearing, and he understood her desire to check other criminal databases to see if Rusty popped up. During Simpson's hearing, the Nevada parole board had relied on the National Crime Information Center's database of records to see if Simpson had any prior convictions. Outside of the acquittal in the murder of his ex-wife and her boyfriend, nothing had shown up, and the parole board had voted to let Simpson go free. Unfortunately, O. J. had been arrested for beating up his wife in 1989 and had pleaded no-contest to the charges. The omission of this crime from the NCIC's database had highlighted a serious problem: There were major gaps in the information sent by the states to the feds.

While Rusty was being processed, a check had been run on his driver's license, which had revealed that he'd previously lived on Cape Cod and on the south shore of Long Island in the town of Long Beach. Daniels would call the police departments in both areas and have them run a background check. It was the only way to be fully certain that Rusty was telling the truth when he said he had no prior arrests.

Daniels's rental sat beneath a lonely palm tree. He popped the trunk to find a soft-sided leather briefcase lying atop a clothing bag. The briefcase's flap had come open, and papers were spewed across the trunk. He started putting them back until a name across the top of a page caught his eye.

His own.

CHAPTER 31

SOMALIA

The hairs went up on the back of his neck. He got into the rental and started the engine, and with the AC blowing in his face, read the file Daniels had pulled on him.

She had left no stone unturned. There was a report dating back to his high school days that included his report cards plus write-ups of several disciplinary problems, including the time he'd toilet papered the school with his pals.

Next up were his service papers. His missions with the SEALs were classified and would remain that way, but Daniels had still managed to get her hands on psychological evaluations that had been conducted when he'd enlisted and the week before he'd been discharged, when the navy doctors had determined him mentally fit to return to society.

The navy doctors had taken a hard look at his last mission in Somalia. He'd embraced every part of being a SEAL and had hoped to be promoted to commander, until that fateful day when he'd shot a little Somali boy with explosives strapped to his body. While a member of his team dismantled the bomb, he'd tried to stop the boy from bleeding to death. The boy hadn't pulled through and died in his arms.

He had been overcome with grief. In war, there were two options—you could run away, or you could fight. Only this poor kid didn't have those choices. Either he would be blown to bits by the bomb strapped to his body, or a SEAL would shoot him to death.

It had haunted him. For days he'd lain awake at night, replaying the scenario to see if he could have handled things differently. He'd decided that he'd done the right thing. He'd saved the lives of his team, and no one could fault him for that. Yet it had still felt like he'd passed through the gates of hell, and he'd decided to leave the military.

Next were his police files. These were extensive. He'd worn a uniform for five years, and his performance had been reviewed by his superiors every six months. He'd been an undercover detective for ten more, where he had also faced six-month reviews. Daniels had gone through these reviews thoroughly and dog-eared the pages that contained complaints filed against him by citizens where there had been hearings. In each case, a panel had ruled in his favor, and the charges against him had been dismissed.

The last pages of his police files listed the various commendations he'd received during his time on the force. Being a SEAL had given him an edge when dealing with crisis situations, and he'd been decorated for bravery on three occasions. When he'd retired, his boss had written a letter praising his heroism and unselfishness. That was in his file too.

Last up were the missing kids' cases he'd worked for Team Adam in the past two years. The team's director had reviewed each of the investigations he'd handled and given him high praise. Except for the toilet paper incident, there were no black marks against him.

He stuffed the pages into the briefcase and went back inside. The elevator was temperamental, so he took the stairs to the second floor. As he reached the landing, he had an unpleasant thought. Daniels had read his files while flying to South Florida from DC. She knew that he'd served his country with distinction as a SEAL and been an exemplary policeman, yet had treated him like a criminal while she'd trashed his condo. Those two things didn't go together, and made him wonder what her motivation had been.

- - -

He found the special agent by the vending machines on the second floor and handed her the briefcase.

"Anything turn up?" he asked.

"Yes. Rusty worked as a substitute teacher on Long Island twenty years ago and got caught fondling a kid," she said. "The town where it happened is still in the process of transferring their paper records to digital, so it wasn't in the NCIC database."

"How does that change things?"

"It means I'm not going to cut him a deal."

"Are you going to tell him that?"

"Hell no. I'm going to show him the torture photos of a young black girl, and get him to confirm they're the same as the ones that Creepie sent to him. Then I'm going to search his place and get my hands on his computer. If I'm lucky, I'll get an email address for Creepie and hunt him down."

"Is Creepie the prize?"

"Yes, he is."

"He's a serial killer, isn't he?"

"Right again."

"And he has a partner."

"Go to the head of the class."

"You've been chasing this guy for a long time, haven't you?"

"Too long."

Every sting was designed to catch a certain criminal or groups of criminals. The Cassandra videos had been created with the sole purpose of catching a serial killer, and he finally understood what was behind

Daniels's fury. Serial killers never stopped killing, and each wasted hour or day could result in the loss of a victim's life.

"What kind of soda did Rusty say he wanted?" Daniels asked.

"Diet Pepsi," he said.

She bought a Diet Pepsi and then perused the snack selections.

"What do you think he likes to eat?" she asked.

"Get him a bag of Fritos," he said. "If he doesn't want them, I'll eat them."

Daniels bought the chips, and they walked down the hall to the interrogation room. She punched a code into the keypad, and the door clicked open. Rusty sat in his chair wearing the same dead expression. Daniels placed the snacks on the table, and his demeanor changed. Ripping open the bag, he began stuffing the chips into his mouth.

"You must be hungry," Daniels said.

"Starving. I haven't eaten since this morning," Rusty said.

"Here's what I'm going to do. When we're done, I'll buy you a sandwich from the Subway down the street. Does that sound like a plan?"

"That works for me."

Rusty finished the chips and washed them down with the soda. The walls of resistance had lowered, and he was ready to play ball. Rusty mistakenly believed that by cooperating, Daniels would ask a judge to go light on him, but in fact the only deal he had was the one he'd made with the devil long ago.

Daniels opened her briefcase and removed a manila envelope. Out came five photographs of the black girl who'd been hog-tied. She placed them in a row on the table so they faced their suspect.

"Let's get started," the FBI agent said.

CHAPTER 32

TRUST

Daniels got a search warrant, and they set out for Inverrary Resort, where Rusty rented a one-bedroom. Lancaster was hungry, and he persuaded Daniels to pull into a McDonald's, where he ordered a quarter pounder with cheese and a large fry.

"You sure you don't want anything?" he asked.

"I'll just pick at yours." She filched a french fry and pulled out of the drive-through. "I noticed that you looked through my briefcase. Find anything of interest?"

"It wasn't intentional. Your papers were all over the trunk, so I put them back."

"You must have seen the background check I did on you."

"As a matter of fact, I did."

"You're quite the Boy Scout with all those medals and citations," she said.

He placed the french fries beneath her nose. She grabbed several more and stuffed them into her mouth. She couldn't talk with her mouth full, so he pressed her.

"You knew that about me before you came to my condo this morning," he said. "Yet you still chose to treat me like a common criminal. I'd like to know what you saw in those reports that made you think I was a bad guy."

She chewed silently and stared at the road. He unwrapped the quarter pounder and bit into it. He offered her a bite, and she shook her head no.

"I didn't see anything in those reports," she said. "The red flag was the voice mail you left me. You referenced the Cassandra videos, and that was all I needed to hear to hop on a plane and come down here."

"You mean because I'd seen them."

She nodded. "You've got a stellar background, but that doesn't mean you couldn't be a predator. You should see some of the guys I've arrested. Lawyers, doctors, I even busted a circuit court judge once. They were all leading double lives. In public they were very respectable people. In private they were monsters."

"How many guys have you busted because of those videos?"

"I've personally busted sixteen. Other agents around the country have also made busts. The last time I checked, the total number was over forty."

"That's a big haul."

"It is. And we're not done yet."

"Creepie and his partner are the prize."

"Yes, they are."

He finished his meal. The Cassandra videos were bait, and the men that took that bait deserved no sympathy. But he still wasn't clear on why an agent in their local office hadn't paid him a visit, instead of Daniels doing it herself. Something in his background reports had raised a red flag that had made her personally fly here from Washington, and that bothered him.

She pulled into Inverrary Resort and parked in front of a deserted valet stand. She got out and grabbed her briefcase before they headed inside. Inverrary had once been a playground for the rich and famous, with fine dining and sprawling golf courses, but it had fallen on hard times and now rented rooms to drug addicts and assorted miscreants.

"This could be the set for a horror movie," she said.

"Wait until you see the rooms," he said.

"You've stayed here before?"

"When I was in uniform, we got called here every night."

The desk manager was a gaunt Pakistani wearing a white dress shirt. He studied Daniels's ID and search warrant before handing it back.

"Is Rusty in trouble?" the desk manager asked.

"He's in a lot of trouble," Daniels replied. "Are you friends with him?"

"We are not friends. I ask because he's behind on his rent."

"That's too bad. I need to see his apartment."

They all took a creaky elevator to the third floor and were soon standing in Rusty's one-bedroom. The overhead light didn't work, and Daniels drew the blinds so that sunshine flooded the interior. "I guess housecleaning isn't included in the daily rate," she said under her breath. The carpet was torn, the wallpaper was peeling, and a sink ran in the bathroom. The desk manager tried to turn the water off and cursed under his breath.

"I will have to call a plumber and get this fixed," he said.

"Not so fast," she said. "We're going to have a look around, and then a team of FBI agents is going to pack everything up and take it away to be analyzed. I don't want any workers in here until that's done. Am I making myself clear?"

"Yes, ma'am," he said.

The desk manager made himself scarce. Daniels placed a call on her cell phone to the local FBI office and requested a team be sent to pack up Rusty's things. Ending the call, she unzipped the side pocket on her briefcase and removed two pairs of white latex gloves, one of which she tossed to Lancaster.

"Put these on before you touch anything," she said.

"Will do. What else do you have in that briefcase?"

"You'd be surprised."

A laptop computer sat on a small desk that was bolted to the wall. Daniels pulled up the room's only chair and powered up the laptop. The screen saver was a beach at sunrise taken from a lifeguard's high chair, and Lancaster guessed that Rusty had taken the shot. He wasn't going to be seeing many more of those where he was going.

Daniels tried to gain entry and was denied. The laptop was password protected.

"I know a good hacker," he said.

"So do I," she said.

From her briefcase she removed a black box with an electrical cord and a USB connector, and she connected the box to the back of Rusty's laptop. Soon the device was running tens of thousands of passwords per second through the laptop. Daniels leaned back in her chair and crossed her arms in front of her chest.

"Where did you get that?" he asked.

"The FBI hired a hacker to build them for us. It's now standard equipment, just like the firearms we carry."

"Can I get one?"

She shook her head.

"What if I help you catch this guy?"

The device beeped, indicating it had found the correct password. Daniels brought her face up to the rectangular screen and began her search.

"Do you mind if I look around?" he asked.

"Go ahead," she said.

He searched the room and discovered that Rusty had little in the way of material possessions. There were assorted articles of clothing, a boom box, a pair of flip-flops, a pair of sneakers, and a jump rope. On the floor of the closet was a cardboard box that begged a closer look. It was heavy, and he popped the lid to find it filled with old laptops. He carefully removed each one and placed it on the bed. There were eight in all, with models by Dell, Gateway, Sony, and Apple. Their combined value was more than all the other items in Rusty's possession.

"What do you think of this?" he asked.

Daniels glanced at the bed out of the corner of her eye. "Isn't that a nice collection. Don't bother turning them on. The hard drives have been erased."

"How can you be sure?" he said.

"Because that's what guys who share kiddie porn do."

He sat down on the edge of the bed. He thought he understood but wanted to be sure. "Is that the game? Rusty buys a new laptop every six months and transfers his porn library before erasing the hard drive on the old one. He gets a new IP address with each new laptop, which makes it harder to catch him. He also moves around a lot, just in case the law gets him in its crosshairs."

"That's the game," she said. "The smart ones also get new email addresses."

"How does that work?"

"Gmail lets a user create multiple email addresses under different aliases. There's a tutorial on YouTube that explains how to do it."

"The internet is heaven for these sick bastards, isn't it?"

"Yes, it is. We still catch them, it just takes longer."

The minutes dragged on. He went to the room's only window and gazed down at the rear of the property. A narrow concrete sidewalk ran alongside the brown fairway of the resort's eighteen-hole golf course. The golf course was no longer in use, and a family with several small children sat on a blanket enjoying a late-afternoon picnic.

The sidewalk was busy with residents of the hotel having a cigarette or taking a stroll. An elderly man pushing a wheelchair came into view. He wore an orange tracksuit and was pushing an emaciated woman who appeared to be in the final stages of life. As the wheelchair got close to the others on the sidewalk, they moved out of its path but did not speak to the elderly man or the dying woman. Watching this happen gave him pause, and he thought about the near-abduction of Nicki at the Galleria mall. Nicki's abductors had used a wheelchair, and now he understood why.

Daniels slapped the desk. She pulled out her cell phone and typed in a text message, then punched the screen with her forefinger.

"You found Creepie's email," he said.

"Yes, and I just sent it to FBI headquarters in DC," she said. "The FBI has an unwritten agreement with the country's internet service providers. When we want to find out who an email belongs to, the ISPs will tell us without a subpoena. It comes in real handy during investigations." Her fingers tapped the desk impatiently. "We've been searching for these monsters for a long time. Let's hope this leads us to him."

He hoped she was right. In his experience, two criminals working as a team could go for years without getting caught. One member of the team committed the crime, while his partner cleaned up the incriminating evidence.

They waited for Washington to get back to Daniels. She wasn't very talkative and continued to search the contents of Rusty's laptop. He sat down on the bed and rubbed his wrists. They were still chafed from Daniels's handcuffs.

"I've got some extra-strength ibuprofen if you need it," she said.

"I'll live," he said.

Her cell phone rang. She glanced at the caller ID and answered it.

"What have you got for me?" she said, unable to hide her excitement. She listened, and her face crashed. "There's no record? How can that be?"

She got her answer and ended the call.

"God damn it," she swore. "There's no record of the email address in any of these ISP databases. It's as if it never existed."

"How does that work?"

"The hell I know."

There was a knock on the door, and Lancaster went and answered it. The Pakistani desk manager and a team of FBI agents wearing hazmat suits stood in the hallway. He turned and spoke to Daniels.

"Your boys are here," he said.

- - -

Back in the car, Lancaster decided to play his hand. Daniels had refused to share any meaningful information with him except by accident, and he thought he knew why. She still didn't completely trust him. Her distrust had little to do with him, and was a byproduct of her investigation.

"Tell me how to get back to your place," she said.

"Are we done?" he asked.

"Yes, Jon, we're done. Thanks for your help."

"Can I buy you a cup of coffee? I'd like to talk with you."

"About what?"

"Your niece. These stalkers aren't going away. One is going to get his hands on her, and Nicki's going to get hurt or killed. You don't want that to happen, do you?"

"I'll deal with Nicki's situation in due time. Meanwhile, you can keep protecting her. My sister and her husband have plenty of money, and can afford your services."

"That's pretty callous."

Her jaw tightened, and she stared at the road. "Don't judge me without knowing all the facts." The rental sped up. She was itching to get rid of him. It was time.

"Creepie's a cop, isn't he?" he said.

Daniels pulled onto the shoulder and slammed on the brakes, then turned in her seat to stare at him. "How the hell did you know that?" she asked.

"The way you handcuffed me gave you away."

"Why? I always handcuff suspects."

"You left them on for too long. Your sister told you that she'd hired me, yet you didn't make a move to release me. You were still suspicious."

"That's pretty flimsy reasoning," she said.

"I'll agree with you. It was flimsy reasoning until we questioned Rusty and you took the cuffs off him in the interrogation room. Rusty was a pervert, yet you didn't feel threatened by him. You knew Rusty wasn't Creepie because you ran a background check and saw that he'd never been a cop."

"That's still flimsy reasoning."

"There's more."

"Keep talking."

"Creepie and his partner are the same pair that tried to abduct you at Dartmouth College. I read *The Hanover Killers* before I called you. The book's author said that every male in Dartmouth submitted to DNA testing and it didn't do any good. In the book's epilogue, the author speculated who the killers might be. One theory was that it was two cops from a nearby town, since the cops never submitted to DNA testing. Well, those cops are still abducting young girls and killing them, and you're chasing them."

"That's very good, Jon. I'm impressed."

Her opinion of him had changed. He could see it in her face and especially in her eyes. He'd demonstrated enough deductive reasoning to put them on equal footing.

"Come on, let me buy you dinner," he said. "There's a place nearby called Country Walk that serves really good food. We can talk in private there."

"I'm sorry, but I can't. I've got to get back to DC."

"But I want to help you."

Daniels shook her head. She was as stubborn as a mule, and he decided to play the last card in his hand. "If I told you that I have a video of Creepie and his partner trying to abduct your niece, would you change your mind?"

Her eyes grew wide. "What are you talking about?"

"Did your sister tell you about what happened at Galleria mall?"

"Melanie said two men tried to grab Nicki, but Nolan stopped them."

"I have a surveillance video taken at the mall. Let me show it to you, and explain why I think it was them. You can judge for yourself."

"All right. But I need to pay for my own dinner. Bureau rules."

"Whatever you want," he said.

She asked her phone for directions to Country Walk, and an automated voice gave her instructions. Then she merged into traffic and got back on the road.

CHAPTER 33
WHEELCHAIR ETIQUETTE

"I want to be straight with you about something," Daniels said as she pulled into a parking space at Country Walk and silenced the engine. "I had no idea how identical Nicki looked to Cassandra. Had I known, I would never have posted the videos."

Her voice was riddled with guilt. Lancaster had worked stings as a cop and never liked them. There were often unintended consequences to setting a trap that no one ever saw coming. As he started to get out, she grabbed his wrist.

"You believe me, don't you?"

"I don't think you'd do anything to hurt your niece," he said. "But you must have realized that another teenage girl might bear a resemblance to Cassandra. And that by posting those videos, you'd put that girl in harm's way."

Her lower lip began to tremble.

"That never occurred to me," she said.

"I find that hard to accept," he said.

He was roasting without the AC and tried to get out. She kept holding his wrist.

"Please believe me," she said.

"But I don't," he said. "If you were an ordinary cop, that would be another story. But you're an FBI agent and you also went to Dartmouth, which is Ivy League. You've got to be pretty smart to get into that place. The sting you created had the potential to hurt an innocent girl. You knew that, but you still went full steam ahead."

A single tear ran down her cheek. She wiped it away and took a deep breath.

"All right. I knew there was a risk, and so did my superiors," she said. "But we took it anyway. We didn't really have a choice, considering the circumstances."

"You've lost me. What circumstances?"

"If I tell you, you have to promise you won't talk about it."

"You have my word."

She reached into the back seat and grabbed her briefcase. Holding it in her lap, she unzipped an inside compartment and removed a large manila envelope with a drawstring, which she spent a moment undoing. From within came a handful of old-fashioned square photographs that was an inch thick. She passed the stack to him, and he thumbed through them. They were a collection of different young women taken before and after their lives were extinguished. In the before photos, the women were clothed and had smiles on their faces and looked either high or drunk. In the after photos, they were naked and tied up, their lifeless faces etched with anguish and pain. Unable to process anymore, he handed the photos back to her.

"That's beyond horrible," he said.

"Welcome to my world," she said.

- - -

Dinner no longer sounded appealing. She found a Starbucks, and he went inside and bought two grande cups of Pike Place and brought them out to the car. He placed a handful of sugar packets and artificial sweetener on the seat between them, along with a pastry.

"Only one? Talk about showing a girl a good time," she said.

"We can split it," he said.

She leaned against her door and blew the steam off her drink. "I joined the FBI right after I graduated from Dartmouth and worked my way up the ranks. Maybe because of what happened to me in college, I became adept at catching sexual predators. I would stay up all night running them down. My bosses noticed, and in 2012, I was promoted to running the Violent Crimes Against Children/Online Predator Unit. I wasn't on the job two weeks when the first photographs landed on my desk."

"The killers sent them to you?"

"They were more clever than that. The victim's photographs were taken on an old-fashioned camera, and the film was dropped off at a pharmacy to be developed. When the pharmacy processed the film and saw it was of a murder, the local police were contacted. The cops didn't know what to do with the photos. They didn't have a body or know the victim's identity, so the photos were forwarded to the FBI. Since the victim was a young girl, the photos were passed on to me."

She tore a piece off the pastry and popped it into her mouth.

"You can have all of it," he said.

"Thanks. The first photos came from a pharmacy in Houston, so I flew in and worked with our office there trying to identify the victim. We eventually matched her to a body that had been found in a field on the side of a highway. She was an illegal Mexican immigrant who left her job at the mall one afternoon and never arrived home. There were no real leads in the case, so I went back to DC."

"Those were the photos you showed Rusty," he said.

"Yes. She was the first victim."

Half the pastry was gone. It seemed to help her relax.

"Six months later, another set of murder photos showed up on my desk," Daniels said. "Same scenario as before. Taken on an old-fashioned camera and dropped off at a pharmacy to be processed, this time in Atlanta. Again, the cops didn't know what to do with them, so they were sent to the FBI, and I got them. I flew to Atlanta, and worked with our office there to identify the victim. She was another teenage girl who worked at a mall and never came home. The body was found in a field while I was there. It struck a nerve."

"The killings in Hanover," he said.

She nodded. "The Hanover killers also discarded their victims' bodies in fields. It made me wonder if the murders were connected, so I had a forensics team compare the evidence from the Hanover killings to the killings in Houston and Atlanta. All four of the victims had worked in malls. They'd also been fed a meal before they were killed. There were enough similarities with the cases that forensics concluded the same pair of killers had murdered all four victims."

"That must have freaked you out," he said.

"It was very upsetting, to say the least. I went to my bosses and asked them to open an active investigation into the Houston and Atlanta killings. An active investigation means the bureau devotes a portion of its budget to a case, and is required to report its findings to the Justice Department every six months. My request got approved, and I've been chasing the killers ever since."

"How many victims are there?" he asked.

"Fifteen so far. The photos show up like clockwork every six months. They rotate between Houston, Atlanta, and Fort Lauderdale. The killers have a unique calling card. In the before photo, the victim is wearing a gold Saint Jude medal, in the after photo, she's not. Just when I get ready to shut the investigation down, I have to start it back up."

"Why would you shut it down?"

"Bureau rules. If there's no movement in six months, the case is put on the back burner, and the agent handling the case is given a new assignment."

"Are you telling me that you've been working this case continuously since 2012?"

"Afraid so."

"That's seven years working one case. You must be frustrated as hell."

"I am. But I can't stop. I look at the photographs of these dead girls, and it rips me apart." She turned her head and stared through the windshield. "I can't remember the last time I had a decent night's sleep."

She fell silent. The pastry was a memory, so he got out of the car and went into the Starbucks and purchased an apple fritter the size of a softball. He brought it to her, and she immediately started picking at it. Sweets were definitely her weakness.

"We caught a break two years ago," she said. "The photographs were dropped off at a Walgreens pharmacy in Plantation in South Broward. I flew down and interviewed the photo processor who'd been on duty that day. His last name was Daniels, so of course we hit it off. Daniels remembered the guy who'd dropped the film off, and told me that he'd seen the guy at a Fourth of July fireworks celebration on the beach."

"So our killers live in Fort Lauderdale," he said.

"At least part of the time. They may also have residences in Houston and Atlanta as well. You want some of this fritter? It's really tasty."

He tore off a small piece to be sociable. "Where are we in the rotation?"

"What do you mean?"

"You said that every six months there's another victim. Are we due for another killing? If the way you ransacked my condo is an indication, I'm guessing we are."

"Yes, we're due. The last victim was killed five months and three weeks ago. I should be getting another packet on my desk any day now."

"From Fort Lauderdale?"

"Correct. It's next in line. We think the killers kidnap a girl and keep her doped up for a few days. They feed her a last meal, and then it's lights out."

"What's the significance of the last meal?"

"We don't know. Maybe it's a way to calm her down."

He chewed on the fritter and washed it down with his coffee. "If your math is right, these guys are going to kill another girl very soon. Do you have any other leads?"

"No. I'm running blind." She gave him a weary look. "Can you help me save her?"

The question caught him off guard. Saving people had been his specialty as a SEAL. His pot belly and small stature had made it easy for him to blend in just about anywhere in the world. That had come in handy during hostage rescues.

"I'm happy to try. You want to take a break first? Go for a walk?"

"I'm okay, but thanks for offering," she said.

"I have a theory about your killers," he said. "Before I share it with you, I need to ask you a question. How many of the victims worked at malls or in retail centers?"

"All of them."

"So the victims were around groups of people when they were abducted."

"Yes. Except for me. I was walking home from a class."

"You were different."

"How so?"

"Our killers saw you walking by yourself and decided to be opportunistic and grab you. They put ski masks on, jumped out of their car, and abducted you. It was a rushed job, and they botched it. That's why you managed to escape."

"That makes sense. What's your theory?"

He thought back to the elderly man in the tracksuit pushing the dying woman in the wheelchair, and how every person they'd encountered had avoided them. "Our killers have come up with a unique way to abduct their victims from public places," he said. "They use a wheelchair. I first thought the wheelchair was for distraction, but there's another reason. Let me show you how it works."

He took out his cell phone and pulled up the surveillance video of Nicki's near abduction at the Galleria mall. Daniels held the phone up to her face and stared at the screen. Her mouth grew taut with rage.

"My brother-in-law saved the day," she said.

"Yes, he did," he said. "Nicki was the killers' next victim. They connected her to the Cassandra videos and decided to abduct her, knowing it would destroy you when the photos of her landed on your desk."

"How can you know that for certain?"

"I know because of how hard they tried. The abduction at the Galleria mall failed, so they tried to grab her from home and escape in a boat. When that failed, they parked a van across the street and started watching the house. They were on a mission."

"You may be right. So what's your theory?"

"I'll show you. Watch the video again. This time, focus on the people in the mall."

Daniels watched the surveillance video a second time.

"None of them are paying attention," she said. "Why do you think that is?"

"It's the presence of the wheelchair," he said. "From the time we're little kids, our parents train us not to stare at people being pushed in wheelchairs, who are either handicapped or sick. It's considered bad manners, so we avoid making eye contact when we see a person in a wheelchair. That's our killers' trick. They approach their victim from behind. One pushes a wheelchair, while the other holds a bottle of chloroform and a rag. They knock their victim out and strap her into the wheelchair, which they push through the crowd while people deliberately avoid looking at them. Outside in the parking lot, they put the victim in their vehicle, and load the wheelchair in the trunk."

"You're saying that there are witnesses, but they're not paying attention."

"Correct. There were plenty of people present when Nicki was nearly abducted at the Galleria mall, yet none of them helped your brother-in-law. That's because they were looking the other way. Which leads me to my next theory."

"Which is what?"

"You've been looking for a pair of cops. That makes sense, since the police from the nearby towns didn't submit to DNA testing during the investigation of the Hanover killers. But what if this wasn't a pair of cops? What if it was a pair of nurses or paramedics? They would have experience handling a wheelchair and also access to chloroform at the hospital where they worked."

"Jesus. I never considered that," Daniels said.

She fell silent. Her fist punched the dashboard.

"Don't be hard on yourself," he said. "People in the medical profession rarely commit crimes and hardly come up on law enforcement's radar. But there are always exceptions. Did the employees at the hospitals in Hanover submit to DNA testing during the investigation?"

"I don't know. There's only one hospital near Hanover, and that's the Dartmouth-Hitchcock Medical Center in Lebanon, which is three miles from the college."

"How hard would it be to find out?"

"Not hard at all. I stay in contact with the FBI agent that handled that case. He's retired now and lives in a community in central Florida called The Villages. Every time I get new information, I share it with him, hoping it might spark a memory."

"You should call him. I'm willing to bet that the employees at Dartmouth-Hitchcock didn't submit to DNA testing either."

"You think our killers are male nurses," she said.

"Yes, I do," he said.

CHAPTER 34
KEEP MOVING FORWARD

Daniels placed a call to the retired FBI agent who'd handled the Hanover killers case. His name was Mark Eberbach, and he confirmed to her that the male employees at Dartmouth-Hitchcock Medical Center had not submitted to DNA testing during the investigation. Daniels thanked Eberbach for his time and promised to stay in touch.

"I need to go to the FBI's office in North Miami Beach and get on a computer and do some digging," Daniels said. "Want to tag along?"

He'd finally gained her trust. He nodded, and she pulled out of the Starbucks parking lot and drove west toward I-95. The FBI had three facilities in South Florida: one in Miami, a newly opened office in Miramar, and an office in North Miami Beach. The NMB office was the closest, but that was a relative term when driving in South Florida, where a ten-mile journey could take between ten minutes and an hour.

Traffic was at a standstill a mile from the entrance ramp to I-95. He opened the traffic app on his phone and saw that I-95 was a parking lot. Daniels punched the wheel in frustration. Every wasted minute might lead to another young woman being lost.

"Why don't you work out of my place," he suggested. "I do consulting work with Team Adam, and have access to all the major databases on my computer."

Daniels answered him by doing a U-turn and heading back to the beach. He gave her instructions as she drove. Daniels had a wire in the blood and was seeing things in a new light. It was how many investigations went. Months or years of tedious searching were rewarded by a sudden revelation that propelled the case forward.

"How long have you consulted for Team Adam?" she asked.

"Two years," he said.

"What do you think of them?"

"They have a ninety-two percent success rate."

"Wow. How does that work?"

"I asked myself the same question when I started with them. Why is Team Adam more effective at solving difficult cases than other law enforcement agencies? After working a few cases, I saw what it was. They never stop moving forward. If a team working an investigation hits a wall, a fresh pair of eyes is brought in to review the evidence and offer a different perspective."

"Keep moving forward," she said. "I'll have to remember that."

Three blocks from his condo, they hit another deterrent. The King Tides were unpredictable and often flooded roads without warning. A pair of metal detour signs had been placed in the middle of the road, forcing drivers to seek alternative routes.

"What's with all the water? Have you had a lot of rain recently?" she asked.

"It hasn't rained in weeks," he said. "The flooding is a strange phenomenon called the King Tides. No one really knows what causes it."

"I'm assuming there's an alternative route," she said.

"Of course. Back up, and I'll get you there."

She threw the rental into reverse. Turning in her seat, she looked over her shoulder, hit the gas, and expertly drove backward down the block until she reached the intersection, where she made a sharp turn, then hit the brakes, threw the rental into drive, and headed off in the direction that his finger was pointing. He'd been trained in defensive driving while in the SEALs, but this was a cut above.

"Where did you learn to drive like that?" he asked.

"Impressed?" she asked.

"You're way good. I'm very impressed."

"I'll take that as a compliment, coming from a former SEAL."

"I trained in Southern California. We didn't spend a lot of time learning to drive in reverse. Most of our missions were conducted on foot or using small boats. No cars."

"I learned on a course at TEVOC at Quantico. That's short for Tactical and Emergency Vehicle Operations Center. The FBI teaches its agents how to drive every vehicle you can imagine in an emergency situation. We're required to go back every six months for a refresher."

"Do they take outsiders?"

"Help me solve this, and I'll put in a word for you."

Soon they were at his condo. He brewed a fresh pot of coffee while Daniels sat at the desk in his study and spoke with the head of human resources at Dartmouth-Hitchcock, with whom she was on a first-name basis. The head of HR agreed to email Daniels the names of all male employees at the hospital during the time of the Hanover killings, and the call ended. He placed a steaming mug in front of her.

"Sounds like you're making progress," he said.

"One step at a time," she said. "Dartmouth-Hitchcock is an academic facility and has several thousand employees. There are a lot of male nurses working there. I'll need to run background checks on each one to see if they have criminal records. We could be here for a while."

Running criminal background checks was problematic since there was no single database that contained every criminal record.

"I think there might be a simpler way to track down our killers," he said.

Her eyebrows lifted. "I'm listening."

"We know these guys have a residence in Fort Lauderdale and live here part of the year," he said. "I'd suggest that you run the names of the male nurses the hospital sends you against the Department of Motor Vehicles database to see what pops up. The DMV database includes address changes and name changes and is always current."

"That's an interesting angle," she said. "What if our killers are still using their out-of-state driver's licenses? Your idea wouldn't work then."

"That's unlikely. If our killers have a residence here, they've probably applied for a homestead exemption, which saves them a bundle on property taxes. They'd also want to establish residency so as to not pay state income tax."

"There's no state income tax in Florida?"

"Nope. It's why so many people retire here. Once a person establishes residency, they have thirty days to get a new driver's license. If they don't, and get pulled over by a cop for speeding, they'll get arrested."

"Good thinking. Do you have access to the DMV database?"

"I sure do. And I have a Team Adam password."

"I'm willing to give it a try."

They drank more coffee waiting for the head of HR's email. Daniels got up from the desk and moved around the study, admiring the collection of art hanging on the walls. There were paintings, glass work, ceramics, and a black-and-white photograph of the Everglades at sunrise taken by the state's answer to Ansel Adams, Clyde Butcher.

"You have good taste," she said. "There was an exhibition of Clyde Butcher's work at a gallery in Georgetown, where I live. The prices were through the roof."

"I actually have lousy taste," he said. "Just about everything in my place was given to me by one of my clients. It's how I do business. I don't take cash."

She sat on the edge of the desk and looked him in the eye. "Is that the deal that you have with my sister and her husband?"

"Yes. Your brother-in-law agreed to buy me a new refrigerator. I'm got my eye on a make by Bosch with all the trimmings."

"So no cash. Are you hiding it from the government and not paying taxes?"

"No. I declare everything and pay taxes on it."

"Okay, I'm hooked. What's the story here?"

"I need the memories."

Daniels shook her head, not understanding.

"While I was a SEAL, I performed a hundred and fifty missions in all parts of the world. Most were rescues and were done in secret. They weren't written down, and our government will disavow that they ever happened. The people I rescued were kidnap victims that worked in our embassies or undercover CIA agents whose cover got blown. Except for my first mission, where we were given bad information, I got every single one out alive."

"That's some record. Good for you, Jon."

"Thanks. There was only one problem. I wanted to know what happened to the people I rescued later on. Did their lives go back to normal? Did everything work out okay? Because the mission was never officially acknowledged by the government, I couldn't contact them and find out. It bugged the hell out of me."

"You got attached to the people you rescued."

"In a way, yes. I wanted to know if they were okay. That way, I could move on and stop worrying about them."

"You wanted closure," she said.

"Yes, closure. Over time, the missions faded from memory, which bothered me even more. I had nothing to remember these people by. Not even a selfie."

Daniels was a quick study and nodded understanding. "You make your clients pay you in material objects so you have something to remember them by. Does it work?"

"Yes, it does. It all started with Jimmy Buffett."

"The singer? What's your connection?"

"I saved his life once."

"Is that how you got the autographed guitar hanging in your living room?"

"Yes. I was a cop and assigned to protect him while he was giving a concert. When the show was over, we drove back to his hotel in a limo. As we pulled up, I got out first. There was a guy inside the lobby who struck me as suspicious."

"What caught your eye?"

"It was summer, and he was wearing a long-sleeve Nike athletic shirt and jeans. Nobody wears long-sleeve shirts in the summer unless they're hiding something."

"Was he?"

"A knife, two guns, and a stun grenade. He was planning to ambush us and take Buffett out. He'd been stalking him for a while and wanted to kill him."

"Jon to the rescue."

He smiled at the memory. "It was one of my better moments. I took the crazy bastard down and the other cops on the detail whisked Buffett into an elevator and took him upstairs. Nobody got hurt. We arrested the perp and took him down to the station to book him. A couple of hours later I got a phone call from Buffett's manager asking me to come back to the hotel. I went, and Buffett was in his suite waiting for me with the autographed guitar. He shook my hand so hard I thought he was going to break my fingers. Every time I look at the guitar, I'm reminded of that night."

"Do you like Buffett's music? I saw that you had a lot of his CDs."

"I'm a big fan. That night had a lot to do with it."

"If you don't take cash, what do you live on?"

"I have a navy pension and my cop pension. That keeps me in groceries and pays my condo association fees."

Daniels started to ask another question when her laptop made a noise indicating that an email had arrived. She went around the desk and had a look.

"It's from the head of HR at Dartmouth-Hitchcock and it has an attachment," she said. "Looks like we're in business."

The email's attachment contained the names of every nurse employed by Dartmouth-Hitchcock during the time of the Hanover murders. There were over eight hundred names, and the list included both male and female nurses. With his help, she printed the list on the HP LaserJet printer that was stored in the closet.

They spent a half hour parsing the list and running a black line through the female nurses' names. When done, slightly less than half the names remained, which were in random order. He got on the DMV site and used his password to gain entrance.

Daniels took the chair at the desk and faced the computer while he stood next to her and stared over her shoulder. The first name on the list was a male nurse named Ronald Colley. Daniels typed the name into the DMV search engine and hit "Enter." A second later Colley's driving record appeared on the screen. Ronald Colley had moved from Hanover six years ago and now resided in Boston.

"Not him," Daniels said.

She repeated this process for the next fifty names on the list. There were no hits. It was an exhausting process, but she did not tire. People on a mission rarely did.

"You hungry?" he asked.

"Starving," she said. "What's on the menu?"

"Uber Eats. Name your pleasure, and it'll be here in thirty minutes."

"I like Chinese, no MSG."

"I'm partial to a joint called the Rainbow Palace. Any preferences?"

"I'll let you pick."

A half hour later, there was a knock on his door. They had run two hundred names of male nurses through the DMV's database and not gotten a single hit. If she was frustrated, she refused to let it show. He excused himself and went to meet the driver.

Uber didn't want customers to tip their drivers, but he slipped the guy ten bucks anyway. Taking the food to the kitchen, he doled out fried lo mein and crispy duck onto two plates, stuck some cutlery into his pocket, grabbed two paper napkins, and returned to the study. Daniels glanced up from the computer and thanked him with a smile. She balanced the plate on her lap and dug in.

"This is good," she said. "Want to bet we find our guys at the end of the list?"

"Is that how it usually works?" he said.

"It does for me. When I do a search, the needle is always at the bottom of the haystack. I must have been born under an unlucky sign."

"Nothing good ever comes easy," he said.

The food was soon a memory. He stacked their empty plates and was heading to the kitchen when his cell phone rang. It was Karissa. He didn't have time to speak with her right now and hoped she would understand.

"Can I give you a call back tomorrow?" he asked.

"Oh my God, Jon, he's going to kill me," she replied.

CHAPTER 35

Dark Journey

Karissa was screaming, her voice so loud that it came through the speaker in Lancaster's cell phone. Daniels looked up from the computer.

"Who the hell is that?" the FBI agent asked.

"One second." Holding the cell phone against his chest so Karissa couldn't hear, he said, "Her name's Karissa Clement. She helped me get my hands on her ex-boyfriend's cell phone with the Cassandra videos, which led me to you. I'm guessing the ex-boyfriend found out and is threatening her."

"Do you need my help?"

"I just might. Let me talk to her and find out what's going on. I'll be right back."

He walked outside to the balcony and shut the slider behind him. He had lost track of the time, and it took a moment for his eyes to adjust to the night. There was a storm churning out in the Atlantic, and an invisible moist cloth swept across his skin. He brought the cell phone up to his ear and said, "Sorry about that. You still there?"

"Yes, Jon," Karissa said. "I'm still here. Who were you just talking to?"

"There's an FBI agent in my condo. We're working on a case together."

"Sounds important. I don't mean to interrupt whatever you're doing, but I need your help. Zack figured out that I spoke to you, and now he's after me."

"Tell me what happened."

"Zack was waiting when I got off work. The hospital parking area is being paved, so everyone has to park across the street in an empty lot. I came out to my car and he appeared out of nowhere, and started talking to me in a low voice so no one else could hear. He said that someone had gone online and downloaded pornographic videos that he kept stored on his cell phone. Zack said that you'd confronted him and mentioned my name, and he put two and two together. He said that he was going to kidnap me and rape me and then he was going to kill me. He promised to make me suffer."

"Did you call the police?"

"I sure did. They went to see him, and he denied the whole thing. There aren't any surveillance cameras in the lot, so it's my word against his."

"Meaning the cops aren't going to do squat."

"That's why I called you. What am I going to do?"

He stood at the balcony railing and wrestled with how to handle her question. Karissa had gone out of her way to help him, and now she was being repaid by a madman's threats. He had to make this right and prove to her that she'd done the right thing. "You need to leave Fort Lauderdale right now. I have two gay friends in Marathon that own a motel called Captain Pip's Hideaway. Go there and hide out. You'll be safe. I'll deal with Zack."

"But I don't have the money for a motel," she said.

"You won't need any money. Roger and Frankie used to be cops. Tell them I sent you, and that I want you to stay in the guest bedroom in their house. Zack won't be able to find you there, and if he somehow did, their dogs would rip him apart."

"Your friends have dogs?"

"They raise German shorthaired pointers and always have a pack."

"What about Zack? I can't hide in Marathon forever."

"I'm going to have Special Agent Daniels arrest Zack for being a pedophile."

"She'll do that for you?"

"I'm sure I can talk her into it. You need to jump into your car and get on the road right now. Call me when you get to Marathon and are at Captain Pip's. Does that sound like a plan?"

"It sounds like a great plan."

"One more thing. Special Agent Daniels is going to need evidence so she can arrest Zack. Can you remember any other devices that he used to store his porn?"

"I sure can. Zack had an iPad that he kept locked in a desk at his apartment. He told me that he used the iPad for work, only it never left his place. I'm certain that's where he keeps most of his dirty pictures and videos."

"That works. Now, get out of there."

"I've got one foot out the door."

"And call me when you get there."

"I will. Thanks, Jon. I knew I could count on you."

He ended the call and stared into the darkness, hoping that Karissa would be safe. A tapping sound broke his concentration, and he went to the slider. Daniels stood on the other side of the glass wearing a triumphant look on her weary face. The DMV database had come through, and he pulled back the glass and stepped inside.

"You found our killers," he said.

"They were the second-to-last names on the list, if you can believe that," she said with a tired laugh. "You were right about their driver's licenses being like a trail of bread crumbs. They've moved around a lot, and every time they relocate in a new state, they get new licenses."

"How long have they been in South Florida?"

"They both got their Florida driver's licenses on the same day seven years ago. Did I mention that they both have criminal records for being perverts?"

"You have their rap sheets?"

"Yes indeed. Want to see them?"

"I do. Before you show them to me, I need to ask a favor."

"Let me guess. You want me to arrest your girlfriend's ex-boyfriend."

His face grew warm. "She's not my girlfriend."

"Let me rephrase that. You want me to arrest your soon-to-be girlfriend's ex-boyfriend. What have you got on him?"

"Why do you keep saying that?"

"You care about her. I could hear it in your voice when you answered her call. And she called you because she trusts you and knows she can depend on you. Sounds like the start of a beautiful relationship."

Daniels was reading the situation wrong. He kept his personal life and his work separate, and didn't date women he met during investigations, even if he found himself attracted to them. His mission was to serve and protect, not sleep with. He decided to move on and said, "Her ex-boyfriend's name is Zack Kenny and he has an iPad in his apartment filled with porn of young girls. I can give you the address."

"Consider it done."

"Thank you. Can I ask another?"

She lifted an eyebrow suspiciously.

"During my investigation, I stumbled across some dirty cops stealing cocaine from the sheriff's office property stockade and selling it on the street. I can't go directly to the sheriff's office with the information without revealing my source, and that would put his life in jeopardy. I was hoping you could help me out."

"Do you know how they're getting the coke out?"

"It's pretty clever. The thief is using the coke to train a drug-sniffing dog, then he's switching it with flour before returning it to the property unit."

"Okay. I'll see what I can do."

He followed her through the apartment to the study. His hunch that the Hanover killers were male nurses had paid off. It was a satisfying feeling, but it didn't match the elation that he knew Special Agent Daniels was experiencing. Not only was she about to capture a pair of elusive serial killers, she was also going to bring to justice the two men who'd tried to abduct her when she was a college student. He couldn't think of a more satisfying outcome and looked forward to experiencing it with her.

On his desk was a pile of papers she'd printed off his laser printer. She triumphantly handed him the top two sheets. "Our killers' names are Jack Butler and Brandon Rhoden, and they both worked as ER nurses at Dartmouth-Hitchcock during the time of the Hanover killings," she said. "These documents are their work history, courtesy of my HR friend at the hospital."

He studied the two pages. Butler and Rhoden had started at the hospital at the same time, and they'd left their jobs at the same time as well. He strained his memory and realized they'd left their jobs three months after Daniels's failed abduction.

"Did your HR contact know if they quit, or if they were fired?" he asked.

"My contact said it was by mutual agreement. She said that they both showed a lack of compassion for patients in need of critical care."

"Are they sociopaths?"

"That would be my guess."

From the pile, she removed two sheets that were paper clipped together and handed them to him. The logo at the top of the first page said NCSBN, which stood for National Council of State Boards of Nursing. "I contacted the NCSBN to see where Butler and Rhoden went next," she said. "The NCSBN keeps data on every registered nurse in the country and has five million active names in its database. They spent a year working at a hospital in Dayton, Ohio, another year at a hospital in Asheville, North Carolina, and then stints in Atlanta, Baton Rouge, and Houston, with each job never lasting longer than twelve months."

Atlanta and Houston were two of the three cities where the killers had dropped off film of their female victims to pharmacies to be developed, the third being Fort Lauderdale. The circumstantial evidence against Butler and Rhoden was building.

"Moving is expensive," he said. "Is there any way to find out why they didn't stay for more than a year at any of these hospitals?"

"Not easily," she said. "It's personal information, and those hospitals won't release it without a court order. I'm sure it was for the same reasons as Dartmouth-Hitchcock. The staff realized they weren't normal, and they were pushed out."

"But the staffs didn't report them, so Butler and Rhoden continued to find work."

"Correct. As I'm sure you're aware, people in the medical profession are loathe to turn on bad doctors and nurses, even when they're monsters."

"You mean like Michael Swango."

"Exactly. Just like Swango."

Dr. Michael Swango was living proof that the medical profession did not know how to police itself. Over a span of seventeen years, Swango had been instrumental in the deaths of several patients, first while working as an ambulance attendant, then as a doctor. He had poisoned numerous patients and coworkers, yet had managed to keep his license and was employed as a doctor overseas at the time of his arrest by the FBI.

"Now here's the good stuff," Daniels said.

In her hand was a rap sheet, courtesy of the National Crime Information Center. NCIC documents were instantly recognizable due to their distinct dark font and logo being prominently stamped on the top of every page. He traded her the NCSBN documents.

"That's Rhoden's arrest record," she added.

He studied the page. Rhoden's journey to the dark side had started in Dayton, where he'd been arrested for accessing child pornography off a computer at the hospital where he was employed. His second arrest had occurred at a hospital in Asheville, where he'd also been caught downloading illegal images of kids. He'd been a good boy in Atlanta and Baton Rouge, but then got caught with his hand in the cookie jar in Houston, where he'd been arrested for attempting to procure sex with an undercover cop posing as a teenager in a chat room, also on a hospital computer.

"Why does Rhoden use computers at hospitals?" he asked. "He would have to know that he'd lose his job if he got caught."

"It's a ploy that many predators use," she said. "Their lawyer can claim that the computer in question was used by other people at the hospital, therefore making it impossible to prove beyond a reasonable doubt that their client actually did it."

"Does it work?"

"It worked for Rhoden. His attorney got the charges against him reduced in every case. Bastard never did time, just house arrest."

"But he does have a record. So how did he keep getting hospital jobs?"

"I asked myself the same question," she said. "If you look closely at his work record, you'll see that he slightly changed his last name on his job applications. He added an *r* and spelled his name *Rhorden* on each application. That way, his rap sheet didn't come up when the hospital did a background check on him."

He found himself nodding. It was the type of ingenious trick that could allow a serial predator to work at a respectable job and fly beneath the radar.

"What about Butler?" he asked. "Does he have a record?"

"Yes, and it's ugly."

She passed him Butler's rap sheet, and he spent a moment reading it. Butler had the same number of arrests as Rhoden and for similar offenses, ranging from downloading illegal images to trying to procure sex with a minor. The crimes had taken place on computers where he worked and in one case on a computer at a public library.

"Let me guess," he said. "He kept being employed by altering his name on his work applications."

"Correct, only he altered his first name," she said. "On his work applications, he goes by Jack. His actual first name is Jace. That's what's on his driver's license, and that was what got recorded each time he was arrested, only he calls himself Jack."

"Were his convictions also pleaded down?"

"Correct again. Believe it or not, he and Rhoden used the same lawyer. I wouldn't be surprised if they have him on retainer."

He handed the rap sheets back to her. Rhoden and Butler had created a subterfuge that allowed them to commit heinous crimes while remaining employed. Each time they got caught, they moved to another city and went right back to breaking the law.

"You're sure they're our killers?" he asked.

Daniels pulled back in her chair. It was not the response she was expecting.

"You sound skeptical," she said.

"There's a hole here that needs to be filled," he said. "If Rhoden and Butler are our guys, why is there a gap in their killings? The two murders at Dartmouth College took place twenty years ago. The new killings started seven years ago. That's a gap of thirteen years. Why did they stop?"

She took a deep breath before replying. When she did answer him, the words were filled with pain. "They stopped because of what happened in the forest when they were chasing me. I'm pretty fast, and they must have realized they weren't going to catch me because they were both cursing under their breath. I heard one of them fall, and the other fell on top of him. I spun around and saw them lying in the dirt. The one on top was looking right at me. I could see his eyes through his ski mask. His right eye had a milky discoloration, either from a scar or an infection. I shook my fist and said, 'I know what you look like, you dirty motherfucker! I'll get you one day!' Then, I bolted. I didn't tell the author of *The Hanover Killers* that part, so it didn't end up in the book."

"You can identify one of them," he said.

"That's right. I'd heard their voices and could identify one of them. They went dark for thirteen years, and satisfied their cravings in other ways. Then I got promoted at the FBI. They found out, and decided to enact a payback."

"The Saint Jude medal they put on their victims' necks before they kill them is to taunt you. It's their way of saying that your investigation is a lost cause."

She nodded solemnly. "Correct. That's not just my opinion. It's also the bureau's. Our profilers looked at the evidence and determined that's their motivation."

"I'm surprised they left you on the case."

"In the beginning, I was too. But then I realized how much sense it made. If anyone was going to catch them, it was going to be me."

The study was starting to feel claustrophobic. He rose and soon was standing with his stomach pressed to the balcony railing, breathing sweet salt air. She joined him holding two glasses of OJ and handed him one. She clinked her glass against his.

"What are we celebrating?" he asked.

"I've been chasing these fuckers for a long time, and now I'm going to take them down," she said, unable to hide the satisfaction in her voice.

"How? You don't have any evidence."

"No, but I can still arrest them, and get a DNA swab, and make a match."

"On what charges?"

"When Rhoden and Butler moved to Fort Lauderdale they didn't register themselves as sexual predators. The Sex Offender Registration and Notification Act requires that all sexual predators register when they change addresses. They're also required to make in-person appearances with local law enforcement to verify and update their information.

"They didn't do that. The authorities in Atlanta should have checked up on them, since that was the last place where they lived, but it never happened."

"They slipped through the cracks."

"Uh-huh. I'm guessing they moved here and waited to see if the law would catch up with them. When it didn't, they went on their killing spree."

She had made the pieces of the puzzle fit. Rhoden and Butler had lived in Hanover during the first killings and also lived in the cities where the subsequent killings had taken place. And, they were sexual predators with criminal records. All the road signs pointed to them, which 99 percent of the time meant it was them. It was a solid piece of investigative work born out of years of frustration and failure. He hardly knew her, but that didn't lessen how proud he felt for her. She had gone down the long road, and now the finish line was in sight.

"I have their current address," she said. "Got it from DMV and reconfirmed it on the property appraiser's website. They live in a house in Oakland Park they bought seven years ago. I've asked a team of agents from our North Miami office to help me bust them. I'd like you to join us. I think you deserve it."

For a cop, there was no greater honor than to be asked to join a bust. Whatever lingering bad feelings he'd had for her evaporated, including her breaking his grandmother's ladle.

"Count me in," he said. "Would you like me to draw them out? It's my specialty."

"How do you plan to do that?"

"Easy. I'll pretend I work for Amazon."

245

CHAPTER 36

KARMA

In Lancaster's experience, there was no better way to get a suspect inside a dwelling to drop their guard than by posing as an Amazon delivery person. This was especially true in South Florida, where Amazon was the preferred online retailer for many residents.

Delivery people for Amazon did not wear uniforms but did their jobs in street clothes. The vehicles they drove were their own, and had no decals or roof signs. Best of all, they did not have assigned routes but constantly moved around. A customer might receive a package from an Indian gentleman wearing a turban one day, a fetching college coed with purple hair and a brass ring in her nose the next. Customers were accustomed to not seeing the same delivery person, and as a result, they did not become suspicious when a stranger showed up on their doorstep holding a clipboard and carrying a cardboard box with the iconic Amazon logo stamped on its sides.

There was another plus. Amazon delivered every day of the week, including Sundays, often at odd hours. No other delivery company did that.

"Are you sure you want to do this?" Daniels asked.

They sat in Daniels's rental a block from Rhoden and Butler's residence in Oakland Park. The neighborhood was a testimonial to sub-
urbia, with two cars parked in every driveway and landscaping so well
maintained that it looked artificial. It was just past nine o'clock in the
evening. It had taken two hours for Daniels's team of local FBI agents
to assemble. The backup unit consisted of five male agents ranging in
age from early thirties to late forties. Apparently, Daniels liked them big,
and the men looked like the offensive line of a college football team.

A few minutes earlier, Daniels had done a drive-by of Rhoden and
Butler's house. An older vehicle sat in the driveway, and the windows
were lit up. Through a filmy curtain covering the front window, dancing
images on a TV screen were visible.

"Of course I'm sure," he replied. "Drawing suspects out is my specialty. When I was a SEAL, my unit commander always sent me in first.
My appearance threw people off, and they'd let their guard down."

"I still want you to wear a vest," she insisted.

"Beneath my shirt? That won't work."

"You could get shot."

"I've dealt with worse people than these two, and no one's put a
bullet in me so far," he said reassuringly. "Stop worrying."

"Don't tell me not to worry," she said.

The concern in her voice was not the professional kind. She cared
about him. He had helped her find her adversaries, and now there was
a bond between them. He reached across the front seat and gave her
arm a squeeze.

"I'm also good on the draw," he said.

"You're carrying?" she asked.

He lifted the front of his shirt to reveal the Ruger tucked beneath
his belt.

"When did you put that there?" she asked.

"When you weren't looking," he said.

"How good a shot are you?"

"I've won medals for my marksmanship, and I don't miss at close range. If Rhoden or Butler get Western on me, I'll take them both out of the picture."

"Let's hope it doesn't come down to that. Promise me you'll be careful."

"I promise." He paused. "Now let's get these monsters."

They got out. He walked around to the driver's side where she stood. She handed him the keys and crossed the road to where a pair of matching black sedans carrying the backup unit were parked. She gave him a parting nod before climbing into the lead sedan.

"Good luck," her lips said.

He got into the rental and started the engine. Adrenaline was pumping through his veins, and his face was burning up. The world was filled with clever killers who mistakenly believed that they'd never be caught. This was not true. Karma had everyone's address, and it was only a matter of time before a killer tripped up and was apprehended. He knew of no greater pleasure than of seeing the shock register across a suspect's face when the cuffs got slapped on his wrists. He did a U-turn in the street, drove down the block to their suspects' house, and made the front tire kiss the curb. Killing the engine, he found the button to pop the trunk and pressed it. Then he got out.

From the trunk he retrieved the brown cardboard Amazon delivery box that he'd gotten from his apartment, along with a clipboard. He was a Prime member and regularly got shipments sent to his condo. The Amazon box was the size of a hardcover book. He held the box in his left hand next to his body. He placed the clipboard on top of the box so it faced him. On the clipboard was a sheet of paper that contained blurred photographs of Rhoden and Butler, which he'd printed off their Facebook pages. Rhoden had a bald crown and a reddish discoloration on his neck that suggested he might suffer from eczema. Butler had a full head of hair and wore a pair of shades, which Lancaster guessed he wore when having his photograph taken to hide his discolored eye. Both men's faces were soulless.

The backup sedans pulled in behind him and went silent. The front sedan flashed its brights, indicating they were ready to roll. He walked up the brick path to the front stoop. There was a screen door, which he tested and found locked. He pressed the buzzer and waited. The front door swung in, and a man holding a metal cane stood before him. The man wore a bathrobe that hung off his body like a tent. Lancaster glanced at the driver's license photos on the clipboard and determined it was Rhoden.

"Good evening," he said. "I have an Amazon delivery that needs to be signed for."

Rhoden's eyes narrowed, inherently suspicious. "I didn't order anything from Amazon. You have the wrong address."

"This is the right address. I checked the mailbox." He consulted his clipboard. "Does Jack Butler live here? The package is for him."

"Jack didn't order anything either."

His eyes returned to the clipboard. "It's a gift."

"A gift? From who?"

"I have no idea, sir. Is Mr. Butler here? I need to give him his package, and have him sign for it. Or you can sign for it."

"Who's that?" came a man's voice from within the house.

"Guy from Amazon has a package, says it's a gift for you," Rhoden called over his shoulder.

"That must be from my sister. Sign for it."

"What would your sister be sending you?" Rhoden asked.

"My birthday present," said the voice.

"Your birthday was last month."

"She's always late. Sign for it."

Rhoden didn't want to open the screen door. Intuition was the messenger of fear, and Rhoden's instincts were telling him that something was wrong with this picture. Maybe it was the nervous sweat matting

Lancaster's brow that tipped Rhoden off. Or maybe it was something else. It didn't really matter; Rhoden knew something wasn't right.

Only the voice inside the house was insistent. *Sign for it.* Rhoden went against his better judgment and unlocked the screen door and pushed it open. Lancaster passed the box through the opening. As it touched Rhoden's hand and he felt its weight, his eyes grew wide in surprise.

"Wait a minute. This box is empty," Rhoden said.

Lancaster grabbed the screen door with his left hand and pulled it wide open. His right hand lifted the front of his shirt and drew the Ruger. He pointed it at Rhoden's chest.

"Lift your arms into the air," he said.

The empty box fell from Rhoden's hand. He continued to lean on his cane, while his other hand remained in front of his chest. His big bathrobe was a problem. Just about anything could be hidden behind it.

"Do it," Lancaster said.

Rhoden didn't comply. He was plotting his last stand. The bad ones often did, preferring to die by cop than rot away in a prison cell.

"Last chance," he said.

Behind him he heard pounding footsteps on the lawn. Rhoden shifted his gaze as the FBI agents closed in. Bad thoughts flashed through his eyes. Lancaster used his free hand to grab the lapels of Rhoden's bathrobe and hold them closed. He didn't want to discharge his weapon and have to deal with all the legal crap that would follow. If Rhoden needed to be shot, he preferred to let Daniels or one of the other agents do it.

The FBI agents took over. Rhoden was pulled from the house and put on the ground. Daniels handcuffed him behind his back before frisking him. He was clean.

"FBI. You're under arrest," she said.

"For what?" their suspect asked indignantly.

"Failing to register as a sexual predator. Get up."

"I can't. I was in a car accident. I can barely walk."

"That's nonsense. Get up."

"I told you, I can't."

Daniels barked a command, and two of the agents pulled Rhoden to his feet.

"I've been looking a long time for you," Daniels told him.

The other three agents had entered the house to arrest Butler. An agent named Moore appeared in the doorway with his sidearm held loosely at his side. It was a sign that Butler had been contained. The situation was under control, and Lancaster felt himself relax. He had expected Rhoden and Butler to put up more of a fight.

"Special Agent Daniels, you need to come inside and see this," Moore said.

Rhoden noticeably stiffened and stared at Daniels. The two agents holding Rhoden's arms sensed he was going to attack, and they tightened their grip. Daniels shot their suspect a contemptuous sneer before heading inside.

"Care to join me?" she said to Lancaster.

Daniels was savoring the moment and had a real spring to her step. Lancaster followed her into a foyer, which led to a low-ceilinged living room with a collection of matching chairs and a sofa that had grown old together. A porno movie played on the muted TV starring a barely legal Asian girl. On a TV dinner tray sat a laptop computer on which a second porno movie played, the girl clearly not legal. Moore and the other two agents who'd come into the house stood on the far side of the room in a circle. With them was a shriveled man in a wheelchair with a plaid blanket draped over his legs.

Daniels stopped so quickly that Lancaster nearly ran into her from behind.

"Where's Butler?" she asked.

"You're looking at him," Moore said.

"This can't be him. You searched the rest of the house?"

"Yes, and we didn't find anyone else. This is Butler," Moore said.

Daniels drew closer to the suspect, as did Lancaster. The man in the wheelchair resembled Butler but wasn't a perfect match, his face a sickly yellow as if jaundiced. There was no life in his eyes, neither of which was discolored, and he did not acknowledge the FBI agents' presence.

"Are you Jack Butler?" Daniels asked.

The man in the wheelchair gazed at the pornographic images on the TV and smiled. Daniels picked up the remote off a coffee table and killed the picture.

"Answer the question," she said.

The man in the wheelchair wasn't going to play ball, and Daniels angrily tossed the remote onto the coffee table. It slid off and went under the couch. A black Persian cat bolted out and made for the door. Daniels intercepted the animal and scooped it off the floor, holding it by the nape of the neck. The cat let out an ear-piercing yowl.

"You're hurting her," the man in the wheelchair protested.

"What's her name?" Daniels asked.

"Her name is Samantha. Stop hurting her."

"Does Samantha like to play in traffic? If you don't start talking, I'm going to take her outside, and let her loose in the street."

"You can't do that."

"Oh yes, I can. In fact, I can do any damn thing I please."

"Give her to me."

"Will you answer my questions?"

"Yes. Just give her to me."

Daniels passed him the screaming feline. The man in the wheelchair held the pet against his chest and lovingly stroked its fur while talking to it in a tender voice.

"Is your name Jack Butler?" Daniels asked.

"It was the last time I checked," the man said.

"Did you once live in Hanover, New Hampshire, and work as a nurse at Dartmouth-Hitchcock Medical Center?"

"I did."

"Have you ever been arrested for possession of child pornography and for soliciting sex with a minor?"

"Yes, I have."

It was him. Daniels paused before asking the next question. The expression on her face bordered on defeat, but she still asked it.

"Why are you in a wheelchair?"

"I was involved in a car crash seven years ago, right after we moved here," Butler said. "A drunk kid ran a red light and T-boned our car. I was driving, Rhoden was in the passenger seat. He recovered, I didn't."

"You're saying you don't have the use of your legs," she said.

"I'm paralyzed from the waist down."

A tiny scream escaped her lips. They all heard it, but no one acknowledged it.

She yanked away the blanket covering Butler's waist. He wore a pair of green shorts, and his legs were visible. They were milk white and sickly thin, with no muscle hanging off the bone. She spent a long moment composing herself. "You're under arrest for failing to register as a sexual predator and for the possession of child pornography." She gave him his rights, reciting them from memory. When she was done, she said, "Do you have anything to say?"

"Screw you, bitch," Butler said.

Daniels raised her arm as if to strike him. Lancaster stepped between them and escorted her out of the house and onto the front lawn. The darkness was a shield to hide behind, and she dropped her chin onto her chest and began to weep.

"It's not them," she said.

"I know," he said.

"What do we do?"

"Our killers are nurses who worked in Hanover," he said. "They have to be. There are no other suspects that could have done this. We must have missed them in the list the hospital sent you. We start over."

"Are you going to help me?"

"Yes. We're in this together, Beth."

In times of defeat the simplest things often give us strength. Daniels straightened her shoulders and sucked up her rage.

"Okay. Let's go back to your place," she said.

They went to her rental parked at the curb. Rhoden stood on the sidewalk in his bathrobe holding his handcuffed wrists by his waist with two of the FBI agents guarding him. Rhoden stepped forward. The agents grabbed his arms and pulled him back.

"You're Elizabeth Daniels," Rhoden said.

It had been a night filled with surprises. Daniels cautiously approached him.

"How did you know that?" she said.

"I guess you don't remember me. I treated you at Dartmouth-Hitchcock after those two men tried to abduct you. You were in shock and crying hysterically when you came into the ER. I stabilized you and got you calmed down. While we waited for the police to come and take your statement, I asked you if you wanted anything. You told me you were hungry, so I went to the hospital kitchen and got you a cup of chicken noodle soup and a roll. I stood next to you while you ate it. Do you remember?"

Daniels swallowed hard. "I do. You were very kind to me that night."

"That's why you came here, isn't it," Rhoden said. "Because of what happened in Hanover. You think that Jack and I had something to do with those girls' killings."

"Did you?"

Rhoden visibly shuddered and shook his head.

"No," he added for emphasis.

"Do you know who did?" she asked.

"I have no idea," Rhoden said. "A local reporter wrote a book about the killings. His theory was that a pair of cops were behind them. I think he was right."

"Why do you think that?"

"I dealt with the cops often in the ER. A couple of them were real sick bastards. They liked to hang around and watch patients suffer."

"Do you remember their names?"

"No. It was a long time ago."

"What did they look like?"

"They were white, in their late twenties. One had a scar on his chin and blond hair. The other, I think it was his partner, was Italian and had a mustache."

"That's it?"

"Like I said, it was a long time ago."

Daniels shot Lancaster a look that said they were done. He removed the rental's keys from his pocket and tossed them to her, knowing that she would want to drive. She pressed the unlock button on the keys, and the rental's doors popped open.

"Wait." Rhoden lowered his voice. "We're obviously not the men you're looking for. Can't you show some pity, and let us go?"

"Not happening," Daniels said.

"But I *helped* you," Rhoden said, his voice trembling. "I didn't have to buy you that cup of soup, or show you compassion, but I did. You were more than just a patient to me, Elizabeth. You were a terrified young woman, and I went out of my way to help you. Doesn't that count for something?"

Daniels looked ready to explode. "I saw a laptop in your living room. A video of an underage girl having sex with a man was playing on it. Was that your laptop?"

Rhoden nodded. He did not act the least bit ashamed.

"Did you download that video to your laptop?" she asked.

Again, Rhoden nodded.

"Then you're going to prison," she said.

"But it's just a video," he protested. "It's not like Jack and I are molesting young girls. We know that's wrong, so we watch videos to keep our fantasies in check, just like men who watch S&M and bondage videos. Can't you see the difference?"

"I do see the difference," she said. "No young girl willingly has sex with a strange man twice her age. She's either drugged or is being held against her will. She's a slave and has no say in the matter. If it weren't for people like you downloading those videos, they wouldn't exist, and that young girl wouldn't be exploited. That's the difference."

"You're not going to help me," Rhoden said, sounding defeated.

"On the contrary. I'm going to do everything in my power to make sure you never get out of prison. That goes for your friend Jack too."

"But we're invalids."

"Tough shit."

The monster lurking just below the surface showed its ugly head, and Rhoden lunged at her. Lancaster stepped between them and put him on the sidewalk. Rhoden grabbed his hip and howled in pain.

"You broke my leg," he said.

"It was nice catching up," Daniels said.

CHAPTER 37

REVERSE

Every agent of the law wore two faces. There was the face that they wore in public while performing their job, and there was the face they wore in private when no one was looking. Daniels drove out of the Oakland Park neighborhood and headed south to where Lancaster lived. They came to an intersection with a RaceTrac service station on the corner, and she pulled in and parked. Lancaster assumed she was going to use the john or buy a drink, and was surprised when she placed her head on the wheel and shut her eyes.

"Do you mind?" she asked.

He went inside and got two large coffees and an assortment of doughnuts. The store was quiet, and he killed a few minutes chatting with the manager about the flooding and did he think it would end anytime soon? He returned to the car to find Daniels wiping her cheeks with her palms. Both of her eyes were bloodshot. He placed the coffees in the holders on the dash and opened the bag and offered her a doughnut.

"No, thanks, I'm not hungry," she said.

"Eat one anyway. It'll make you feel better," he said.

She chose a chocolate-covered doughnut and took a giant bite out of it. The sweetness brought a tiny smile to her lips, and she washed it down with coffee.

"Do you know how many times this has happened to me?" she asked. "So many that I've lost count. Every time I think I've found these bastards, the rug gets pulled out from under me. It's like God's punishing me, and I have no idea why."

"It's eating you alive, isn't it?" he said.

She finished her doughnut and pulled another out of the bag. "These are delicious."

"Have you thought about asking for a reassignment? I'm sure your superiors would say yes, considering how long this has been going on."

"I've thought about it plenty of times," she said. "But then a new envelope of photographs gets dropped on my desk and there are new leads to run down. I'm so immersed in the case that it would be impossible to bring another agent up to speed and expect they'd be able to put all the pieces together. Do you think I'm a bad person?"

"It doesn't sound like you have enough time in your life to be a bad person."

"Then why is God doing this to me?"

"God isn't doing this to you. There's a lot of evil out there. When it touches people, they get hurt. No one's immune, not even good people like you."

His answer seemed to satisfy her. Back on the road, he asked a question that had been bothering him. "The author of *The Hanover Killers* speculated that a pair of cops might be behind the killings at Dartmouth. Rhoden said the same thing. Is that an angle you checked out?"

"The FBI was all over that," she said. "The bureau interviewed the Hanover Police Department and the departments from the neighboring towns. The neighboring towns were quickly ruled out. That left the Hanover Police Department, which employed sixty-eight full-time officers at the time of the killings and fourteen part-timers. Each officer worked ten-hour shifts, four days a week, and had to attend roll call before they went on duty. The station supervisor was responsible for keeping track of each officer's hours and sick days. The officers were responsible for keeping logs that showed when they issued tickets or made arrests. The FBI reviewed everything and determined that there were six officers whose whereabouts weren't accounted for during the times of the killings and when I was abducted. Two of the officers were female and ruled out. The FBI interviewed the other four officers, and they had airtight alibis."

"If it wasn't the local cops, what about guys with military backgrounds or retired cops who lived in Hanover?"

"We checked out as many of those as we could."

"But you couldn't check out all of them because there's no database that contains all of them," he said. "That's why you were suspicious of me. It could still be a cop."

"It could be."

"You must have a theory as to who these guys are."

"My theories have all proven false. I'm positive I've run across them during my investigation, but I didn't realize it was them. It eats at me."

Two blocks from his condo building they hit more flooding. The street hadn't been flooded when they'd left, and Daniels weighed driving through the water.

"You never know what's underneath," he cautioned.

"Spoilsport."

She threw the rental into reverse and drove backward down the street until she came to an intersection and masterfully turned the vehicle around. Her skill was admirable, and it made him want to enroll in a tactical driving class.

Ten minutes later they were in his condo ready to start over. Earlier, they had separated the list of names of male nurses at Dartmouth-Hitchcock and searched the DMV database to see which ones now lived in Florida, believing that the killers had established residency here. They decided to take a different approach, and run each name against the National Crime Information Center's database to see which of the nurses on the list had criminal records. Daniels sat on the living room couch, working on her laptop. Lancaster sat across from her, holding the list.

"Ready when you are," she said.

He read aloud the first name to her. "Ronald Colley."

He spelled the name to ensure that she entered it into the NCIC's search engine correctly. Daniels hit "Enter" and tapped her fingers impatiently as she waited.

"The computer's running slow tonight. That happens when a lot of agents are running checks at once. Wait, I've got a response. Negative. Who's next?"

"Wayne Heinrich."

He spelled the name, and she entered it into the search engine.

"What did we do before computers?" she asked.

"We guessed more," he said.

Heinrich also came up negative. The next twenty names on the list produced the same result. She raised a hand to her mouth and smothered a yawn.

"I need more coffee," she said. "I'm starting to crash from all the sugar in those doughnuts."

"Coming right up."

He fixed another pot in the kitchen. He made it extra strong and filled two mugs. Searching the NCIC database one name at a time was a painstaking process, but he was convinced it would pay off. The Hanover killers had to be nurses for the simple reason that every other suspect had been eliminated. Daniels's willingness to start over was assurance that she believed he was right. He returned to the living room with the mugs.

"Any luck?" he asked.

She did not reply. Her head was tilted back, and she was snoring. He cleared his throat but did not rouse her. He put the mugs on the coffee table, then gently removed the laptop and also put it on the coffee table. With her eyes still closed, she mumbled thanks, then lay sideways on the couch and slipped into dreamland.

He got a blanket and covered her. It was time to take a break. Before he did, he glanced at the laptop's screen to see if they'd gotten a hit. Her latest entry had come up negative. He grabbed a mug and went outside. He needed to check in with the troops.

- - -

Sometimes late at night when the city was asleep, the light pollution dimmed and the stars came out. Tonight was such an event, and he stood at the railing and beheld the flickering dots in the night sky with his cell phone pressed to his ear, talking to Carlo.

"How are things at the Pearls'?" he asked.

"About the same," Carlo said.

"You still seeing a lot of strange cars?"

"Yeah. Too much traffic for a residential street. That was some scene at the beach. In the old days, you would have torn that lifeguard's arm off."

"I guess I'm getting soft in my old age. How are the Pearls holding up?"

"They're hunkered down inside watching a movie. I wouldn't be surprised if they never came outside again."

"I should probably call and calm them down."

"Not a bad idea. Later, brother."

The building had a visitor. Down below, the security gate rose, and a yellow taxi entered the property. It parked by the entrance, and the driver hopped out and removed a suitcase from the trunk and gave it to his female passenger, who paid him. The driver was familiar, having brought many residents home from the nearby airport.

The driver started to leave. The area around the entrance was having new pavers installed, and the driver had to back out in order not to hit any of the equipment. It was a struggle, and he finally got clear and left. Lancaster watched the taillights disappear and realized his skin was tingling. The driver knew how to handle the wheel, yet when it came to driving in reverse, he had struggled, much in the same way most people who drove a car would struggle. Driving in reverse was difficult, unless you were trained to do it.

Daniels had been trained to drive in reverse at the FBI's training facility in Quantico. She was so skillful that he wanted to learn himself. He'd never seen anyone else drive in reverse that well—with one exception.

Two days ago, two of Nicki's stalkers had been parked in front of the Pearls' house in a white van, casing it. When Lancaster had chased them, the van's driver had gone in reverse down the street and escaped. There were several vehicles parked on either side, yet the van hadn't scraped a single one.

Based upon their use of a wheelchair at the Galleria mall, he felt certain they were the same pair of monsters who'd terrorized Dartmouth College twenty years ago. And now he knew something else about them. One of the stalkers knew how to expertly drive in reverse. Which could only mean one thing.

He'd been trained.

CHAPTER 38
BAD EYE

Lancaster went inside and shut the slider. Daniels was sprawled on the couch and mumbling in her sleep. He stifled the urge to awaken her so he could explain what he'd discovered. It was just a theory, and he needed to write it all down and make sure it held water before he rousted her.

He went to his study and shut the door. Sitting at his desk, he found a legal pad and a pencil in a drawer and wrote the words MISSED CLUES at the top of the page in bold letters. Before he could write any more, his cell phone vibrated and he removed it from his pocket. Karissa had texted him. She'd encountered a problem during her drive to Marathon and had just arrived at his friends' motel and was getting settled in. He felt like a jerk for not reaching out to her to make sure she was okay, so he called her.

"Hey, there," she said. "I didn't know if you were still up."

"Burning the midnight oil," he said. "Tell me what happened."

"I blew a tire on the Florida Turnpike just north of Miami and had to pull off on the shoulder. When I went to replace it, I found the spare was flat, so I called Triple A. Luckily, a highway patrolman came by and babysat me until a repair truck showed up."

"I'm sorry. I hope you're not too stressed out."

"I'll live. Look, Jon, I need to ask you a question. You told me that you have an FBI friend who could arrest Zack. What if your FBI friend doesn't come through? What then? It wouldn't be the first time the law has let me down."

He leaned back in his chair and considered how best to respond. He knew from his years as a policeman that victims of sexual crimes rarely felt protected by the law and did not trust the police to follow through when it came to protecting them from their attackers. He'd promised Karissa that he'd have Zack put away so he couldn't harm her, but until he actually did something, she was going to fear every shadow and strange noise.

"If that happens, then I'll deal with Zack," he said.

"Deal with him how?" she said.

"You don't want to know."

"Yes, I do. Deal with him how?"

"I'll put a bullet in him if I have to. You have my word."

The line went quiet. He'd never made a promise like that before. But the fact was, he'd screwed up when he'd confronted Zack and let Karissa's name slip. He was responsible for the mess she was in, and he needed to fix it.

"I hope it doesn't come to that," she said.

"Neither do I. But if it does, I'll deal with him. He won't hurt you again."

"Thank you. You have no idea how much that means to me. Good night."

He said goodbye and ended the connection. He could only deal with one problem at a time, and he shoved Karissa out of his mind and went back to his legal pad.

- - -

Writing down all the clues they'd missed took twenty minutes. The reality of most criminal investigations was that the truth was hidden in the facts, and if the investigator looked hard enough, the truth would reveal itself. The truth was beginning to reveal itself with the Hanover killers, and he booted up his computer and continued his search.

Three hours later he was done. He'd found the bastards and now understood how they'd managed to evade Daniels for such a long time. He also felt certain that they were about to claim their next victim, and that he and Daniels needed to act quickly.

He found Daniels in the living room still talking in her sleep. Her words were anguished, and her body twisted uncomfortably on the couch. She led a tortured life. During the day she chased the men who'd tried to abduct and kill her, and at night, they chased her. Putting down his legal pad, he knelt next to the couch, wanting to wake her as gently as possible.

"Beth, wake up."

She remained asleep, still talking to herself. He tried a different approach.

"Special Agent Daniels, wake up."

That didn't produce the desired result, so he gave her a gentle shake. Her eyes snapped open, and she grabbed his wrist. Within seconds he was lying on the floor.

"Hey, cut it out!" he said.

She released him and shot him an angry look. "God damn it, Jon. I have a hard enough time sleeping as it is. Please don't ever do that again."

"You got it."

He pulled himself off the floor and collected himself. Then he sat down on the couch beside her. He picked up the legal pad and passed it to her. She spent a long moment staring at what he'd written. She shook her head, not understanding.

"I was wrong," he explained. "Our killers aren't nurses. It took me a while, but I figured out who they are, and why they've evaded you for so long."

"I'm listening," she said.

"We missed several important clues, which I've written down. Let's start from the top." He pointed at the top of the page where he'd written DRIVING IN REVERSE. "One of our killers is trained in tactical driving. I saw him drive a van in reverse on a street outside your sister's house in order to get away from me. The street had cars parked on the curb, but he didn't hit any of them."

"He could have learned that anywhere," she said skeptically.

"I disagree," he said. "I was a SEAL and also a cop for fifteen years, and I took my share of driving courses. I don't remember any time devoted to driving in reverse. The only other person I've ever seen do this was you."

"You think there's a connection," she said.

"Yes, I do."

"It's flimsy. What else have you got?"

He pointed at the second line on the page where he'd written TIMING OF FIRST KILLING/APPEARANCE OF PHOTOS. "Two weeks after you were promoted to run the Violent Crimes Against Children/Online Predator unit, the first envelope of photographs was sent to the FBI and given to you. That's when the investigation officially began. Correct?"

She nodded. "And I've been chasing them ever since."

"You also told me that profilers at the FBI's Behavioral Science Division believe the photographs are payback because you escaped from the killers at Dartmouth."

"Right again. What's the significance?"

"Think about the timing of the first photographs. They appeared two weeks after your promotion. During those two weeks, the killers abducted a victim, kept her in a house, killed her, photographed her body, then dropped the film off at Walgreens to be developed. An employee developed the film, saw it was a murder, and contacted the police, who in turn sent the photos to the FBI. Each one of these things took a few days. If you back them up, it appears the first victim was abducted right after you were promoted. Call it the first payback."

She spent a moment processing what he was saying. Then it hit her.

"The killers knew I'd been promoted."

"They did. Which leads to my next question. How did they know? The FBI doesn't issue press releases, and the names of its agents and their job titles aren't posted on its website. I know because I tried to look you up."

"They must have found out through some other channel."

"What channel? Let me show you something."

He took out his cell phone and got on the internet. Opening the Google app, he typed in "Special Agent Elizabeth Daniels FBI" and hit "Enter." A page of links appeared on the screen, and he clicked on the first one. It was the story from the *Boston Globe* of Daniels and her team busting a child-trafficking ring and included her photograph and job title. It was the same story that had led him to finding her.

"If you go on the internet and type in your name and the word 'FBI,' this is the oldest story that pops up," he said. "This bust in Boston took place three years after you got promoted. The information about your promotion wasn't available for public consumption. Yet our killers somehow knew. They knew the day you were promoted, which led them to abduct and kill their first victim."

She took a deep breath. "I admit, it's a strange coincidence, but it still doesn't prove anything."

"There's more."

"Lay it on me."

He pointed at the next line on the page. It said FUNDING. "You told me something interesting yesterday that I didn't know. You said that every six months, the FBI reviews its active investigations and decides which should be continued and which should be put on the back burner.

These investigations are also reviewed by the Justice Department. If an investigation has stalled, the funding usually stops."

"Correct," she said. "My bosses prioritize investigations based upon forward progress. If there isn't any, the money dries up."

"You also said that for the past seven years, your investigation into the Hanover killers has hit a wall every six months, and that you were just about ready to lose funding when another envelope of photographs landed on your desk, which led to the investigation being continued."

"Correct again. The photos usually showed up a week or two before the review process would begin."

"How many times did this happen?"

"Fourteen. If the killers hold true to form, the bureau will receive a new envelope of photos from a pharmacy in Fort Lauderdale in the next week or so."

"That can't be a coincidence."

She shook her head, not understanding.

"The photographs showing up every six months was a ploy by the killers to keep your investigation going so they could torture you."

"Where's your proof?"

"My proof is that it worked, and it did torture you."

"But how would they know about the review process?"

"I asked myself the same question. How could the killers know about the review process or how funding worked in the FBI? I did an exhaustive search on the internet and couldn't find a single mention of it anywhere. The information simply isn't available."

"So how did they know?"

"They work for the bureau as field agents. Or I should say 'worked.' I'm pretty sure they're semiretired now."

Daniels rocked back on the couch and gave him a condescending look. "That's ridiculous, Jon. The vetting process to become an FBI agent includes a battery of psychological exams that are meant to weed out people with mental disorders, which our killers certainly have. You're barking up the wrong tree."

"No, I'm not. And I can prove it."

"You can prove these are FBI agents?"

"Yes. You may even know them."

Her expression bordered on hostile. She had become blinded to the clues. It happened to even the best investigators when they spent too long working a case.

"Go ahead," she said.

"Eighteen months before the killings at Dartmouth, two girls were kidnapped and murdered in Bedford, New Hampshire, which isn't that far from Dartmouth," he said. "There were a number of similarities between those killings and the Dartmouth killings. The victims were teenagers who were abducted coming home from work. Their bodies were also dumped in fields."

"I'm well aware of the Bedford murders and the parallels to the Dartmouth killings," she said. "On their face, they appeared to have been committed by the same killers. Only that couldn't have happened, because the man responsible for the Bedford killings was a house painter named Clyde Bessemer, and he was caught before the Dartmouth killings started. He's serving a life sentence."

"I know," he said. "I read it online."

"Then what's your point?"

Lancaster reached into his shirt pocket and removed a square of paper, which he carefully unfolded. It was a twenty-two-year-old newspaper article from the *Bedford Bulletin* that he'd printed off the internet on the laser printer in his study. Its headline screamed BEDFORD MURDERS SOLVED! KILLER CAPTURED. Beneath the headline was a mug shot of a man in his forties with a handlebar mustache and the hardened eyes of a killer. The caption identified him as Clyde Bessemer of Bedford.

"This article from the *Bedford Bulletin* said that a pair of FBI agents broke the case," he said. "Their names were Special Agents Don Mates and Troy Holloway, and they worked as field agents out of the FBI's Bedford field office. These two guys are your killers."

"That's utterly ridiculous," she said.

"No, it's not. Their office was an hour-and-ten-minute drive from Dartmouth. As field agents, they could come and go as they pleased and not arouse suspicion. They used the Bedford killings as a blueprint for the Dartmouth killings. After your escape, they decided to rein it in. Then you were promoted to run the Violent Crimes Against Children unit, which I'm guessing was announced internally. Is that right?"

"It was announced on the FBI's intranet, which is only available to staff," she said.

"That explains it. Seeing that you were promoted infuriated Mates and Holloway. You were the one that got away. So they decided to pay you back."

"Do you think I'm stupid?" she asked.

"No, I just think you missed them."

"The FBI didn't miss Mates and Holloway, and neither did I," she said, unable to hide the indignation in her voice. "The bureau recognized that there were parallels between the Bedford killings and the Dartmouth killings right away. Two agents that worked the Dartmouth case interviewed Mates and Holloway to see if they could shed any light on who the killers might be. It didn't lead to anything."

"Mates and Holloway had time to get their stories down and fooled your agents during the interview."

"Be quiet and let me finish. When I graduated from the academy, I got my hands on the interview with Mates and Holloway, and I studied it. There was nothing there. But I still wanted to look them in the face, and make sure they weren't the killers. If either one of them had a discolored right eye, I'd know it was them."

"Your gut was telling you something."

"Would you please let me finish? I couldn't just demand an interview since they'd already been cleared. So I bided my time. Three years after my promotion, my team busted a child-trafficking ring working out of Boston. When the bust was over, I decided to take my shot, and I called Mates and told him I was in the area, and would he and Holloway be willing to meet with me? I explained that I'd gotten a firsthand look at the Dartmouth killers, and was hoping it might jar a memory or two. Mates was pleasant over the phone and said he'd talk to Holloway. He called me back an hour later, and said yes. So I drove up to Bedford."

"You actually met with them. Wow."

"Are you insinuating that I made a mistake?"

"They could have killed you."

"Damn it, Jon, it's not Mates and Holloway. They took me out to lunch to a really nice place, and we sat at a corner booth and discussed the two cases. I was as close to them as I am to you right now. Neither Mates nor Holloway has a discolored eye."

"Mates has a discolored eye. He got injured playing lacrosse in high school."

Daniels acted like she might slap him. "Haven't you heard a word I just said? It's not them."

"You're wrong. It is them. Mates either had surgery to fix his eye, or he's now wearing contact lenses that hide the discoloration. He probably did this right after you escaped from him and Holloway in the woods in Dartmouth."

"You think they fooled me?"

"Afraid so."

"Prove it."

He again used his cell phone to get on the internet. Earlier, he'd found Mates's Facebook page, and learned that the special agent had grown up in the town of Montague in western Massachusetts. Working off the assumption that Mates had attended the local high school, he'd done a yearbook search using a site called e-Yearbook, which he'd used before to hunt down suspects. It had taken a while, but he'd eventually found Don Mates's photograph and profile in the class of 1988's yearbook. Mates had been captain of the lacrosse team in his senior year, and Lancaster now pulled the team photo up, and used his thumb and forefinger to enlarge it. He passed the cell phone to her.

"That's the Montague lacrosse team circa 1988. Mates was the team captain. He's standing in the front row on the very left. Look at his right eye."

She raised the phone to her face. "He's wearing an eye patch."

"If you read the posts, his teammates mention him getting hurt during the final game of the year. Mates took a stick in the eye."

"That still doesn't prove anything."

"There's more."

He took the cell phone and pulled up Mates's graduation photograph. He put the cell phone in front of her face. In the photo, Mates's right eye was scarred, the discoloration rectangular-shaped in the lower part of the iris.

"Is that the bad eye you saw?" he asked.

Her hand came up to her mouth. "Oh my God."

Her face was pale, and she was at a loss for words. She'd looked the murderous bastards right in the eye and not recognized them. It was going to haunt her, and he hoped she was strong enough to recover from it.

"I found Mates's and Holloway's Facebook pages and searched the postings. Mates relocated to Fort Lauderdale eight years ago, while Holloway followed a month later. They must work out of one of the FBI's Miami offices."

"Do you think they're a couple? The FBI has an open policy on gays, lesbians, and bisexuals becoming agents, so it wouldn't be unusual."

"I think they're both straight. A coworker at the Bedford office posted a photo from Mates's going-away party. There was a handpainted sign that said To The Last Confirmed Bachelor. I think Mates and Holloway are serial killers who realized they were less likely to get caught if they stuck together. I found their address on the DMV database. They share a house in an area called Sistrunk. It's a slum."

"They live in a slum?"

"They're not the first serial killers who've done that. Your neighbors are less likely to bother you in a bad neighborhood. We need to take a ride over there and case the place. If my hunch is correct, they're holding a girl there now."

"What are you basing that on? Because I'm expecting a new set of photos? If we show up and start snooping around, they'll get suspicious and get rid of any incriminating evidence. We need to handle this by the book."

"There's no time for that. We need to move fast."

"Why? What did you find?"

"The National Center for Missing and Exploited Children keeps a database of all children that are reported missing. I have access through Team Adam, and reviewed the most recent cases. One stuck out. An eighteen-year-old girl named Ryean Bartell was reported missing yesterday. Ryean works as a server at the Jamba Juice in the Coral Ridge Mall. When she didn't show up to work, her manager contacted the sheriff."

"She's only been gone a day. How can you be sure it's an abduction?"

"Yesterday was payday. The manager thought it was strange that Ryean didn't come in to collect her paycheck, so she called Ryean's roommate to see if there was a problem. The roommate said that Ryean didn't come home the night before and had disappeared." He paused and then said, "She fits the profiles of the other victims. Mates and Holloway abducted Ryean after she got off work two nights ago, and took her to their house in Sistrunk. They're going to go through their ritual, then kill her and snap photos and drop them off at a local pharmacy so they can keep torturing you. Or, we can stop them."

He rose from the couch and pulled out his car keys.

"Come on. Maybe we'll get lucky and save some poor girl's life," he said.

CHAPTER 39

SISTRUNK

Broward County was a vast place, with two million inhabitants spread across 1,320 square miles and thirty vastly different communities. Of those neighborhoods, none was more dangerous than Sistrunk, in the central part of the county.

Sistrunk was a slum filled with crack dens, Section Eight housing, and badass drug dealers staking out their turf on every corner. Of the cops that Lancaster had worked with, he did not know a single one that would answer a distress call from there at night.

The address showing on the DMV site for Mates and Holloway was on NW Ninth Street in an area called Washington Park. Northwest Ninth was a four-lane road with residences taking up one side and a line of businesses on the other. The most prominent was a Fast Stop Food Store that also sold hard liquor and lottery tickets.

It was late morning when they grabbed coffee from McDonald's and sipped it while sitting in the Fast Stop's lot. They were both running on fumes and knew that a jolt of coffee would trick their bodies into staying alert for a few more hours. They had a clear view of their suspects' residence, a one-story concrete-block house with iron bars on the windows and a fenced-in yard. It was a depressing place with equally depressing neighbors.

"This is a rat hole," Daniels said. "Are you sure it's the right address?"

"This is the place," he said. "Let's wait and see if anybody's home."

"Why would they live here? It's dangerous."

"It *is* dangerous," he admitted. "But it also offers them protection. Team Adam did a study of abductors who held their victims for extended periods. This included Jaycee Dugard, Elizabeth Smart, and the three women held in a house in Cleveland—Michelle Knight, Amanda Berry, and Gina DeJesus. The study concluded that these women's abductors had chosen to live in economically depressed communities because people who lived in those areas often have criminal records. Neighbors won't call the police if they see suspicious activity because they don't trust the police."

"You're saying the neighbors know something bad is going on inside the house, but don't want to get involved."

"That's right. Jaycee Dugard was a good example. Her abductor kept her imprisoned in a tent behind his house for eighteen years. The neighbors on either side could clearly see Jaycee, and the two children she had by her abductor, but they never raised a stink or called the police."

"Do you think Mates and Holloway's neighbors know what they're up to?"

"I'm sure they've had their suspicions. Mates and Holloway have been abducting and murdering young girls for over seven years. Someone must have heard something."

"The FBI received the first photos from Houston and the second set from Atlanta. How do you explain that?"

"I think they did that to throw the FBI off the scent. They flew to Houston and Atlanta for a long weekend, killed the girls in a rented house, took photographs of them with their camera, and dropped the film off at a Walgreens to be developed. Miami is their home base."

"That's a lot of work, don't you think?"

He turned in his seat and stared at her.

"It worked, didn't it?" he said.

They finished their drinks in silence. Movement on the other side of the street caught his eye.

"Looks like we've got some activity," he said.

A pair of binoculars lay in Daniels's lap. She lifted them to her face and had a look. "I see a white male wearing cargo pants and a sleeveless T-shirt coming out the front door. He's walking down the front path."

"Is it Mates or Holloway?"

"It looks like Mates. Same haircut, but grayer. Looks like he still works out. He's crossing the street. His destination appears to be the Fast Stop."

Mates came into view. His arms were tight, and he had a weight lifter's thick neck. They watched their suspect step onto the sidewalk and enter the grocery store. Daniels started to get out of the rental, but Lancaster stopped her.

"Where are you going?" he asked.

"I want to tail him, see what he's doing."

"What if he recognizes you? What are you going to say, that you came to Sistrunk on a vacation? Stay put."

She was chomping at the bit to nail Mates and Holloway, and she reluctantly fell back in her seat. Several minutes passed as they waited. The silence was unbearable.

"You never explained how the Cassandra videos were created," he said.

"We used the Reality Thief," she said.

"Is that a person?"

"Yes, he's a person, and my boyfriend. It's a long story."

He thought back to Daniels's Facebook page and the shadowy figure of the man running beside her posted in her photo album. Had she met the love of her life while conducting her investigation? She deserved a reward considering what she'd been through, and he felt happy for her, even if he hardly knew her.

"You'll have to share it with me one day," he said.

"I'll do that," she said.

Five minutes later, Mates exited the grocery store carrying a brown paper bag overflowing with groceries. Sticking out of the top of the bag was a loaf of Cuban bread and what appeared to be a head of lettuce. Mates went to the curb, halted, and glanced suspiciously over his shoulder before crossing. Years of criminal behavior had instilled a sixth sense in him, as it did in many criminals. Mates sensed that he was being watched, and his eyes scanned the street and the lot but did not touch upon the rental.

Mates shrugged it off and crossed. He opened the gate to his property and walked up the brick path. As he reached the front door, it swung in, and a man with silver hair greeted him. They briefly spoke before Mates went inside and the door was shut.

Daniels watched through her binoculars, which she now lowered.

"That was Holloway," she said. "He hasn't changed."

"They're both home," he said. "Is that usual? I would think they'd need to be at work."

"They may be part-timers. Many senior agents do that before applying for full retirement. It sweetens their package."

"They're working cases when they're not abducting girls and killing them. That's really sick."

Daniels pulled out her cell phone and started to make a call.

"What are you doing?" he asked.

"I'm calling my boss in DC to ask them to grant me permission to run a surveillance on the house," she said. "We can't just barge in there and search the place without probable cause. We need to build a case."

"But what if they're preparing to kill Ryean Bartell?" he said. "Waiting isn't an option."

"I have to follow the law, Jon. There's no other choice."

She made the call. Her boss was tied up in a meeting, so she left a message asking that he call her back immediately. Lancaster's mind was racing, and as she ended the call he undid his seatbelt, opened his door, and started to get out.

"Where are you going?" she asked.

"Inside the grocery store. Care to join me?"

She caught up to him halfway across the lot.

"Would you mind telling me what you're doing?" she asked.

"Did you see the bag of groceries Mates was carrying? There was a loaf of bread sticking out of the top and a head of lettuce. Like he was getting ready to cook a big meal. Isn't that part of the ritual? To feed their victim a last meal before the lights get turned out? I want to see what else was in that bag."

"How do you plan to do that?"

"I'm hoping the owner will show us the receipt of what Mates purchased."

"Will he do that?"

"He should. Many of the groceries around here run illegal numbers games. If we tell the owner you're with the FBI, he should play along."

"I'm the leverage."

"Yes, you're the leverage."

An annoying buzzer rang as they stepped inside the store. There were aisles of canned goods and nonperishable items, while produce was kept in bins in the back. Behind glass counters were the meats and poultry and freshly caught fish. The husky Cuban manager working the register wore a white guayabera shirt with a big fat cigar sticking out of the pocket. He eyed them suspiciously as they approached the counter.

"Good morning," Lancaster said. "My name's Jon Lancaster and I'm a private investigator. This nice lady is Special Agent Daniels with the FBI."

The manager stared at Daniels. Lancaster nudged her with his elbow.

"Show him your badge," he said.

Daniels took out her wallet and flipped it open. A silver badge rested inside. She held the wallet in front of the manager's face and let him have a look.

"What's your name?" Lancaster asked.

"My name is Alejandro. My friends call me Alex," the manager replied. "Is something wrong?"

"There was a man in here a few minutes ago," he said. "We need to see the receipt from the items that he purchased."

"You mean Don?" Alex said.

"Yes, Don. You know him?"

"He's one of my best customers. What did he do?"

"Nothing. We just need to see a copy of the receipt. Can you print out one for us?"

"Do you have a warrant?"

In Lancaster's experience, only people who broke the law asked to see warrants. He leaned over the counter and put on his best mean face. "Do you want trouble? We can give you trouble, and shut you down for running an illegal numbers operation. Or you can play along, and print the god damn receipt."

"I don't want trouble," Alex said.

"Prove it."

Alex quickly typed a command into the keyboard on his register. A receipt was spit out of the printer, and Alex tore it off and placed it on the counter. Lancaster and Daniels read it at the same time. Mates had purchased a loaf of bread, a head of lettuce, three New York strip steaks, mushrooms, Hungry Jack instant mashed potatoes, a quart of chocolate Breyers ice cream, a box of brownies, and a product called U by Kotex.

Lancaster pointed at the last item. "What's this?"

Alex acted embarrassed. Instead of explaining, he came out from behind the counter and walked down an aisle. They both followed him. He stopped at a section that sold feminine hygiene products and pulled a box off the shelf and showed it to them.

"Here you go," the manager said.

It was a box of tampons.

CHAPTER 40

NEW YORK STRIP

Alex was a problem. He'd admitted that Mates was an excellent customer. They may have even been friends. There was a good chance he would call Mates and alert him that an FBI agent and private investigator were asking questions about him the moment Daniels and Lancaster walked out of the grocery store.

It was a risk Daniels and Lancaster weren't willing to take. Mates and Holloway were keeping a girl against her will inside the house across the street, and it was their responsibility to make sure no harm came to her. They moved away from the counter and stood in the chips aisle, talking in hushed tones.

"This guy could ruin our investigation," Daniels said, referring to the manager.

"I was thinking the same thing," he said. "We need to get someone in here, and watch him while we figure out how to deal with Mates and Holloway."

"I can do that." She took out her cell phone and started to make a call.

"Who are you calling?" he asked.

"Special Agent Moore. He's dependable."

"He works out of the FBI's North Miami office, doesn't he?"

"What are you thinking? That Moore might know Mates and Holloway, and tip them off? Come on, Jon. Don't be so paranoid."

"Mates and Holloway have been living in South Florida for eight years. They've probably made plenty of friends and established allegiances with the other agents working here. They're con men. It's one of the reasons they've lasted so long."

She stopped dialing and lowered the cell phone. "Do you have a plan B?"

"I want to call Carlo, and ask him to come over."

"All right, call him. You don't need my permission."

"Yes, I do. It's your investigation, Beth."

"Fuck it, call him."

He made the call. Carlo answered on the first ring.

"How are things at Camp Pearl?" he asked.

"Pretty quiet," Carlo said. "Karl's been standing in the driveway, giving menacing looks to passing cars, while Mike's on the dock, watching boats in the Intracoastal. I think they've scared off the sickos stalking Nicki."

"Nice going. Do you feel comfortable leaving and helping me out for a few hours? I need you to watch a grocery store manager for a little while."

"A grocery store manager? What did he do? Sell someone spoiled milk?"

"He didn't do anything. I'm just afraid he might make a phone call, and ruin a stakeout I'm on. Are you in?"

"I'll have Karl take over for me. Give me the address."

He gave him the address of the Fast Stop Food Store. Carlo voiced displeasure that the store was in Sistrunk, and chastised Lancaster for not telling him before hanging up. The front door buzzer went off, and a customer came in and went straight to the section of the store where grilling supplies were displayed. Daniels's mouth dropped open. Lancaster looked at her, then at the customer.

"Holloway?" he asked under his breath.

"The one and only," she whispered.

"Go hide."

Daniels went to the rear of the store where the produce was kept and started squeezing the tomatoes. Lancaster bellied up to the counter and grabbed a pair of cheap shades off a display and put them on. Then he pulled a copy of *People en Español* out of a rack and thumbed through it. Alex was caught in the crosshairs and gave him a nervous look.

"Keep your damn mouth shut," he whispered.

"Yes, sir," the manager whispered back.

Holloway was making his way to the front of the store. He stood a half foot taller than his partner and also had a gym physique. He was a seasoned FBI agent and would realize the man at the counter wasn't a normal customer if Lancaster didn't handle things right.

"Give me a pack of Marlboros," Lancaster said as he fitted the magazine back into the rack.

The cigarettes were stored in a plastic display behind the register. Alex pulled out a pack and tossed it on the counter. Lancaster took out his wallet and reached for a five-dollar bill. He didn't smoke and had no idea how much a pack cost. If he put down too little, it might set off an alarm, so he threw down a twenty.

"That will be seven dollars," Alex said.

Alex rang up the sale and counted out his change. Lancaster stuffed the money into his pocket and headed for the exit, then stopped and came back. Holloway had put a bag of charcoal on the counter and had his wallet out.

"Forgot my matches," he said. "Go ahead. I'll wait."

Holloway settled up and left the store. Daniels returned to the counter.

"Did you think he suspected anything?" she asked.

"No, he was in the dark." He returned the shades to the display. To the manager he said, "Good job."

Alex was not happy with the situation, and frowned. Ten minutes later, Carlo walked into the grocery and joined them at the counter.

"I got here as fast as I could," Carlo said.

"Much appreciated." He addressed Alex. "I want you to listen to me. This man was a SEAL and can kill you with his bare hands. If you do anything stupid, he'll tear one of your arms off, and beat you to death with it. Got it?"

"You don't have to threaten me," the manager said.

"Just trying to make myself clear. Are we good?"

Alex nodded. Then he said, "This is about the girls, isn't it?"

Daniels nearly leaped over the counter. "What girls? What are you talking about?"

"The girls that stay with Don and Troy in the house across the street," Alex said. "They bring them into the store late at night. The girls are drugged out and can hardly stand up. I have wondered what happens to them, but I've learned not to ask."

Daniels looked ready to strangle him. "How many times has this happened?"

"Too many," he said.

"Were the girls young?" she asked.

"Yes."

"Did you know any of them?"

"No. I'd never seen any of them before. I felt bad for them."

"Then why didn't you call the police?"

"Because the police don't give a shit," Alex said. "Bad things happen in Sistrunk every day, and the police look the other way. Why would these guys be treated any differently?"

Daniels was enraged. Mates and Holloway had paraded their victims in front of the manager and probably his customers and no one had acted. Fighting evil was hard; fighting it alone was nearly impossible. Lancaster pulled her away from the counter and told her to calm down. She unclenched her fists and took a deep breath.

"You have no idea how angry this makes me," she said.

"Yes, I do," he said. He turned and addressed Carlo. "We're leaving. Keep your cell phone handy. I may need you."

"Will do. Be careful," Carlo said.

They went to the front door. Daniels hadn't calmed down, and he felt like he needed to do something. He started to speak, and she shut him down. The door was made of glass, and she pointed across the street. A column of black smoke rose in the air behind Mates and Holloway's house.

"What do you think that is?" Daniels asked.

They ventured outside. The smell of grilling meat filled the air, and Lancaster realized that Mates and Holloway were grilling the three New York strip steaks they'd just purchased as they prepared Ryean Bartell's last meal. Ryean would be photographed before they ate, and when the meal was over, she would be killed and her corpse photographed on a camera with film that would later need to be developed.

"Looks like we're just in time," he said.

CHAPTER 41

DIVIDE AND CONQUER

"We need backup to do this right," Daniels said. "Do you have a contact at the sheriff's office that will help us?"

"I'm still friends with my former supervisor," he said.

"Call him."

He called his former supervisor to request a SWAT team. The Broward County Sheriff's Office had a twenty-four-hour SWAT team at its disposal to deal with active shooters and possible terrorist activity. The only issue would be traffic, which could seriously delay their arrival. An automated receptionist answered, and he punched zero to speak to an operator. Canned music filled his ear.

"What's taking so long?" she asked.

"Must be a busy day," he said.

A minute passed. He sniffed the air.

"They just put the steaks on," he said. "Mates bought three New York strips, which take about ten minutes to cook. We're running out of time. What do you want to do?"

"I've never stormed a house before," she said. "You were the SEAL. Make the call, and I'll back you up."

He pocketed his cell phone, marched over to his car, and popped the trunk. The floor panel and spare tire had been removed, making the compartment extra deep. Three long plastic storage boxes were arranged side by side. He popped the lid of the first box, where a bulky bullet-proof vest lay inside. He handed it to her.

"Just one?" she asked.

"I usually run solo," he explained.

"You should wear it."

"I insist. Don't argue with me, Beth."

She fitted on the vest and tightened the belt. He opened the second storage box. Inside was a Beretta Tx4 Storm 12-gauge shotgun, which he also gave to her.

"This is a Beretta. It's gas operated and absolutely deadly at close range," he said. "It also won't take your shoulder off with the recoil."

"What's the load?" she asked.

"One-ounce slugs. They're perfect to take down a door."

"Gotcha."

The third box contained four handguns arranged on a piece of carpet. It was always best to match the equipment with the goal. He chose the Luger with the double stack magazine that held seventeen rounds and slammed the trunk shut.

"Ready when you are," he said.

Daniels took her badge from her wallet and pinned it to the shoulder strap on the vest. They moved to the sidewalk in front of the grocery and looked both ways. Sistrunk was a nocturnal community, and there was not a soul to be seen.

"What's our plan of attack?" Daniels asked.

"Divide and conquer," he said. "One of them is in the backyard grilling the steaks, and the other is inside preparing the meal. We'll deal with them individually. I'll go around back while you count to sixty. When you reach sixty, go to the front door and blow it open. I'll deal with the guy in back and enter the house through the back door. That will let us trap whoever's inside. That sound good to you?"

"I like it," she said. "When should I start counting?"

"When we reach the other side of the street."

They crossed. Lancaster said a silent prayer. He didn't believe in God but always said a prayer in tight situations, just in case. Daniels started counting as her foot touched the sidewalk. The moment she did, he dropped into a crouch and scurried around the side of the house. The property had a waist-high chain-link fence that would be easily jumped. He saw no sign of a guard dog or security cameras. Mates and Holloway obviously felt safe living here, the bad neighborhood a perfect deterrent.

He stopped at the corner of the house and peered through the fence. Holloway stood at a charcoal grill with a cell phone in his hand. He was gazing at the cell phone's screen and did not see his visitor. In the back of the property was a carport, where the white van they'd used to case the Pearls' house was parked.

Lancaster waited. He had dealt with serial killers before. What always surprised him was their ordinariness. They were not cannibals who wore flesh masks and danced naked beneath the full moon. They went to ball games, ate fast food, and wore regular clothes. They were as dull as dirt, except when that inner alarm clock in their heads went off, telling them to kill again. Then the monsters came out.

He heard a thunderclap. Daniels had taken down the front door. Holloway put the cell phone away and moved toward the house. Lancaster rose to his full height and took aim.

"Freeze."

Holloway's mouth dropped open. "Who the hell are you?"

"You heard me. Put your hands up."

Holloway didn't obey. Instead he came toward Lancaster in slow, measured steps. With each step, his arms lowered another few inches. There was a handgun hidden somewhere on his body, and he was planning to use it.

Lancaster had given him a chance. It was a lesson that had been drilled into his head during SEAL training. You gave your adversary a chance to save himself, and if he didn't take it, you took him out. Without another word, he pumped three bullets into Holloway's chest and saw him fly backward and knock over the grill on his way down. Burning charcoal covered his body, and he quickly caught on fire.

Lancaster jumped the fence and entered the house through the back door. The kitchen had an island where a salad was being prepared. Instant potatoes were cooking on the stove, and a loaf of bread sat waiting to be cut. There was also an old Kodak camera sitting on the island for when the meal was done. It was called a Brownie and this particular model was small enough to slip into a man's shirt pocket. Every serial killer had a ritual that was religiously followed, and he wondered if it was part of the flawed wiring in their brains.

He passed into the dining room. The table had three place settings and an open bottle of red wine. Mates stood across the room, pressing the barrel of a handgun to the head of a freckle-faced teenage girl, who he guessed was Ryean Bartell. Mates's other arm was around her throat, from which hung a gold Saint Jude medal.

Ryean begged Mates not to kill her.

"Shut your fucking mouth," Mates told her.

The dining and living rooms were connected. Daniels stood in the center of the living room, pointing the shotgun. She wasn't backing down, and neither was Mates.

"Let her go," Daniels said.

"Fuck you," Mates said.

Lancaster decided to change the odds. He aimed at Mates's head and closed one eye. He'd put a bullet into the head of an al-Qaida militant in Yemen and managed not to hurt the hostage, and was willing to try it here.

"Do you want one of us to shoot you?" Daniels asked.

"I'll take my chances," Mates said.

He took aim. Mates realized he was being sized up and jerked Ryean from side to side so Lancaster couldn't get off a clean shot. Ryean started to sob.

"How did you figure out it was us?" Mates asked.

"Blame him," Daniels said.

Mates gave Lancaster a murderous look. It was eating at him.

"You left a lot of clues," Lancaster said, trying to rattle him.

"Bullshit. You just got lucky," Mates said.

Mates was buying time while formulating a plan. He was going to make a last stand and hope it paid off. Ryean would either get killed in the crossfire or Mates would put a bullet in her before he ran out the door. Either way she was a goner. Lancaster decided to tell her, and see where it led.

"They were going to kill you after lunch," he said. "You knew that, don't you?"

Ryean blinked. She was drugged and having a hard time focusing.

"But I didn't do nothing," the girl sobbed.

"Doesn't matter. They were still going to kill you."

"Shut the fuck up," Mates said.

"They've killed fifteen girls," Lancaster told her. "Each victim was abducted from a mall and brought to a house. She's pumped up with so many drugs that she loses her will. Then she's fed a nice meal and murdered. You were number sixteen."

"But I didn't do nothing," she said again.

"Doesn't matter. Your time was up."

"I said, shut the fuck up," Mates roared.

Ryean had reached the breaking point. She sank her teeth into Mates's forearm, and her abductor momentarily loosened his grip on her neck. Throwing her weight forward, she grabbed a steak knife off the table. Her arm came straight back and she blindly plunged the tip into Mates's eye. Mates screamed and discharged his handgun.

Ryean wrestled free. Instead of running, she pushed Mates into the wall and stabbed him repeatedly. Mates tried to protect his face, and she went straight for his jugular. It was over in seconds, and Mates fell to the floor and did a death crawl.

Lancaster went to Daniels's aid. The stray shot had caught her thigh, and there was a pool of blood on the floor. He tore off his shirt and made a tourniquet, getting the blood to stop. Ryean hovered behind him, still clutching the steak knife.

"You okay?" he asked.

She said yes. He tossed his cell phone to her.

"Call 911."

Ryean made the call. She went outside to read the address off the mailbox to the dispatcher, then returned. The wait was unbearable. Lancaster held Daniels's hand and said another prayer. The FBI agent stared at the ceiling, her eyes unblinking.

"Tell my sister that I love her," Daniels said.

"You're not going to die," Lancaster said.

"Just in case. Will you do that?"

"Of course."

Daniels sniffed the air. "I smell something burning."

He lifted his head and glanced into the kitchen. He'd left the back door open, and smoke was pouring into the house.

"I shot Holloway. He fell on the grill and caught on fire," he said.

"Good going," she said.

CHAPTER 42
THE REALITY THIEF

If you believed what you read in the newspapers, the decline in the national murder rate was due to a less violent population. Fewer people were dying of gunshot and knife wounds each year, which could only mean that the populace was becoming less violent.

Only half of this statement was true. The citizenry was as violent as ever, the number of people being shot and stabbed at an all-time high. What had changed was the medical profession's ability in dealing with the victims. First responders kept the victims breathing, and emergency rooms saved their lives.

That was why Daniels survived. Ten years ago, this would not have been the case, and she would have died from loss of blood and the shock. But the emergency medical attendants were pros, and they had kept her alive until they reached the hospital.

Daniels's status as an FBI agent earned her a private room in the ICU of Broward Health Medical Center. She was weak and needed time to regain her strength before starting rehabilitation. To anyone who came to visit, Daniels vowed that she would be back running within six months. No one had doubted her.

Lancaster came to visit a few days later. Melanie, Nolan, and Nicki Pearl were gathered around her bed sharing a story. Melanie hugged him.

"And to think I didn't want to hire you," Melanie said.

"It all worked out in the end," he said. "How's our patient doing?"

"My sister's a tough little shit. She's going to be fine."

"I heard that," Daniels said. "What did you bring me?"

Lancaster handed her the gift bag. Daniels undid the bow holding it together and removed a picture frame in distressed gold. Instead of a photograph, there was a quote from the Irish poet Samuel Beckett written in bold calligraphy.

"What does it say?" Nicki asked.

"It says, 'Ever tried. Ever failed. No matter. Try again. Fail again. Fail better,'" Daniels read aloud. "Is that what we did, Jon, fail better?"

"We didn't quit," he said.

She placed the frame on the night table. "No, we didn't. How's our victim?"

Ryean Bartell was also a patient in Broward Health Medical Center. Mates and Holloway had given her so many sedatives that she was lucky to be alive. Ryean hadn't understood the mortal danger she was in until Daniels had blown down the front door and come charging in. The newspapers had nicknamed her "The One That Got Away."

"The kid's a survivor," he said. "She's going to be okay."

Daniels started to reply but instead shut her eyes. Melanie reached over the bed and hugged her sister. The bad moment passed, and Daniels reopened her eyes.

"I need to tell all of you something," she said. "I'm sorry for all the grief I caused Nicki and the rest of you by creating those videos. I have a way to make Nicki's stalkers go away so your lives can return to normal. It will take a few weeks to work, and then everything will be good again."

"You're going to make these bad men leave me alone?" Nicki said.

"I sure am, honey," Daniels said.

Nicki kissed her aunt on the cheek. Then it was Melanie's turn, then Nolan's.

They were a family again. There was a silver lining in every tragedy. This was theirs.

"Would you guys mind leaving the room for a few minutes?" Daniels asked. "I need to speak with Jon in private."

The Pearls filed out. Before leaving, Nicki gave Lancaster a hug. She wore a pink T-shirt that said CAUTION! THIS PERSON MAY TALK ABOUT HORSES AT ANY MOMENT!

"Thank you for helping us," she said.

"You're welcome, Nicki," he said.

"My dad says that now he has to buy you a new refrigerator. Do you have one picked out?"

"I do. Every time I open it up, I'm going to think of you."

"That's cool."

Nicki left, and Lancaster pulled up a chair and rested his elbows on the metal guardrail on Daniels's hospital bed. He'd held up his end of the bargain, and now it was time for Daniels to fulfill hers and make good on the two things he'd asked of her.

"I've got good news and bad news," Daniels said. "My boss came by this morning, and brought along the director of the bureau's North Miami office. I told them about the two detectives dealing in stolen coke. The North Miami office is aware of the situation. Turns out, there are other detectives involved. They're going down soon."

"How soon?"

"Next week. The director told me that the coke is passed to the detectives at a Mexican restaurant. The FBI plans to secretly videotape the detectives receiving the stolen coke, and bust everyone at once."

The news made him feel better, but only a little.

"What about Zack Kenny?" he said. "He threatened to kill the woman who helped us blow this thing open. I promised her that I'd deal with Zack."

"I'm afraid that's the bad news. Kenny's situation will take longer to resolve. My boss did some digging. Zack had a restraining order put on him by an ex-girlfriend, but is otherwise clean. We need hard evidence to bring him down, and that takes time."

"Zack has a library of kiddie porn on an iPad in his apartment. That should be enough to put him away for a while, don't you think?"

"It should, except the tip came from his ex-girlfriend, who obviously hates him. A judge will want to know why the ex-girlfriend took so long to tell the police, considering they broke up a while ago."

"You're saying the judge might turn down a request for subpoena."

"Unfortunately. We need another angle."

He rested his chin on the cold metal bar. He had promised Karissa that he'd fix this. Karissa had opened the door that had led him to Daniels. Her bravery had made the difference, and he was not going to allow that selfless act to go unrewarded.

"I need to think about this," he said. "I'm going to the cafeteria to get a drink. You want something?"

"I'm craving sweets. Get me a chocolate doughnut," she said.

"Coming right up."

At the doorway he stopped and turned around. Zack Kenny had kept a teenage runaway in his condo, and he wondered if it might be enough to convince a judge to issue a warrant. He started to pose the question, but Daniels had drifted off to sleep.

In the hallway he tried to remember his way to the elevators. A Middle Eastern man wearing designer clothes acknowledged him with a smile. It took a moment to place him. It was Cassandra's partner from the videos. He'd shaved his goatee, but his dark eyes gave him away.

"I'm Jon Lancaster," he said.

"My name is Fadi. Beth has told me all about you," the man said.

"Are you the Reality Thief?"

"I'd rather think of myself as Beth's boyfriend."

"You and I need to talk."

"I really need to see Beth. I just flew in on the red-eye."

"She's taking a nap. You want something to eat? My treat."

"Beth said you were very persuasive. Lead the way."

- - -

They paid a visit to the hospital cafeteria in the basement. Fadi hadn't eaten on the plane, and Lancaster's offer to pay for lunch was enthusiastically received. He was a good-looking guy and spoke English better than most Americans.

"How did you make the Cassandra videos look so real?" Lancaster asked.

Fadi blew on a spoonful of chicken soup. "The ability to age-regress photographs isn't new. I figured out how to transfer the technology to video so each frame was age-regressed and resembled the previous frame. The process is not perfect, by any means."

"Is that why the videos were shot in muted light?"

"They were actually shot through a soft lens that hid the imperfections."

"It sure fooled me. Do you work in Hollywood making movies?"

Fadi laughed under his breath. "Hardly. I live in Silicon Valley. My parents moved here from Lebanon to work as engineers for Apple. I grew up creating avatars on my computer. When I graduated from Stanford, I started my own animation video company in my apartment. I called it BTTF, which stands for *Back to the Future*, which is one of my favorite movies. We produce videos that use age-regression technology that turns adult actors into children and shows them revisiting their childhood. It was a huge hit on YouTube, which Beth tells me you know something about."

"I've heard of BTTF. It was bought out by Google, wasn't it?"

"Yes, it was, although I still run things. Two years ago, we were approached by the FBI. They wanted us to create videos using an adult actress who we'd age-regress to look like a teenager. The goal was to lure sexual predators out of hiding, and arrest them.

"At first I refused. I did not want BTTF associated with pornography. Then Beth paid me a visit. She told me about what happened at Dartmouth and how the killers were taunting her with the photographs of their latest victims. She practically begged me to help her.

"Beth and I share a passion for running. The next day, we ran five miles together. At the end of the run, I realized I was attracted to her, so I agreed to create the videos using Beth, who would be age-regressed in my studios.

"Men who download kiddie porn are not stupid. They download the video to a computer, then transfer the video to another device, and scrub the hard drive of the original computer. When the police search the original computer's hard drive, they won't find evidence of the download, and cannot make an arrest.

"Beth asked me if there was a way to put a permanent cookie on a site that downloaded a kiddie-porn video. It took a while, but my engineers came up with a solution. Do you know what a cookie is?"

"Cookies are code that sites attach to the IP address on a computer," Lancaster said. "It allows the site to retarget the viewer with ads."

"If you scrub a computer's hard drive, it erases the cookies. My company created a code that we call zombie cookies. A zombie cookie becomes embedded in the hard drive and cannot be erased. Beth was convinced that zombie cookies could be used in court to show that a deviant had downloaded a porn video.

"Unfortunately, the courts didn't allow it. The technology was new, and no one understood it. The fact that a zombie cookie was embedded on a pervert's computer didn't give the FBI the right to make an arrest. It was a huge setback.

"By then, Beth and I were dating. Every month, we would get together for a long weekend. During one of these visits, Beth told me that the age-regressed videos were a failure. She asked me if we could make a video of the two of us having sex, and then have my team age-regress her in the video. She thought this would create greater interest and draw out the killers who were taunting her."

"Because of the sex," he said.

"Exactly. Beth called it the honey pot. The bear sticks its paw into the honey pot, and cannot pull it out. And that's how the Cassandra videos were created."

Fadi tore apart his roll and cleaned the bottom of his bowl. If Lancaster remembered correctly, Google had paid $1 billion to acquire BTTF. Fadi was one of those rare individuals who'd gotten rich but remained humble.

"You didn't like it, did you?" Lancaster said.

"No, I didn't. Making the Cassandra videos made me feel dirty. Then, a few days ago, Beth called me and said she thought she'd found the Dartmouth killers, and that the videos had helped draw them out. It made the whole thing seem worthwhile."

"Beth's niece has been stalked by men who think she's the girl in the Cassandra videos," he said. "Beth said there was a way to fix this. How?"

"Beth knew the Cassandra videos might be harmful," Fadi said. "She asked me to create a final video that would repulse the perverts. She planned to release it when the sting was over. It was designed to make the perverts stop fantasizing about Cassandra."

"Can I see it?"

"I really should ask Beth first."

"I'm sure she'd say yes, don't you think?"

"You're probably right."

Fadi took out a cell phone as thin as a playing card. He opened an app and hit a command, then turned the screen. The last installment of the Cassandra videos began to play. It had been shot in a hotel room with muted lighting. An age-regressed Beth lay naked in bed, talking to the camera. A naked Fadi entered the picture. He joined her and they began to kiss. Then Beth reached beneath a pillow and pulled out a pipe, which she began to beat him with. Each blow was accompanied by a loud cracking sound. Fadi jumped out of bed, fearful for his life. Beth followed him around the room and continued to inflict punishment. Bleeding from the mouth and nose, Fadi sank to the floor. The video ended with him begging for mercy.

"That's brutal," Lancaster said.

"It's intended to be brutal," Fadi said. "The other videos portray Cassandra as a victim. Here, she is clearly the aggressor. Beth showed it to the profilers at the FBI's Behavioral Sciences unit. The profilers said that once the perverts watch it, they will never see Cassandra the same way again, and will stop fantasizing about her."

"When are you going live with this?"

"As soon as Beth tells me to."

"I hope your solution works. Nicki and her parents have been through hell because of those videos."

"I know. Beth told me what happened."

Fadi looked sad. He'd done something against his better judgment, and now appeared unhappy with his decision. Lancaster went to the cafeteria's bakery section and bought a chocolate doughnut. He walked Fadi to the elevator and handed him the bag.

"Please give this to her."

The elevator came, but Fadi did not board. His conscience was eating at him, the way it did to moral people. It was hard to do good, as he now painfully understood.

"I want to fix the harm I've caused," he said. "How do I do that?"

That was a good question. It was true that time healed all wounds. But there would always be psychological scars. Whenever Nicki saw a strange man staring at her, she would be fearful. All the money in the world couldn't fix that.

"I'm sure you'll think of something," he said.

CHAPTER 43
THE DEVIL YOU KNOW

The best thing about not being a cop was that the rules changed. As a private investigator, Lancaster didn't have to concern himself with a suspect's rights or the protections afforded him or her under the Constitution. Those things stopped mattering.

Leaving the hospital, he drove to a trendy eatery on Las Olas called YOLO, which stood for You Only Live Once. It was not the kind of place where he usually hung out, and he didn't expect to run into anyone he knew. The lunch crowd had thinned out, and he found a parking space on a side street and called the sheriff's office main switchboard. He asked to speak to Detective Vargas and was patched through to voice mail.

"Good afternoon, Detective Vargas. This is your old pal Jon Lancaster," he said. "I hear you've been going around town saying nasty things about me. Well, I'm going to pay you back for your trouble. You and your asshole partner are in a world of trouble. I'm talking prison, loss of pension, and having your bank accounts seized. If you'd like to hear more, meet me at YOLO. I'll be at the bar."

He was into his second beer when Vargas came in. She was breathing hard and had worked up a real sweat. She refused to sit down. He settled his tab and picked up his beer. They walked to the back of the dining room and took a booth.

"Where's your ugly partner?" he asked.

"Booking a suspect," Vargas said. "I was at my desk typing up an arrest report when your call came in. I didn't like the sound of it, so I dropped what I was doing and came over. What the fuck are you talking about?"

Vargas was playing dumb, wanting to see how much he actually knew. A waitress pretty enough to model materialized at their table.

"You want a drink?" he asked.

"Can't, I'm working," she said.

"You're going to want a drink after you hear what I have to say."

Vargas waved the waitress away. "Spit it out, Jon. The less time I have to spend in your company, the better."

There was no love lost between them, and he decided to let her have both barrels.

"The FBI is onto you," he said.

The corner of her mouth twitched.

"I don't know what you're talking about," she said.

"Let me refresh your memory. The FBI knows that a police dog trainer is stealing blow out of the stockade in his cowboy boots, and that he's passing it on to detectives with the department who are moving it for him. The FBI also knows that you and your partner are strong-arming strippers into moving it for you. Is this ringing any bells?"

Vargas looked like she might puke. She got the waitress's attention.

"A shot of Jameson and a beer chaser," she said.

They shared a long, uncomfortable silence. Her drink came. Vargas belted the whiskey back and chased it down. It brought the color back to her face and helped her regain her composure.

"How did you find out?" she asked.

"That's none of your god damn business," he said. "What's important is that I know, and I can help you."

"You can make this go away?"

"I didn't say that. There's going to be a bust, and it will be ugly. What I can do is protect you and your partner. You won't go down with the rest of them."

"But the others will take the fall."

"That's right."

"They might think we ratted them out."

"Who cares? They'll be in prison, and you won't."

Vargas was having a hard time dealing with the reality of what he was saying. Most criminals accepted that they might get caught and face prison. Vargas hadn't considered this, and it was turning her inside out. She flagged the waitress and ordered another whiskey.

"What do you want in return?" she asked.

"There's a guy named Zack Kenny I want you to bust. He has a library of kiddie porn stored on his iPad in the study of his condo. I'll give you the address."

"That's it?"

"He needs to go down hard. You can't screw it up."

"We won't screw it up. But we'll need a good reason to get a warrant to search his condo. Otherwise, whatever we find will get tossed out of court."

"Kenny kept a teenage girl in his condo for a few months," he said. "The condo association found out about it, and there was a big ruckus. Everyone in the building knows, including the guard at the front gate."

"Did Kenny screw her?"

"I'm sure he did."

"Then it was statutory rape. Is the girl still there?"

"I don't think so."

"Then how does that help us get into his place?"

"It establishes that Kenny has a history of dealings with underage girls. You need to coerce another teenage girl to say that Kenny lured her to his condo. Get her to say that she saw kiddie porn on his iPad. Then go to a judge for your search warrant."

"That's a tall order. If the girl trips up, I'm screwed."

"Would you rather get arrested for dealing coke? The feds will take everything you have. When you get out of the joint, you'll be broke. Pick your poison."

Vargas was twisting on the end of an invisible rope. The waitress brought her a fresh shot. She belted it back, and would have probably licked the glass if he hadn't been looking. She wiped her mouth with her sleeve and took a deep breath.

"Give me this asshole's address," she said.

CHAPTER 44

50 OCEAN

They ended up killing him.

It happened the next day. Lancaster was stuck in traffic on I-95 when he heard the news. He'd just left the FBI's North Miami office and was heading home. He'd spent three hours explaining to a roomful of agents how he and Daniels had discovered that Mates and Holloway were the Hanover killers, and his throat was raw from the retelling. His cell phone buzzed, and he picked it up off the passenger seat and stared at the screen. He subscribed to the online version of the *Sun-Sentinel* and received breaking news stories over his phone. A pair of Fort Lauderdale detectives had attempted to arrest a suspect in a parking lot and had ended up shooting him dead. The story was developing with more details to follow. Neither the suspect's nor the detectives' names were given, but his gut told him that the deceased was Zack Kenny.

He made it home and got on his computer to see if there were any updates on the shooting. There was nothing. He considered calling one of his friends with the sheriff's office to get more details but decided not to. If Zack Kenny was dead, he didn't want his name associated with it, even in a casual way.

Four different TV stations served the Fort Lauderdale market. Each had a six o'clock news program devoted to that day's events. At the stroke of six, he parked himself in front of the TV with a cold beer and surfed between them. The ABC affiliate, Local 10 News, opened with the story, so he picked them.

A deeply tanned newscaster read off a prompter. A pair of Broward detectives had attempted to execute a search warrant to a suspected sexual predator in the parking lot of an upscale apartment complex in Coral Ridge when the suspect suddenly attacked one of the detectives, who was female. The detective's partner had drawn his weapon and shot the suspect multiple times, killing him instantly. The sheriff's office had released the dead man's name. It was Zackary Lawrence Kenny.

He raised his beer to the screen. The world was a safer place with Zack gone. He tried to imagine how Karissa would react to the news. She would be relieved but maybe saddened. She'd been in love with Zack, and those feelings were hard to erase. He was about to call her when he got a call from Vargas.

"I just saw the news on TV," he said. "Did he hurt you?"

"Bastard broke my nose," Vargas said.

"I'm sorry to hear that."

"No, you're not."

He sipped his beer and smiled. "How did you get the search warrant so quickly?"

"I decided that your idea of fabricating a story was a bad one," she said, "so I went to the brokerage house where Zack worked and spoke to the head of human resources. Guys like him usually can't keep their hands off women they work with. Sure enough, I was right. An intern had filed a complaint saying Zack had tried to molest her in the copy room. I got a copy of the complaint, then went to his apartment and spoke to the head of the homeowner's association. She confirmed that Zack had shacked up with an underage runaway. Her statement and the complaint were enough to sway the judge to issue a warrant."

"Sounds like you did everything by the book."

"Damn straight. Assholes like that know their rights. Last thing we wanted was to have it thrown out of court on a technicality."

"What happens now?"

"There'll be two investigations. One internal, the second criminal, to make sure we didn't break any laws. A surveillance camera on the apartment building videoed the whole thing, so we should be fine. I'm going to take time off to let my face heal."

"What about your partner?"

"He's been put on administrative duties. He'll have to sit at a desk alphabetizing three-by-five cards and going through OD death certificates. You know the drill." She paused, then said, "We kept up our end of the bargain. Now it's your turn. I want you to tell me how you're going to save us from getting busted. And don't you dare screw us."

He put the beer down, thinking hard. Daniels had confided that the FBI planned to bust the ring of drug-dealing detectives next week. The detectives would be caught receiving the coke at a restaurant and secretly videotaped in the act. This would provide a rock-solid case in court, and the ring would go down hard. All Vargas and her partner needed to do was not be present at the restaurant that day.

But sharing this information with Vargas was a problem. She might alert the other detectives in the ring, and ruin the bust. The FBI would realize the detectives had been tipped off, and that might find its way back to Daniels, and hurt her. His loyalty was to Daniels, not Vargas, so he chose his words carefully.

"Does your partner have any accrued vacation time?" he asked.

"I'm sure he does," Vargas said.

"Tell him to take it, and leave town for a few weeks."

"All right. What then?"

"When the two of you return, your problem will be gone."

"You're going to fix it?"

Her question gave him pause. Vargas didn't suspect that the bust would be going down soon. She was in the dark, and the less he said, the better.

"Yes, I'm going to fix it," he said.

"You still haven't told me how this is going to work," Vargas said.

"Enjoy your time off."

He ended the connection feeling relieved. He'd made good on his promises to Vargas without harming his relationship with Daniels. Playing both sides of the fence was never easy, especially when people's lives and reputations hung in the balance. Karissa was still holed up in Marathon, and he texted her, saying that it was safe to come home. Then he called Daniels to see how things were going. Daniels had been discharged from the hospital and was at her sister's house recuperating.

"I'm doing shitty, thanks for asking," Daniels said.

"What's wrong?" he said.

"Fadi came by earlier. He wanted to talk to me in private, so I grabbed the walker I'm using, and we went onto the dock. He got down on his knee and gave me the biggest diamond ring you've ever seen. Then he asked me to marry him."

There was a long pause, and she began to cry.

"You said no," he said.

"Yeah, I said no. Fadi got really upset, and accused me of using him to make the Cassandra videos to capture Mates and Holloway. He took the ring back and threw it into the water. Then he said he never wanted to see me again and left."

"I'm sorry, Beth."

"So am I. Do you want to know the stupid part? I'm in love with him."

"Then why did you turn him down?"

"Because he wanted me to relocate to California and leave the bureau. I'm not ready to do that. Does that sound crazy?"

"He wanted you to change."

"Yes, he wanted me to change."

Some cops couldn't change but had to continue to fight crime and chase down evil. They were on a mission that often precluded them from having normal lives. He knew the deal because he'd been living it for most of his life.

"It doesn't sound crazy at all," he said.

- - -

Two weeks later, he took Daniels out to dinner. She was going to physical therapy every day and was already strong enough to walk without assistance. He showed up at the Pearls' place at a few minutes before six. He'd gotten a haircut and bought himself a new pair of chinos and a Tommy Bahama dress shirt with fancy buttons.

The first thing he'd noticed was how quiet the neighborhood was. The street in front of the house hardly had any traffic. The last Cassandra video had been posted, and like magic, Nicki's stalkers had crawled back under their rocks and stopped pursuing her.

The Pearls greeted him at the front door with hugs and smiles. Nicki told him how her parents had agreed to let her start taking horseback-riding lessons and how excited she was. Then Daniels came downstairs dressed in a pair of designer jeans and a shimmering gold blouse. Her hair was pulled back in a ponytail, and the makeup she wore made her look like an actress. Before they left, Melanie snapped a photo on her cell phone.

"Where are you taking me?" Daniels asked in the car.

"I made a reservation at 50 Ocean. The views are amazing," he said.

"Sounds wonderful," she said.

A bootleg Jimmy Buffett concert played on the car's stereo, and she hummed along while he drove. Something had changed, and he sensed that she wanted to talk about it but didn't know how to begin. If they didn't get past it, the night would be ruined.

"You seem different," he said.

"How so?" she asked.

"Like a dark cloud's been lifted. You almost seem happy."

"I am happy. The nightmares I've been having since college have stopped. I'm waking up in the morning feeling great. It's an amazing feeling."

"That sounds like cause for celebration."

"What are we celebrating? That Mates and Holloway are dead? That seems a little morbid, don't you think?"

He stopped at a traffic light and faced her. "Mates and Holloway were evil, and evil never wins. That's what we're celebrating."

"Do you really believe that?"

"I sure do. The world is a good place, and so are most of the people who live in it. Evil people are a minority, and they're not supposed to win. When they go down, we have every right to pop a bottle of champagne and cheer."

She took his hand and gave it a squeeze.

"I knew there was a reason I liked you," she said.

50 Ocean was located on the same block as Boston's, across the street from the ocean. He decided to park in a public lot a few blocks away to avoid the flooding.

"You strong enough for a little walk?" he asked.

"I did a mile today on the treadmill," she said proudly.

As they walked to the restaurant, she talked about her childhood, and how she'd aspired to be a surgeon like her father and save lives. That dream had carried her to Dartmouth, and she would have gotten a medical degree and gone to work doing research had Mates and Holloway not abducted her. Lying in the trunk of their car, her life had flashed before her eyes, and she'd accepted that she was about to die. When the trunk had sprung open, bright sunlight had flooded over her, and she'd felt like she'd been reborn.

They came to the restaurant. The road in front looked different, and it took a moment for him to realize why. The water had receded, and the pavement was bone dry.

"What are you looking at?" she asked.

"This road had six inches of water the last time I was here."

"That's so strange. Does anyone know what causes the flooding?"

"No one knows what causes the King Tides. It screws everything up when it's here, and when it's gone, it's like it was never there in the first place. I guess it's the price we pay for living in paradise."

"I want to stick my feet in the ocean," she said.

They crossed and walked to the ocean's edge. Taking off their shoes, they stood in the wet sand and let the gentle waves tickle their feet. The world felt normal again, and they stayed until the sun went down, knowing the feeling would not last.

ABOUT THE AUTHOR

James Swain is the national bestselling author of twenty mystery novels and has worked as a magazine editor, screenwriter, and novelist. His books have been translated into a dozen languages and have been selected as Mysteries of the Year by *Publishers Weekly* and *Kirkus Reviews*. Swain has been nominated for three Barry Awards, has received a Florida Book Award for fiction, and was awarded France's prestigious Prix Calibre .38 for Best American Crime Writing. When he isn't writing, he enjoys performing close-up magic.